Readers love SJ[
Pony

"Love this book, love the series, love the author... that's just a whole heap of love pouring out of me for this latest instalment in the Guards of Folsom series."

—Sinfully Sexy Books

"I enjoyed this addition to the series and thought it went in ways that I didn't quite expect. I can't wait to see which kink is up next!"

—Guilty Indulgence Romance Review

"I am a huge fan of the Guards of Folsom series by SJD Peterson, and I think this is my favorite book so far. It is a story that manages to be warm and romantic, while at the same time being totally hot and sexy."

—Joyfully Jay

"One of the things I love about this author's writing is just how vividly the characters come to life. They seem like real people that you truly grow to care for. I love this series and love this author's work."

—Hearts on Fire

"I was captivated by this third installment in the series and am now lusting after more. Thank you, again, to the incredible author, Jo Peterson, for giving voices to my guys and another beautiful love story for me to enjoy."

—Rainbow Book Reviews

"For me this was perhaps the best in the series. It had it all, the kinks, the awesome couple, the hot mind-blowing scenes, and joy. Yup, that's mostly my favorite part, the fact that it made me have this stupid grin on my face during the entire read."

—MM Good Book Reviews

"The third installment in the Guards of Folsom series, and it totally renewed my love for the series.... I'd say this was the best Folsom book to date!"

—3 Chicks After Dark

By SJD PETERSON

Beyond Duty*
Leon
Masters & Boyd
Plan B*
Tuck & Cover

WHISPERING PINES RANCH
Lorcan's Desire*
Quinn's Need*
Ty's Obsession*
Conner's Courage*
Jess's Journey*
Riveted (short story)

GUARDS OF FOLSOM
Pup*
Tag Team*
Pony*
Roped*

*Available in paperback

Published by DREAMSPINNER PRESS
http://www.dreamspinnerpress.com

ROPED

A GUARDS OF FOLSOM NOVEL

SJD PETERSON

Dreamspinner Press

Published by
Dreamspinner Press
5032 Capital Circle SW
Suite 2, PMB# 279
Tallahassee, FL 32305-7886
USA
http://www.dreamspinnerpress.com/

This is a work of fiction. Names, characters, places, and incidents either are the product of author imagination or are used fictitiously, and any resemblance to actual persons, living or dead, business establishments, events, or locales is entirely coincidental.

Roped
© 2014 SJD Peterson.

Cover Art
© 2014 Paul Richmond.
http://www.paulrichmondstudio.com
Cover content is for illustrative purposes only and any person depicted on the cover is a model.

ISBN: 978-1-62798-919-0
Digital ISBN: 978-1-62798-920-6

Printed in the United States of America
First Edition
May 2014

DEDICATION

Born of blood and violence and the mind of S.A. McAuley.
Love ya, Boo!

ROPED PLAYLIST

Ludacris—Growing Pains

Judas Priest—Turbo Lover

Three Days Grace—Pain

Greg Holden—The Lost Boy

Joshua James—Coal War

Secondhand Serenade—A Twist In My Story

Anthrax—Madhouse

Incubus—Drive

Molly Hatchet—Flirtin' With Disaster

Alice Cooper—I'm Eighteen

Rock Riot—Carry On Wayward Son

Johnny Cash—Hurt

Oasis—Wonderwall

Scorpions—Rock You Like A Hurricane

Alice Cooper—Poison

The Goo Goo Dolls—Iris

AC/DC—Highway To Hell

Mötley Crüe—Shout At The Devil

Five Finger Death Punch—Bad Company

Life has been known by a series of constants: violence, anger, drugs, sex, death, heartbreak, pain, fear, and, the most common, hunger. Always hunger. Not the kind that can be satisfied with food, but the kind born of circumstance. The kind that not only claws within a gut, but settles into a heart, consumes a mind. Deeper—encircles, penetrates the soul. Hunger for something more, something better, safer. Always just out of grasp—craving—starved.

It's part of me.

Who I am.

Born of blood and violence, hunger is my fate.

Yet, the slightest things can change the directions of a life. An unplanned circumstance, random act—a connection—a chance event, like a lightning strike, fate is trumped.

Jamie is my lightning strike.

Tek Cain

A child is born, brought into the world as a lump of clay. Each hand that touches it, marks it, molds it, creates life. Some of those hands are talented, working the clay as it spins slowly on the wheel into beautiful shapes, flowing lines—art. Other less than talented hands slide awkwardly along the clay, trying over and over to add something good and whole to the piece. Fumbling fingers with good intentions leave their imperfections behind. Yet somehow, these blemishes, these mistakes, add to the uniqueness and yes, the beauty of the art. Then there are those who only wish to defile, destroy. They dig their fingers into the wet clay creating deep, ugly imprints, mangled globs of mud with no shape, no purpose, and no form. But the wheel keeps spinning; new hands begin to work the clay back into some semblance of order, talented hands, good hands. The clay can never be as it was originally, it's irrevocably changed, but art and beauty can still be created.

By the time I was thirteen, I had been touched, shaped, and molded by all three types of hands. I had been touched numerous times by the fingers whose sole purpose was to defile and destroy. In my young life, I had seen evil, been touched by evil, molded by evil, but there were always new hands.

Good hands.

Talented hands.

Jamie's hands.

Tek Cain

Summer of Innocence

GUNNER CAIN pulled his arm back, aimed carefully toward the window on the second floor, and let the pebble fly. He waited. Hiding in the shadows of the bushes that surrounded the Cape Cod-style home, Gunner felt his heart hammering in his chest, seconds were like hours. *C'mon, c'mon, c'mon.* If he were caught sneaking out of the house again, his stepdad would put a boot in his ass sideways. Worse, they were going to miss all the action. Gunner shifted from foot to foot and the muscle in his cheek twitched, the nervousness and excitement not allowing him to hold still.

With a huff, Gunner reached down and grabbed a handful of small rocks, pulled his arm back and—

The window opened and a head full of shaggy brown hair popped out followed by the scowling face of his best friend, James Ryan. Most everyone called him James, Jim, Jimmy, or Junior, but Gunner called him Jamie. Gunner was the only one allowed to call him Jamie.

"Gunner?"

"Yeah," he whispered, tossing the rocks to the ground and wiping the dirt on his jeans. "It's me. Get your ass down here."

"No way," Jamie said, shaking his head. "I couldn't sit down for a week the last time I let you talk me into sneaking out."

Damn, his friend could be dramatic as a bunch of sissy girls. "It was only a day, you pansy ass," he hissed. Gunner rolled his eyes. He'd had his own difficulties with sitting after his stepdad had been done tearing up his ass with a belt, but he wasn't going to let that deter him. "Now get down here. I want to show you something."

"What?"

Gunner didn't answer, simply crossed his arms over his chest and tapped his foot with impatience. Jamie hesitated, his expression unsure, but Gunner had no doubt Jamie would come. And he better hurry it up or they were going to miss the show.

Finally, after what felt like forever, Jamie glanced behind him and then whispered, "I'll meet you on the back porch."

Gunner smiled and moved back into the shadows. He made his way around the side of the house, being careful not to bump into the garbage cans, and peeked around the corner. Satisfied the coast was clear, he moved to the porch and waited.

With only a small squeak from the hinges of the screen door, Jamie stepped out onto the porch in a white T-shirt, running shorts, and tennis shoes in hand. He gave Gunner an exasperated look but jumped off the porch, avoiding the steps—the stairs creaked too loudly.

"If we get caught, I'm gonna beat you silly," Jamie grumbled and then bent to put on his shoes.

Gunner ruffled Jamie's unruly curls. "We're not going to get caught. You worry too much."

Jamie slapped at him, but Gunner pulled his hand out of reach—spinning away. He had to bite down on his lip to keep from laughing at the disbelieving look and glare Jamie threw his way.

"That's what you said last time," Jamie complained quietly.

As soon as Jamie finished tying his sneakers, Gunner grabbed Jamie's shirt and yanked—"C'mon"—and took off running.

Gunner raced across the backyard, Jamie right on his heels. They jumped over the short fence separating Jamie's yard from the neighbor's. They didn't have to worry about trespassing. The few houses that were in this rural area of Chatom, California, belonged to club members—Gunner's stepdad and president of the local chapter of the Crimson VIII motorcycle club, Rocco Lundy, ruled with an iron fist—and outsiders were not welcome.

Gunner didn't slow down—confident Jamie would keep up—until the clubhouse was in sight. From the outside it looked like any country hick bar: weathered clapboard exterior, neon flashing beer signs in the heavily tinted windows, gravel parking lot out front filled with trucks, muscle cars, and Harleys—lots of Harleys. It was the dealings that went down within the walls, the action taking place out back secured by a system rivaling Fort Knox that made this place different. It was a place Gunner Cain, as an only child, would someday rule, just as his grandpa, father, and now stepfather had.

They stopped next to the back end of a rusted Ford truck, keeping their heads low. Gunner was breathing harshly, sweat running down his forehead. He wiped it away with his forearm. Gunner gave Jamie a once-over. He was panting hard too, the neon lights from the club causing the perspiration on his brow to glisten in a multitude of colors. He looked okay, wide-eyed, nervous, unsure, but okay. Satisfied, Gunner nodded to himself. Jamie was his responsibility, one day standing at Gunner's side as his right-hand man. It was his job to protect Jamie, and also to make sure the guy had a little fun. Jamie could be a little bit of a worrywart.

Gunner put a finger to his lips, reminding Jamie to stay quiet, and then gave a curt nod in the direction they were to go. They kept low to the ground and crouched behind vehicles as they made their way through the parking lot and around to the far side of the club. Toward the back was a lone window—Gunner's goal.

Crouched beneath the window, Gunner pointed to it and then placed his lips close to Jamie's ear. "Sully is gearing up for a show."

Sully, whose real name was Claude, got his nickname from the fact his mission in life since he'd been a kid was to soil or stain every woman who crossed his path. Within the club, sex was open, few things considered taboo, but Sully took it to the extreme. He was one sick and perverted bastard.

Jamie turned his head, their noses practically touching, and glared at Gunner. "You got me out of bed for this?" he hissed.

"Don't you want to know what to do when you bang your first bitch?"

"Sure, but not from Sully. The guy is seriously nasty," Jamie whispered. His nose wrinkled in obvious disgust.

"You gotta learn it all, Jamie," Gunner informed him. "Gotta know what the bitches like and don't like."

Hands gripping the windowsill, Gunner rose up just enough to peer into the small hole he'd made in the black vinyl that covered the glass. What he saw in the gloomy bedroom beyond caused his eyes to widen in shock. Naked bodies, male and female, were all tangled together in a jumbled mess of parts. It reminded him of a nest of worms all slithering, wrapped around each other, making it difficult to distinguish where one body ended and another began. The only difference was this mass had arms and legs, faces. One guy was thrusting hard against a big squishy butt, another had his dick between big tits, thrusting hard as he gripped the girl's hair, still another had his head between a girl's legs. Tongues, lips, fingers, private parts, it was…. Gunner wasn't sure what he felt, but mostly confusion.

"Take a look at this and tell me what you think," he told Jamie, moving over to give him room.

His best friend hesitated but did as Gunner asked. It was too dark to see the expression on Jamie's face to tell what he thought of the sight, plus Jamie had his eye to the window, his head turned away, so it wouldn't have mattered if there had been a light. Jamie didn't leave him curious for long.

"Eww! It looks like a big nest of freaky snakes with limbs," Jamie complained.

"Lower your voice," Gunner scolded in a whisper. But Jamie's comment was so close to what Gunner had initially thought it made him grin.

Gunner turned back to the wall and slid down. He pulled his knees up and wrapped his arms around them. Jamie sat next to him in the same position. Neither of them spoke for a few moments. They'd watched some of the other club members banging women before. Cole, Rocco's first lieutenant, was well known for his do-it-anywhere-any-time attitude and cared little for who was around or watching. Gunner and Jamie had done their best to hide the giggles by covering their bright red faces with their hands, but usually ended up in another room laughing hysterically.

However, the scene they'd just witnessed was neither funny nor boner inspiring. He glanced over to his friend, but with the position he was in, Gunner couldn't tell if Jamie had one.

Gunner leaned closer to Jamie's ear and whispered, "Did you pop a boner?"

Jamie shook his head vigorously.

"No tingles or nothing?" Gunner asked.

"Nothing," Jamie admitted. "I don't want to have to do that. It was…."

"Weird?"

"I was going to say gross," Jamie countered.

The distaste in Jamie's tone made Gunner snicker. "That's Sully for ya."

They both went silent, heads leaned together. Gunner had been thinking about sex a lot lately. Well, maybe not the sweaty grunting kind of stuff—Jamie was right, that was kind of gross. But Gunner liked the idea of touching and kissing. There were always a lot of chicks around the club. They made themselves available to the members, and Gunner had no doubt one day they'd make themselves available to him and Jamie. Rocco had drilled into Gunner's head since he was little, though: in whatever he does, he could never show weakness to those he leads.

Gunner had no confidence when it came to the chicks. They kind of…. Well, grossed him out too. He didn't like the thick stench of overly sweet perfume that clung to them, the paint on their faces, and especially the greasy bright red lips he would one day have to press his to. Gunner shuddered in revulsion.

A leader is always confident.

"You know," Gunner said, breaking the silence. "We should practice."

"Practice what?" Jamie asked.

"You know…." Gunner shrugged.

"That in there?" Jamie squeaked, stabbing a thumb over his shoulder. "No way!"

"Shh," Gunner reminded his friend. "Not that, but maybe we should start with… I don't know… the kissing?" he suggested hesitantly. "We're going to be thirteen next month. It's time we start thinking about this."

"I know how to kiss," Jamie huffed.

"Really?"

Jamie nodded.

"Kissing your grandma doesn't count, you dork," Gunner snorted and shoved at Jamie with his shoulder. "I'm talking about real kissing. You know, with a chick. Use your tongue. You gotta practice."

"Who we gonna get to let us practice on them?"

Gunner thought about Jamie's question for a bit. They didn't know any girls close to their own age. Being homeschooled, they were around adults mostly. Sully had a couple of girls who came to the club every now and then, but they were little kids. Gunner couldn't think of anyone except....

Decision made, he turned to his friend. "We're gonna have to practice on each other."

"What?" Jamie gasped.

"We gotta," Gunner insisted. "Ain't nobody else, and no way in hell am I going to have a chick know more than me. We're men, Jamie. We gotta take charge. Can't do that if we don't know what we're doing."

Jamie stared at him. In the darkness it was hard to read the expression on Jamie's face, but Gunner knew his friend well enough to know he was thinking about it. Jamie always thought about everything—worried too much, analyzed and reasoned shit out. He rarely did anything on impulse. That's why Jamie needed Gunner so much, to make sure he did spontaneous, silly stuff once in a while. It was also Gunner's job—no, his duty—to make sure Jamie was ready to stand next to him when Gunner became president.

With that thought in his head, urging him, Gunner grabbed Jamie's face in both his hands and smashed their mouths together. Jamie tensed but didn't pull away. Encouraged, Gunner tilted his head back and forth, their lips rubbing together. He liked the way Jamie's mouth felt against his: warm, soft. Tentatively, Gunner stuck his tongue out, tasted a hint of the mint gum Jamie was always chewing, and Gunner liked it. He wanted to taste more and pushed his tongue past Jamie's lips.

Jamie didn't really kiss Gunner back, he stayed tense, but he opened his mouth, allowed Gunner to kiss him with lips and tongue. Damn. Gunner had no idea what the hell he was doing, but he liked it, liked the taste and feel of Jamie's mouth. He liked the way it made him all tingly inside, as if butterflies had taken flight in his belly and were flying all through his body, their wings tickling him from inside.

Gunner explored Jamie's mouth, licked his teeth and gums, and when he swiped the tip of his tongue against the roof of Jamie's mouth, his friend shuddered and made a small sound he'd never heard Jamie make. The taste of Jamie's wet and warm mouth, the appealing sound coming from his friend, the tingling in his belly, all mingled into heat that raced down Gunner's body, settled beneath the waistband of his jeans and....

Gunner jerked back, gasping. His heart hammered painfully in his chest, pumped blood so fast through his system he could hear it roar in his ears. "I, uh... I...." Gunner licked his lips, could still taste Jamie and the heat increased. "I.... We...." He wiped his mouth on the back of his hand. "We gotta get home," he blurted and jumped to his feet, doing his best to shield his body from his friend. "Let's go!"

Keeping his back to Jamie, Gunner led them back through the parking lot, dodging cars and keeping in the shadows. He wanted to run, but somehow he managed to hold himself back. He was aware of Jamie behind him, had to get his friend home. *Slow, quiet, careful*, he kept repeating over and over in his head. No way did he want to get caught now. How would he explain...?

Slow, quiet, careful.

The second they made it to the tree line, Gunner broke out into a dead run, dodging small bushes and trees, feet pounding against the forest floor, conscious of the familiar presence behind him. Jamie's house came into view. Gunner scanned it as he ran, no lights on inside, quiet. He hopped the small fence, landed in Jamie's yard, and slowed near the porch, but didn't turn around.

"See you tomorrow," he tossed quietly over his shoulder and disappeared around the side of the house, escaped to the cover of darkness with a relieved sigh.

Gunner had done his job; he'd gotten Jamie back home without being spotted, his friend safe. To his greater satisfaction, he'd done it without giving away the giant boner he'd popped from kissing Jamie.

Gunner ran his hands over his face and then looked around him to make sure no one could see before looking down his body. Nope, he wasn't dreaming. *Holy hell! A boner? A goddamn boner from kissing Jamie?*

The best of intentions by some are invariably tarnished by others. Evil is always watching, seeking, waiting. It preys upon weak minds and cold hearts. It silently seeps its way into the smallest of openings, a tortured soul, and a hint of doubt. Evil is a cancer spreading its poison to everything it touches. Some embrace the evil, relish in it, become a servant to it, a pestilence. Others sit passively by, deem it necessary, and in doing so, help perpetrate it.

I read once something by Bodhidharma. "The ignorant mind, with its infinite afflictions, passions, and evils, is rooted in the three poisons. Greed, anger, and delusion."

My poison was delusion.

Tek Cain

Prospects

JAMIE STOOD outside the door to the boardroom—his ear pressed to the wood, straining to hear what was being said. The voices were muffled, but Jamie could pick up enough of the conversation to know they were discussing his and Gunner's fate.

The Crimson VIII motorcycle club was originally founded by Patrick—aka Gunner—Cain. Patrick had been a gunner with the 101st Airborne Division in World War II, hence his nickname. He'd learned what true loyalty and sacrifice meant in such places as the beaches of Normandy and in the trenches of Carentan and Bastogne. The original four members were all veterans and the club was named in memory of those who hadn't survived the war. Crimson spilt defending, sacrificing until the last drop of all eight pints was spent.

Jamie knew the history well. It had been a part of his life as well as that of his best friend Gunner—Patrick's namesake and great-grandson—since the day they were born. Born on the same day in fact; brought into the world on a Friday the thirteenth of July. Jamie was to be the older of the two, but a drive-by shooting that left Gunner's dad dead—a bullet in his head—had sent his mom into premature labor. Blood, violence, and death ushered him and Gunner into existence. Since day one in a shared bassinet, their lives had been planned out. Gunner was to rule and Jamie to protect the ruler, a job Jamie worried a lot about since. While the club was still all about loyalty and sacrifice, it had long ago moved away from its original roots. Running drugs and guns—and sex and violence—were now its main focus.

"They're not even eighteen yet."

Jamie wasn't sure whose voice that was, but apparently, someone wasn't happy about him and Gunner becoming prospects.

"These are not typical prospects off the street. This is Gunner and James we are talking about." Rocco's deep baritone voice was easily recognizable. "They were fucking born for this club."

"I agree," someone confirmed.

"Then we take it to a vote," Rocco said. "All those in favor."

One by one, Jamie listened as eleven of the thirteen members voted in favor of allowing him and Gunner to become prospects. Each "Aye" caused Jamie's heart to speed, and by the end he was sweating and breathless.

"Holy fuck," Jamie muttered under his breath. He and Gunner were officially prospects. The youngest prospects ever! *Gunner.* He had to call Gunner.

Jamie bolted out of the club, nearly knocking down some chick that was coming in. "Sorry," he apologized without slowing down. He fumbled in his pocket for his cell phone, pulled it out, and flipped it open—dialing as he slid behind the wheel of his truck.

"Holy fuck," he repeated. Prospect! He and Gunner were fucking prospects.

"This better be important," snapped Gunner through the phone line. He sounded breathless and irritated.

"Why? Since when do I have to have an important reason for calling you?" Jamie complained.

"Oh.... Um, Jamie, I'm kind of busy here."

"What the hell are you doing?" Jamie asked suspiciously.

Jamie's suspicion flared into anger when he heard a female voice in the background scream, "Oh my God. Seriously, Gunner! You had to answer the phone now?"

Something had shifted in Jamie when Gunner had kissed him over three years ago. Or perhaps it wasn't so much as shifted but fell into place. While Gunner was out trying to bang every chick that walked, Jamie found himself home at night fantasizing about smooth skin over taut muscular chests. It was the one and only thing he didn't share with his best friend. He couldn't. There were no homos in the club. Sully and his drag queens and orgies didn't count. He was a freak, and that was not a title Jamie would tolerate—freaks were not lieutenants.

"I was kind of in the middle of banging...." Gunner's voice was muffled as if he'd covered the phone with his hand. "What was your name again?"

There was no mistaking the outraged shriek of a female, and with it, the anger drained from Jamie. Whatever chick Gunner had in his bed obviously didn't mean anything to him. Jamie still felt the prickling sensation of jealousy; he couldn't help it. Knowing she meant nothing to Gunner, however, let Jamie still live in his fantasy of Gunner only banging girls because it was expected of him, not because he wanted to. That he'd rather be with him and only truly cared about Jamie.

"Hey, calm down, baby.... Put that down...."

Jamie snickered when the sound of Gunner grunting came through the phone. Obviously, what's-her-name had damn good aim. Jamie cradled the phone between his ear and shoulder and cranked the engine to life, smiling as he enjoyed the drama taking place on the other end of the phone.

"C'mon, baby, don't be mad. Hey! Where ya goin'?" Gunner's pleading voice was followed by a loud slam much like the sound of a door connecting with a doorframe. "Fuck you, bitch! Bros before hos," Gunner yelled.

Jamie laughed out loud and pulled the phone from his ear as Gunner cursed and shouted.

"It's not funny, you fucker." Gunner's voice was much clearer and lower through the phone line—apparently, he moved it back to his mouth and was addressing Jamie.

"You're right," Jamie agreed and put his truck in drive. "It's fucking hilarious!"

"I hate you," Gunner grumbled.

"No you don't. Now put your dick away and pay attention. I got some kickass news."

"Bend over, bitch, and I'll put it away. Right up to your fucking gut," Gunner growled. "Would serve you right for the blue balls you're causing me."

Jamie shook his head at his friend's remark. *If only you knew*. But he didn't say it out loud, instead he joked, "You're one sick bastard. Besides, you forget, I've seen your dick, it wouldn't reach."

"Yeah, yeah, yeah. So what's so important you had to interrupt my pussy poking?"

"We got the votes. You and I are the youngest prospects to ever join Crimson Eight."

"Fucking A, right?" Gunner hooted. "Well, that does call for a celebration. Get your ass over here! I got a six-pack and what's-her-name's friend's phone number. Party time!"

"Already on my way."

Jamie ended the call, threw his cell on the seat next to him, and stomped on the gas pedal. It was turning into an awesome night. Not only were he and Gunner going to be official club members, he'd kept his friend from sharing that hot body with anyone else. As he drove, he hummed along to the music with a smile. He didn't feel the least bit of guilt over the color of Gunner's balls.

So many things about a person can easily be changed: hair color, religious beliefs, political views, education, job, and the clothes they wear. Man has free will. Men can decide to be good men or bad men or something in between. Whether to have children, marry, fight, or walk away, the options are innumerable. But no matter how many changes we make, masks we wear, we cannot change nor hide from what we are at our core—our true selves. Sure, appetites can be subdued, but desire cannot be eradicated.

For too long, I tried to live a life being someone I wasn't, but I now realize I wasn't living. I was existing.

Tek Cain

Patched and Pussified

GUNNER STOOD naked, dripping wet from a hot shower, and studied his reflection in the full-length mirror. *Eighteen.* He certainly looked like an adult. He was built like his father. Tall, already hitting six foot three and still growing. If he reached his father's height, he'd end up six eight. Well-defined legs, broad chest and thick arms, he added to his size daily with a strict weight-lifting regiment. His longish blond hair and matching goatee also added to the appearance of being older. Gunner ran his hand over his goatee and smiled as he remembered Jamie laughing when he told Gunner he looked like a badass Jesus. His mood turned somber, smile falling as he thought about what he and Jamie would be doing tonight. Tonight, they'd become full-fledged members of Crimson VIII.

The last two years had stripped away the remaining shreds of innocence from Gunner. He'd seen and done shit as a prospect he wasn't proud of, but reminded himself they'd been necessary evils. When he'd taken the oath and slipped on his vest, he'd vowed to give all eight, every last drop of blood, for the club. Loyalty and sacrifice was his creed. The weight of that statement was already visible in his eyes, the same look he'd seen in Jamie's green eyes: the loss of innocence.

Turning from the mirror, Gunner grabbed his towel and ran it over his hair, then down his body. He tossed it to the floor and snatched up his jeans from the bed. They stuttered over his damp skin as he pulled them on—his T-shirt doing the same. Gunner wasn't too worried about his clothing for the evening festivities. He'd been witness to a number of patch parties, all of which ended in the newly inducted members being trashed and naked within a few hours. He didn't have any doubt he'd be in the same condition soon. With enough alcohol in his system, maybe he wouldn't care this time. Might actually enjoy it for a change.

Gunner's bedroom door flew open, causing him to jump and instinctively reach for his gun.

"You about ready to go?" Jamie asked, a big grin on his face as he stepped into Gunner's room.

"How many times have I told you to fucking knock?" Gunner grumbled and sat down on the edge of the bed, grabbed his tennis shoes, and slipped them on.

"Umm…." Jamie tilted his head, looked thoughtful for a second. "About a million," he responded with a smirk.

"One of these days you're going to end up with a bullet in your smart ass for barging in on people like that."

"Well then you'll need this," Jamie chuckled. He sat down next to Gunner, shoulders touching, and held out a cardboard box with a cheap red bow on it. "Here!"

"What is it?" Gunner asked, narrowing his eyes.

"A bomb. Now open the damn thing," Jamie huffed.

Gunner took the box, still staring at Jamie. He was dressed similar to Gunner, baggy jeans and white K-Swiss tennis shoes, but where Gunner's shirt was black, Jamie's was charcoal gray. Their sizes were almost identical as well, Jamie an inch taller at six foot four but their muscle mass nearly exact. The biggest difference between them was where Gunner's hair was a dirty blond color, Jamie's was dark brown, nearly black like his beard. And Gunner's eyes were a common, boring hazel color; Jamie's eyes were the most stunning shade of blue Gunner had ever seen. But he wasn't going to think about Jamie and stunning in the same thought. Those thoughts were dangerous.

Gunner turned his attentions back to the box, turning it over, examining it, and shaking it. Whatever was inside made a heavy thunk.

"Would you just open the damn thing? We have a party to attend."

Gunner gave a slight roll of his eyes and pulled the box open. "Holy shit! Where the fuck did you find this?" He hooted. Inside was a Tec-9 machine gun, the exact weapon he'd been coveting since he was like five.

"Sully hooked me up," Jamie said proudly. "Bastard actually does something besides fucking once in a while." He laughed.

Gunner carefully took the weapon out and tossed the box aside. The gun was a solid weight in his hand as he ran a finger over the cool steel. He palmed it, pointing it at the far wall, checked the sight.

"I fucking love it. Thank you."

"It fits you," Jamie murmured.

Gunner lowered the weapon and turned to face Jamie. Something in his friend's voice caught Gunner's attention; even more curious was the flush in Jamie's cheeks and the way he averted his eyes.

"What's that look for?" Gunner asked.

"What look?" Jamie asked without meeting Gunner's eyes.

Gunner set the gun on the bedside table and shifted on the bed, facing Jamie. "That one," he said, pointing at Jamie's pink cheeks. "We don't have secrets, so spill it."

"It's nothing."

"Good, then tell me," Gunner demanded and shoved Jamie's shoulder.

"I was thinking it's a good nickname for you, you know, Tek, 'cause you're way more than just a gun." Jamie shrugged, the color in his face deepening. "It's kind of stupid, I know."

"Tek," Gunner echoed. "I like it." He threw his arms around Jamie, squeezed him briefly, and then gave him a manly pat on the back. "Dude! That's two fucking awesome gifts you gave me. Best birthday ever!"

Jamie's brows shot up. "Yeah? You really gonna use it?"

"Hell yeah! Both the gun"—he picked up the weapon and pointed it once again at the far wall—"and the name! Tek is one bad mother fucker, just like me."

"I wouldn't go that far," Jamie sniffed.

"Whatever, dude. You know it's true. And tonight we're both gonna be bad sons a bitches when we get patched and pussified."

"Crude too," Jamie grumbled and rolled his eyes.

"Yup," Gunner said unapologetically and draped his arm over Jamie's shoulder. "And now for your birthday gift." He laid the gun on his lap, snatched up the envelope from the table, and handed it to Jamie.

"Oh, cool, an envelope, you shouldn't have," Jamie drawled sarcastically.

"Don't be an ass," Gunner retorted. "You and I, my friend, are getting our first ink done today."

"Seriously, you got me pain for my birthday? Wow and here all I got you was a gun."

"You can make it up to me later by buying the first round," Gunner teased. "C'mon, let's go!"

"What, now?" Jamie squeaked.

"No time like the present." Gunner released his hold on Jamie and got to his feet. He tucked the Tec-9 beneath his pillow; he'd come back for it later. He couldn't wait to show it off to the other guys. "You're not scared, are you?" Gunner asked, arching a brow. "Don't worry, baby, I'll hold your hand."

Jamie got up and headed out the door without a word, but his reply was obvious with the bird he flipped.

JAMIE LAY on his belly, head resting on his folded arms. Sweat ran down his temples, his gut churning and his back on fucking fire. The first couple of hours hadn't been so bad, but the fourth and fifth had been hell. It felt as if he had a really bad sunburn and some dumbass named Christian was slapping it over and over. A dumbass he so badly wanted to punch in the face, but he didn't dare move. He snuck a peek over to where Gunner lay. The bastard had his headphones on, a blissed-out expression on his face as the tattoo artist added ink to Gunner's broad back.

They had both chosen the club's name—Crimson VIII—in a gangsta style font as was tradition, in an arch from shoulder blade to shoulder blade. Beneath it, the club's logo—a skull with the handle of a blade sticking out of the top, blood dripping from the eye sockets, was surrounded by eight dice with the words "all eight" written in the same gangsta font below the gaping mouth of the skull. To complete the tattoo, each member was required to close the circle by adding something meaningful in a reversed arch. Jamie had chosen "Truth & Knowledge" for personal reasons he'd never reveal to anyone. Gunner had gone with "Cradle to Grave," a fitting sentiment as Gunner was born into the club and would die a leader.

However, at the moment, Jamie didn't care about tradition, clubs, or any such shit. He was in fucking pain, but there was no way in hell he would show any outward signs of it. He knew as soon as he did, Gunner would open his eyes and catch him. He'd been checking on Jamie every few moments since the torture had begun.

Jamie clenched his teeth and held his breath when the needle sawed across his lower back. The areas over the boney prominents of his spine were the hardest to take, and tension built in his muscles until he thought he would burst. His jaw ached, head pounded; an internal battle raged, his need to save face only slightly stronger than his need to cry out in pain, but he was wavering. Jesus, it fucking hurt! When he thought he couldn't take it another second, opened his mouth to utter the words that would stop the madness, he was saved by two sweet words he'd wanted to hear for the last five hours: "All done."

With a heavy sigh of relief, Jamie closed his eyes and slumped against the table, spent. His muscles twitched as a cool cloth was passed over his back. Compared to the fire of the tattoo gun against abused flesh, the cloth was soothing.

"You doing okay, Jamie?" Gunner asked.

Jamie couldn't even muster the strength to open his eyes, he just needed to breathe for a moment, but he forced himself to give a slight nod.

"That was a fucking rush!" Gunner declared.

Yeah, a rush.... Whatever. Jamie sleepily opened his eyes to see Gunner straddling the table, his freshly inked back to Jamie, but his friend was looking over his shoulder with a big goofy smile on his face. He met Jamie's gaze and winked.

Jamie's attention was caught by the movement of the white cloth over Gunner's back as the artist cleaned up Gunner's tat. The thick muscles were flexing and bulging, and heat rushed to Jamie's groin. He'd always found Gunner's body enticing, but with his skin now flushed with a black tattoo standing out in sharp contrast, there was only one word that fit the sight before him—intoxicating.

God, how he wanted to run his hands over Gunner's back, feel the heat against his palms, knead those bulging muscles. Trace each line of ink with his tongue, taste Gunner's skin. Jamie's dick grew increasingly harder, throbbing painfully against the weight of his body pressing it against the table. A small sensual sound escaped him before he could clamp down on it.

"I knew you were a pain slut," Gunner laughed. "Happy Birthday, dude!"

Shit! Jamie hid his lust-filled eyes by pushing up to a seated position, his back to Gunner. He flipped his friend off without turning around. Seemed that was his response to Gunner a lot lately. He had a hard time facing him, Gunner knowing him well enough to read his expressions, and he didn't trust that his voice wouldn't betray him by coming out husky.

"Wow! That is seriously wicked," Christian commented.

Jamie glanced behind him to see Christian inspecting Gunner's tattoo. Jamie took the opportunity to take a few calming breaths. He rolled his neck and shoulders and shook his arms out, trying to relieve a little of the tension that was so tightly coiled. He also adjusted his raging hard-on in his jeans and willed it to please go the fuck down.

"Looks good on you, Gunner," Christian praised.

"It's Tek," Gunner corrected him.

"What? Is that some new code name for kickass?" Johnny, the other artist, asked.

"Damn right it is," Gunner laughed. "My new nickname. Jamie gave it to me. And yeah, I am totally kickass."

"And modest too," Jamie interjected.

After one last deep breath, Jamie pushed up from the table, grabbed his shirt, and hung it from his belt, hiding the evidence of his arousal. If Tek saw it, he'd never let Jamie live it down, assuming he'd gotten a boner from ink. Actually he had, but from seeing it on Tek's sexy-as-fuck back. Either way, it would be bad for Jamie if his friend knew.

"Turn around, let me see," Tek encouraged.

Jamie did as Tek asked; standing next to Tek, he turned and presented his back.

Tek whistled. "Sweet! The chicks are going to be all over you tonight, man."

"I'm doing the doggie, my man. No way am I lying on my back tonight," Jamie deflected. He hated when Tek encouraged him to bang chicks, but he'd learned long ago just to go with it. Play it safe.

Jamie checked his watch—six fifteen. "You ready? We gotta be at the club in forty-five minutes."

Jamie thanked Christian, complimented Tek's artist, and then took his instructions and left Tek to settle up. Jamie stepped out of the shop and inhaled deeply. The warm summer wind felt cool against his sweat-dampened flesh. He was thankful for the few extra minutes to get his shit together. He was finding it harder and harder to hide his desire around Tek. He'd hoped it was a phase, like the hero envy he'd had for Batman when he was eight, but it was getting worse. Jamie scrubbed his hand over his face and rubbed at the throb that was settling into his forehead. Somehow he had to figure out how in the hell he was going to come to terms with the fact he was in love with his best friend. The bigger question was how in the fuck he was going to keep it hidden.

THE WHISKEY flowing through Tek's system had long burned off any discomfort he'd felt on his back. His body tingled pleasantly—his head a little swimmy. He sat on the old worn leather couch at the back of the club. He had the perfect vantage point to take in everything going on around him as he sipped his drink. The club was full, all the members drinking, laughing, playing pool, and having a good time. Plenty of chicks tonight too; some dancing, swaying sensually to the loud rock songs that blasted from the stereo, others clinging to the men, being felt up, kissing, and groping each other. And they were all here to celebrate with him and Jamie—the newest members of Crimson VIII.

Tek grinned and slammed back the rest of his whiskey. *Best fucking birthday, ever!*

Tek sought out Jamie, finding him leaning down to take his shot at the pool table. Jamie was the biggest reason their eighteenth birthday was so perfect. It wasn't just the sweet weapon or the kickass new nickname that the rest of the members approved of or even the matching tats inked across their backs, but because Jamie had been at his side. Setting his glass aside, Tek pushed up from the couch and made his way to the pool table just in time to see Jamie sink the eight ball and win the game.

"That's my boy," Tek praised and raised his hand to slap Jamie on the back.

"Don't you fucking dare," Jamie warned with a brow arched.

Tek yanked his hand back. "Oops, sorry, I keep forgetting," he chuckled. "Congrats." He held out his fist.

Jamie bumped Tek's fist with his own and grinned. "Fourth one in a row," he said proudly.

Tek took the cue stick out of his hand and handed it off to Sully who was grumbling something about Jamie cheating. "Time to give someone else a chance," Tek informed Jamie and slung his arm over his shoulder, mindful of the new ink.

He steered a frowning Jamie toward the bar. "I was—"

"Yeah, yeah, I know. Winning," Tek interrupted. "Best to always go out on top, my man. Besides, I want some attention. I was starting to get a little jealous of all those balls you were playing with." He planted a wet, sloppy kiss to Jamie's cheek and laughed at the way Jamie shoved him and glared at Tek.

Behind the bar, a hot little blonde with big tits spilling from her black leather bra was pouring drinks. She was fairly new to the club, but from the dull look in her blue eyes and lines around them, she wasn't new to the party scene. Tek guessed she was pushing thirty from some of the conversations he'd had with her earlier, but she looked older. Didn't matter, she had a smoking hot body. Obviously, what she didn't spend on booze or drugs, she spent on plastic. Better yet, with this one, he didn't have to try and sweet-talk her or make promises, bullshit her into thinking he liked her for more than just her wet hole. The younger girls irritated the hell out of him with their *tell me I'm pretty, do you really like me, are you going to call again.* None of that stupidity with Miss Big Tits. She'd already told him she'd love to give Tek a birthday present. The seductive tone of her voice left no question as to what she was offering as a gift. The cherry on the top was she had a friend who would love to give Jamie a *gift* as well.

"Hey, sweetheart, how about a drink for the birthday boys," Tek called out and gave her a sly grin he knew worked well with the chicks.

She grabbed two glasses and a bottle of Jack Daniel's and swished and swayed her way to Tek and Jamie. "But of course, darlings," she drawled, batting her long fake lashes. "*Anything* for the birthday boys."

The way she had emphasized *anything* made Tek's grin grow, and he waggled his brows at Jamie. "I got you hooked up," Tek whispered against Jamie's ear. "You want the blonde or that one?" Tek nodded toward blonde's friend at the other end of the bar.

She didn't have as an impressive rack or bod—she was tiny, barely any curves—but she was younger, cuter, with her long flowing dark curls and huge blue eyes. Tek could picture her with Jamie, neither of them seemed to have the hard edge Tek and the blonde chick did. And from their shared stories, Tek knew Jamie was nowhere near as fucked-up kinky as Tek was.

"Dude, I'm pretty sure I can find my own," Jamie hissed and grabbed the glass of whiskey the blonde set in front of him. Jamie took a large gulp and winced.

"I have no doubt you can," Tek assured him and picked up his whiskey. He clinked his glass against Jamie's. "But why turn down a feast when it's spread out in front of you?"

Tek tipped up his glass, drank down half in one large gulp. He loved the way it burned his throat, the way the heat moved down into his gut, warming him from the inside out. Without giving Jamie time to protest or back out, Tek winked at the blonde. "How about you find someone else to work the bar and you and your friend come hang with me and my boy here in the back for a little while?"

"No need," she purred. "Rocco already informed me I was to make sure the birthday boys had a good time and give them whatever they wanted." She topped off Tek's drink and then Jamie's. "I'm all yours."

"And your friend?" Tek inquired.

The blonde set her hands on the bar and leaned forward, putting her impressive tits on display. "Sure, or you both could have all this. It's all about your pleasure."

Another dirty little whore willing to do whatever it took to win favor with the club president. Tek shook his head; he didn't care, and he would be using her for much of the same reason, no guilt. Tek knew what he preferred. The thought of he and Jamie tag-teaming a chick was something he'd thought about, not as often as.... Well, he wasn't going to go there. With the amount of whiskey in his system, he wasn't sure how well he'd be able to keep those desires hidden. But if they were with the same girl and he just so happened to get a good feel of Jamie's skin, taste it, he could blame it on the moment, the close contact. But would Jamie go for it?

Tek glanced over to his friend. Jamie's cheeks were red, and he was looking down at his glass. Jamie had never had much confidence with women, turning them down more times than he accepted their offers. Tek could use that to his advantage in getting what he wanted; he was simply going to help a friend, boost his confidence with sex. *Yeah, that's it, you sick fucker.* Tek ignored the little voice in his head. He felt too good, full of warmth and desire to let this opportunity pass.

"I say we do her in the shower, that way we can wash off that bottle of sweet shit she bathed in. Sound good?" Tek whispered against Jamie's ear.

Jamie swallowed hard, Tek's gaze drawn to the movement. This close he could see the muscles twitch in Jamie's jaw as he clenched, smell the alcohol, clean sweat, and cologne on Jamie's skin. Jamie wasn't looking at him, but Tek could tell he was thinking about it, saw the thoughtful expression in his handsome features.

"C'mon," Tek encouraged. "Let's show this little chick the time of her fucking life."

Jamie swirled the dark amber fluid in his glass, staring at the movement for a second, then tipped it up and gulped down the contents in one drink. He then slammed the glass down on the bar and met Tek's gaze.

"Let's do it," he growled and headed toward the back room.

"Tonight is your lucky night, sweetheart. Let's go," he said with a wink and followed Jamie.

TEK BEGAN washing the dark blonde locks the instant they were under the spray, no doubt trying to wash away the scent he'd complained about earlier. Jamie had zero desire to touch this chick, let alone bang her, but he needed to do something to keep his eyes and his mind from settling on Tek's naked form. It had been pure fucking torture trying not to watch Tek's firm ass as he entered the shower, even harder to keep his eyes averted while the sexy fucker rolled the condom down the length of his impressive shaft. The few glances Jamie had gotten were the only reason he had a hard-on in the first place. He was finding it more and more difficult to… rise to the occasion with a girl.

Jamie grabbed the soap and washed her chest and stomach. The spray washed away the suds until only the water sluiced down her body. Seizing on the distraction, Jamie leaned in and chased the water droplets rolling down her body with his tongue. Down her collarbone to the swell of her breasts, he lapped at her skin until he reached her hardened nipple. He teased one with the tip of his tongue before sucking it into his mouth. It felt strange, too big, compared to the size of Tek's nipples, the ones Jamie had been fantasizing about teasing and tasting. A deep moan as he sucked on the tender flesh caused him to look up. They both stared at him as he suckled, but it was Tek's heated gaze that made Jamie's hard shaft swell even further until he felt as if the skin would split.

"God, that's hot," Tek groaned.

Fuck yeah, it was hot, but he doubted for the same reason Tek thought. He loved having Tek's gaze on him, and without dropping his eyes, he moved across the chick's chest—he still didn't know her name and didn't care—and lavished the other tight nub with teeth and tongue.

There was no way in hell Jamie was going to go any farther down her body. Instead, he pulled off the nipple with a pop and waggled his brows at Tek. "Want a taste?"

"Fuck yeah!" Tek smirked.

Jamie stood up and turned the chick around in his arms, encouraged her to lean back against him without ever taking his eyes off Tek. Jamie grabbed her thighs, spreading them wide as Tek made his way down her body, going to his knees, licking and sucking at her tender flesh. Jamie couldn't stand it; he closed his eyes, imagined Tek going to his knees for him. Tek's lips wrapped around Jamie's cock, the wicked tongue working his flesh. The image sent a thrill racing down Jamie's spine, and he began thrusting against her, pushing her harder against Tek's mouth.

Blondie's whimpers turned to long drawn-out moans, the sound grating on Jamie, ruining his fantasy. He opened his eyes in time to see Tek working his fingers inside her passage, twisting and stroking. A flare of jealousy raced through Jamie, but he clamped down on it. This had been a bad fucking idea, and suddenly, he just wanted it over.

Jamie changed the position of his hands, gripped her thighs, lifted her up off the shower floor and spread her even wider so her legs were draped over his forearms. Tek sat back on his heels, continuing to pump his fingers in and out, but Jamie's jealousy wavered. Tek kept his gaze on Jamie, his eyes dark with lust, and the change in position had exposed Jamie's cock to Tek, who slid his fingers along the top of it. The image before him, the feeling of Tek touching him, nearly knocked Jamie on his ass, it was so powerful.

Without warning, Tek rolled to his feet, and in one swift movement, he removed his fingers and thrust deep inside Blondie. Jamie's cock slid along Tek's sac with each thrust, causing Jamie's eyes to roll back in his head.

"Son of a bitch," Jamie grunted as he was shoved against the tile wall as Tek began to snap his hips with more force.

Tek placed a hand on either side of Blondie and Jamie's head and locked eyes with Jamie. "Best fucking birthday ever, man," Tek groaned and emphasized each word with a hard thrust.

Jealousy and defiance raged in Jamie, mixing and battling with lust and need. Each movement of Tek's body forced Blondie's ass back against Jamie at the perfect angle to ensure that each thrust forced Jamie's hard cock against Tek's balls. The jealousy and defiance was quickly replaced until only the lust and hunger remained.

Jamie stared into those black eyes; his own need pushed higher and higher. His cock was against Tek's sac, the chick forgotten, lost in Tek's lust-filled gaze. Jamie fought to hold back the orgasm rushing down his spine. He was determined to keep his eyes open, wanted to see the pleasure on Tek's face as he fell over the edge into orgasm. Christ, how he wanted to kiss that sexy mouth. Shove his tongue past those full lips, taste him again.

Tek doubled his efforts, thrusting hard and fast into Blondie, the rhythm increasing the friction on Jamie's cock. He wasn't sure he could take much more before he lost it—his cock so fucking hard it was going to burst, his sac full and heavy from the dual stimulation.

"Oh fucking hell," Tek grunted as his spine arched and his head fell back as he gave in to his orgasm.

The blissed-out look on Tek's face, the silky skin of his balls against Jamie's dick ripped his release out of him so suddenly that it consumed every fiber of his being. He could only give in to the pleasure and ride it out as he bathed Tek's balls with each pulse of his orgasm. That was the closest he'd ever gotten to his fantasy, the closest he'd ever dared to get.

It's amazing the cruelties one man can inflict upon another. It's been my experience that next to religious beliefs, the greatest acts of cruelty are done in the name of honor. One man steals from you, you cut off his hand. One dares to step on your turf, you take out his knees. Loss of a tongue the punishment for taking food from your family. The ultimate sin, putting a hand on someone you love, threatening them, the payment is blood and brain matter scattered across a flithy warehouse floor.

When did violence become the norm and the turn-the-other-cheek mentality become the rarity? When did we begin viewing men with the courage to walk away, to be the better man, as nothing more than weak? Has it always been this way? Will it always be this way? Why did I become one of the masses rather than a rarity of courage?

Tek Cain

Gone Cold

CIGARETTE CLENCHED between his teeth, wind blowing his hair back, Tek flew down the darkened highway; the lights of the city in the distance beckoned him. He loved the feel of his hog beneath him, the way it vibrated with power, as it ate up the pavement—the freedom of the road.

The brake lights of the lead bikes flashed red, and Tek eased off the gas. He followed Rocco and Sully, Jamie on his hog to Tek's right, onto the gravel road. The feel-good moment of the open road was washed away with adrenaline as Tek's pulse began to race. This was to be an easy hit, get in, grab the guns, set the C-4 and bye-bye Westside Bangers' warehouse.

The Bangers had been a thorn in the Crimson VIII's side for too fucking long. They'd started out as nothing more than some wannabe gang, running a petty dope operation. No real threat. The club had kept a close eye on them as their numbers began to grow, but as long as they didn't interfere with Crimson VIII Motorcycle club biz, the bastards could grow all the dope they wanted. Fucking potheads were worthless. The law within the MC had zero tolerance for members who did any kind of drugs. Rocco had the club running meth and heroine for about ten years; it had been a very profitable business. But in the end, the loss became too great. They'd lost more members to overdose and pickled brains than they'd ever lost to bullets. When Tek was fifteen, Rocco outlawed all drugs. Members could drown in pussy, drink booze till it was pouring out their arses, but no drugs.

Had the Bangers stuck with smoking, munching, and giggling they would have been fine, but the dumb fucks had to go and get greedy. They just had to start cutting into Crimson VIII's profit. Rocco assured Tek and the others that the run tonight was nothing more than a message. However, Tek knew firsthand how quickly shit could turn ugly. He had a bad feeling in the pit of his stomach as they parked the bikes in the woods.

Rocco crouched down near the end of his bike and pointed at Sully and Jamie and then toward the west side of the warehouse. He then pointed at Tek and gave the hand signal for 'on me.' Tek gritted his teeth against the protest that wanted out as he watched Jamie move off into the dark with Sully. He understood Rocco's reasoning—a veteran with a younger member—but it just didn't sit right with Tek. Jamie was his responsibility.

Tek pulled the Beretta 90-TWO from his waistband at the small of his back and pushed the safety lever into the "fire" position as he followed Rocco to the east. Tek's attention was only half on Rocco as he watched Jamie's familiar form move off to the west. Tek's unease grew. He didn't trust anyone to have his back other than Jamie, and Tek hated not being able to have Jamie's. They were a team, a constant, one incomplete without the other. Still, he pushed the anxiety down, focused on the task at hand. Get in and get out as quickly as possible. The sooner they got this shit done, got back to the clubhouse, Jamie safe, the better Tek would feel.

Rocco came to a stop behind a small group of trees. He pointed two fingers toward his eyes and then to the front door of the warehouse where a lone figure stood smoking. Tek nodded. They'd done recon, and these yahoos never had more than two men on guard duty. No doubt the other was somewhere munching Cheetos. Fuck, Tek hated dopeheads. They were unpredictable.

They eased their way around to the side of the warehouse, Tek's senses hyperaware of his surroundings. The pack on his back was filled with explosives—a solid weight. Constantly scanning the area, Tek strained to listen for sounds within, but it was difficult with the roar of blood in his ears as his heart hammered painfully.

Rocco made a fist, indicating to Tek to stop, and then the president pointed toward a window. Once again Tek nodded in understanding. He tucked his gun back into his waistband and pulled out his blade. Slowly, he eased up from his crouching position, having to trust Rocco to keep an eye out for intruders, and carefully worked at the lock on the window. He was in a vulnerable position; the glass covered in heavy tinting didn't allow Tek to see inside, but anyone from within the warehouse would have a clear visual of him. Tek let out a sigh of relief when the lock gave. He flipped the blade closed and stuffed it into his pocket, then once again grabbed his gun, thumb sliding over the safety.

Tek glanced at Rocco who gave him a curt nod. *Here we go.* Tek eased up the window, finger on the Beretta moving to the trigger, expecting the blaring sound of an alarm. Nothing. *Gotta love druggies.* Tek smirked and pushed the window wide open.

The warehouse that once housed a small upholstery business was now littered with junk cars, boxes, and rubbish. The cloying scent of musk, mold, and gasoline filled Tek's nostrils. A single low-wattage bulb hung from wires near the front door, the rest of the interior dark and in shadow. Tek scanned the area the best he could and listened for any sounds that would alert him to anyone's presence. All was silent and still.

Easing back down to a crouching position and facing Rocco, Tek whispered, "I don't like it. It's too quiet."

"Did you get a visual on the other guy?" Rocco inquired.

Tek shook his head.

"Probably napping," Rocco surmised. "Let's go."

Tek pointed his weapon first to one end of the warehouse and then the other as Rocco made his way in through the open window, before following. They stayed to the shadows, making their way to the back of the building to hook up with Sully and Jamie.

Tek's trepidation grew, his stomach clenching when they arrived at the rendezvous spot with no signs of the other members. From his vantage point behind a large crate, Tek studied the west side of the building, searching out a familiar form. *C'mon, you crazy son of a bitch. Where are you?*

Tek jerked when Rocco tapped him on the shoulder and whispered, "Set the charges."

Tek bit down on the angry snarl of protest that was poised on his lips. Fuck the explosives. Fuck the Bangers. Fuck the guns and the mission and profit and…. Tek stole another glance to the west, willed his friend to appear, but the warehouse stayed still and silent. *Goddammit, Jamie, where are you?*

Obviously knowing what Tek was stressing about, Rocco patted Tek's shoulder. "Get it set and we'll go find them," Rocco assured him.

"Watch for them," Tek demanded, not caring he was ordering around the pres. Fuck him too.

With trembling hands, Tek removed the pack from his back and pulled out the C-4. He had enough material to leave nothing but a crater in the wake of the explosion. If he could just get his fucking hands to work. *Where the hell is Jamie?* Tek clamped down on his fear, pushed it out of his head. He needed to focus on the job, get in and get out.

"Hurry up," Rocco hissed.

Tek was about to tell Rocco to fuck off, but he bit his tongue. The pres was right. Tek set the charges, dumped the pack, and stuffed the detonator in his pocket, careful not to hit the switch. Getting his ass blown into a million little pieces wasn't part of the plan tonight. Tek rejoined Rocco in his hiding spot behind the crates and gave him a thumbs-up.

A loud crash and blinding lights disoriented Tek for a moment. He stared at the front of the building where the disturbance came from. He shielded his eyes from the high beams on the truck that had crashed through the doors. He caught up quickly however when four men jumped out of the truck and bullets began whizzing by his head.

"Told you this looked too fucking easy," Tek snarled at Rocco as they dove for cover.

"I hate party crashers," Rocco growled.

Tek dodged and weaved, following behind Rocco and hoping like hell the sons of bitches chasing him didn't get lucky and hit their mark. Behind a rusted-out old truck, Tek stopped long enough to return fire, unloading all ten shots and switching clips as he moved. Rocco gave covering fire.

Tek wasn't afraid; the rush of adrenaline surging through him was all about survival. He had no time for fear. His pulse was thumping, sweat rolling down his spine, but his focus was narrowed. Looking ahead to the next hidden spot, aware of Rocco, the assholes behind him, and his weapon, there was no room for anything else in his head.

So focused on the next move, Tek wasn't aware that the gunfire had ceased until he slipped behind another junk car and trained his weapon on the area he'd just come from. Nothing. The roar of the truck engine was still loud in the room, but nothing else. No one screaming, no blasts of gunfire. Tek's brow dipped, and he shot a questioning look at Rocco who was crouched next to him.

"I saw them both go down," Rocco assured him.

"Where the hell did the other two go?"

Rocco nodded to the west.

Jamie!

Tek's grip tightened on his weapon, and without a thought for his own safety, he started to move to the west side of the warehouse.

Rocco grabbed the back of Tek's jacket, halting him. "Where are you going?"

Tek glared at Rocco and yanked free. He was on a mission.

"Will you at least stay the fuck down," Rocco pleaded. "Your mom will have my balls if I let something happen to you."

"Then you better watch my back," Tek countered, but he did follow Rocco's orders to stick to the shadows and cover of the various cars, boxes, and machinery. He'd be no good to Jamie if he got a bullet in his head.

Tek stepped around a piece of junk, and his heart stopped in his chest along with his breath. Jamie was on his knees, hands behind his head, and some motherfucker who was about to die had the barrel of a gun pressed to Jamie's temple. Tek saw red.

Just as he started to rush to Jamie's side, his shirt was yanked back and a hand clamped over his mouth. He was going to rip Rocco to shreds.

"Stop! You'll get yourself killed," Rocco hissed against Tek's ear.

"I don't care. Let me go. I have to get to him," Tek snarled, the words muffled by Rocco's palm.

"A bullet will pass through his head and his brains will be splattered on the wall before you can make it halfway there," Rocco said dangerously low against Tek's ear, and he released Tek and shoved him. "So go on, get your stupid ass killed right along with your boy."

Pain ripped through Tek's chest, the agony driving him to his knees. The sobering reality of Rocco's words enough to cut through the fog of rage, and Tek stopped struggling. The image of Jamie with a gun to his head, what that bullet could do was forever seared into Tek's mind. He was trembling, breathless, and so goddamn scared. But he couldn't give in to it. He had to shut down his emotions. There was no place for fear, anger, dread, or love. His heart rate returned to normal, his breath slowed, even the trembling in his limbs ceased as he pushed away all emotion. Locked it down in his gut behind his ironclad determination to save Jamie. He needed to concentrate, form a plan. Tek went cold.

"I know you're in here, mother fuckers," one of Jamie's captors called out. "Show yourselves or your club is going to be less two members."

Tek peeked around the corner. He'd been so focused on Jamie he'd forgotten Sully was with him. He spotted the other brother, also on his knees with a gun to his head. Tek couldn't see Jamie's face, but he could tell by the way Jamie was holding himself he was scared, his muscles tense and bulging. The picture was completely unlike Sully, whose face Tek could see. Sully was downright pissed.

Sully was a loose wire; perhaps insane was a better term. Tek had never seen fear on Sully's face, doubted the stupid fucker had enough sense to be scared. It was only a matter of time before the crazy bastard got tired of being on his knees; his boredom would get someone killed. More than likely Jamie, since no matter the shit that went down, Sully always came out smelling like a rose. Well, Tek didn't care if Sully came out smelling like a fucking rose garden. Tek would be damned if he'd let Jamie fertilize it. But he couldn't see a way to get them out of there without surrendering, which would be suicide. Tek wasn't stupid. He knew if they showed themselves and gave up their weapons, all four of them would be dead. It's what would happen to anyone who stepped on their turf and tried to take over something that belonged to the Crimson VIII.

Tek turned and glared at Rocco. "This was your fucking idea, now how the hell are we going to get them out of this mess?"

"We go back the way we came and get the fuck out of here is what we do," Rocco growled. "Dumbasses got themselves captured by dopers. They're on their own."

Before Tek could even think about the consequences, his hand shot out and he tightened it around Rocco's throat. "You run and I will kill you myself."

Rocco's brows shot up, his eyes going wide, but the shock only lasted a second before he smirked. "I knew you had big balls. Guess we're going with plan B."

"Damn right we are," Tek snarled. He wasn't impressed with the tease or the test or whatever Rocco thought he was doing. He didn't have time for bullshit. Every second that barrel was at Jamie's head was a second something could go wrong. Unacceptable.

Tek didn't wait for Rocco to come up with a plan. Tek had one of his own.

"You're going to go that way," Tek informed Rocco. "You're going to make your way around to the other side of them and scream, jump up and down, do a fucking hula, I don't care. Just cause a distraction. Make it loud." Tek released his hold on Rocco and turned back to check on Jamie and Sully.

"And what the hell are you going to do?" Rocco inquired, sounding skeptical.

Tek didn't care if Rocco had confidence in him or not. Tek knew what he had to do. More importantly, what he was willing to do. He let the cold he'd experienced earlier seep through him, welcomed it as it settled his nerves and brought him a strange kind of peace.

"I'm going to go make some dopers pay," he said adamantly. He and Jamie were either walking out of this place or taking a one-way ticket to hell; whichever the outcome, they were going together. "Now go."

Rocco studied him for a moment, searched Tek's eyes. Tek didn't blink, nor did he waver in his conviction. Obviously, Rocco saw it or realized it was a solid plan; hell, maybe he couldn't think of a better plan.

Whatever conclusion Rocco came to, he nodded and held out his fist. "All eight."

Tek bumped his fist against Rocco's. "All eight."

Rocco brought his gun to his lips and, with one last nod at Tek, headed back the way they'd come. Tek turned his attention back to Jamie and his captors. The asshole holding the gun on Jamie looked twitchy, constantly scanning the area, and Tek hoped like hell Rocco would make it quick. The other doper, the one with the gun on Sully, must have gotten high before they'd arrived. He looked bored.

"I'm going to give you to the count of ten," Twitchy yelled out, still scanning the area.

Good, the ass still didn't have any idea where he and Rocco were. Hopefully, that would play in their favor.

"One."

Tek checked his weapon.

"Two."

Tek trained his gaze on the back of Jamie's head, pulled his knife from the sheath on his hip.

"Three."

Three. Four. Five. Each number ticked off was like a lightning strike to Tek's soul. The urge to rush out into the opening and drop his weapon was huge, but somehow he managed to swallow it down. The panic and need tasted like a poisonous sludge that burned his throat and gut.

"Six."

Tek's muscles coiled, ready to spring, his eyes glued to the gun on his friend.

"Seven."

At nine he would show himself. No way would he let the fucker get to ten and pull the trigger.

"Eight."

"Oh shut the fuck up!" Rocco bellowed, gun trained on Jamie's captor. "If you were going to shoot him you would have already done so, you stupid cunt."

"Drop the weapon, or I'll prove just how wrong you are. This piece of shit means nothing to me," the doper spat.

Tek gritted his teeth, his hand tightening on the handle of the blade as the doper shoved Jamie's head with the barrel of the gun. Tek had to hold on to the coldness for just a few more minutes, keep the rage in check until his hands were on the mother fucker who'd dared to threaten Jamie.

Tek watched intently as Rocco lowered his weapon but didn't drop it. His gaze scanned back and forth between the two rivals.

"Drop your weapon and lace your fingers behind your head. Do it! Do it now!" Twitchy screamed.

Bored Guy no longer seemed so out of it. He inched his way around behind Sully, the gun to Sully's head and his gaze on Rocco. *Good!* Tek figured he had mere seconds to put his plan into action. As long as Rocco kept them distracted, they had a shot of all four of them coming out of this alive.

Rocco held up his free hand in surrender and slowly set the gun on the floor. "I dropped it. Now take those goddamn guns away from their heads."

"You're in no position to tell me what to do," Twitchy sneered. "Now, hands behind your head."

Rocco did as he was ordered, and the moment his hands were behind his head, Twitchy made the mistake of aiming his weapon at Rocco. Tek moved. Keeping low and silent, Tek inched closer, scarcely breathing.

"Happy now?" Rocco taunted.

"Now tell your partner to step out, or the club is going to be looking for a new president."

"Your dumb fucks got a lucky shot and took him out," Rocco accused. "But I got my revenge, and they'll soon be joined by your rotting carcass if you don't turn my boys loose."

Tek saw Jamie stiffen when he heard Rocco confess to Tek's death. Tek could only hope Jamie was smarter than Tek was. If their places were reversed, Tek had no doubt he'd already have lunged for the bastard and ripped his throat out, demand an eye for an eye. *Keep talking, Rocco.* Tek crept up behind a garbage can, ignoring the banter between Rocco and Twitchy, his focus narrowed down to nothing but his goal.

If Twitchy or Bored turned their heads now, he was a dead man or worse.... No, he wasn't going to think of that. Tek ripped his gaze from Jamie and looked toward Sully, who was watching Rocco with interest, a thoughtful look on his face. *C'mon, Sully, turn your head,* Tek pleaded silently. He just needed the man to notice him, and this would all be over.

It felt like forever, but in reality was probably only a few seconds before Sully finally looked Tek's way. Tek nodded toward the man holding Sully, and Sully grinned, then blinked his eyes, obviously comprehending what Tek wanted him to do. Tek sheathed the knife, no longer having to worry about taking Bored out silently. Tek got into position and held up three fingers, lowering one at a time, and as he dropped the last one, Tek lunged.

Bored screamed, causing Twitchy to take his concentration off Rocco, but it was too late. Tek had his hand wrapped around Twitchy's wrist, twisting and rendering him unable to shoot at anyone; with his other hand, he brought his weapon up to Twitchy's head.

"Your first mistake was counting," Tek snarled. "Now drop the gun." He shoved the barrel hard against Twitchy's temple, emphasizing the seriousness of his words.

Bored continued to scream in agony. Tek didn't dare take his focus off Twitchy long enough to see what Sully had done to the man. Tek didn't care. The coldness dissipated, burned off by the fire of rage. This asshole had dared to touch Jamie.

The distinct sound of metal hitting the concrete floor alerted Tek to the fact that Twitchy had followed his orders, and relief surged through Tek. The four of them would be making it out of there after all.

"You lying bastard," Jamie howled at Rocco as he picked up Twitchy's gun. "I should shoot you my damn self for making my heart stop like that!"

"Like what?" Rocco asked with a shrug.

"Don't you ever kid about Tek being dead," Jamie snapped and then turned his gaze on Tek. The fear, sadness, and pain still swirling in Jamie's eyes made Tek's breath hitch.

"It worked," Rocco said unapologetically and moved over to inspect the man writhing in pain.

"It's okay, Jamie, I'm fine," Tek said gently. "Did this piece of shit hurt you?"

Jamie shook his head. "I heard the gunfire, and I tried to get to you. I forgot to watch my back. I'm so sorry, Tek."

"Jesus, I had heard you two were fucking fags for each other," Twitchy spat.

Tek stiffened.

"Next time I catch you with your back to me, I'll make sure my gun is up your ass rather than against your head."

The rage that had been burning in his gut roared and raced through Tek's system. The thought of this man ever getting another chance at Jamie consumed him, and he whispered, "There won't be a next time."

He pulled the trigger.

Tek's ears rang with the explosion of bullet to flesh as he let the dead man slump to the ground without taking his gaze from Jamie's. There was no room inside him for remorse, no care for the man at his feet. He would remove any and all threats to keep Jamie safe.

Lies and secrets are the only way wrongdoers can continue to thrive. Born into a brotherhood, I was taught loyalty and sacrifice. I've discovered they are only pretty words to mask the ugly truth. No matter how you say them, wrap them up in a pretty bow of honor, they are still lies and secrets. I was no better. I was a believer in the pretty words, the fancy dressing. I thought that some things were best kept secret.

I was wrong.

With secrets there is always guilt. The very word secrecy means evasion: evasion of truth?

The guilty conscience needs to confess and as I've learned— should.

Tek Cain

Confessions

CLEANING UP the mess at the warehouse had been easy. Jamie had helped Sully gather and load all the weapons they could find while Rocco had sent the sole survivor of the Bangers back to his club with a warning and Sully's knife still stuck in his nut sac. The explosion Tek had set made sure the only evidence the authorities would find was twisted wreckage and dirt.

Cleaning up the emotional shit Tek was dealing with wasn't going to be as easy. Tek had been silent and brooding since they returned from the warehouse. Jamie had watched him closely as they all sat around the table and clued the other members in as to what went down. Jamie hadn't listened to a word being said—didn't care, his concern for Tek his only focus. Jamie wanted to wrap his arms around Tek, assure him everything would be okay, wipe the crease away that marred Tek's brow, and do anything to remove that haunted look from Tek's eyes. But he couldn't. Not here. Not in front of the others. So he waited. His gut churning and chest aching, he waited, praying the debriefing would be over soon.

The second they were excused, Jamie jumped to his feet and whispered to Tek, "You going to be okay?"

Tek nodded, then turned and walked out of the room.

"Tek."

Tek kept moving through the club, his stride lacking the confidence it normally had, ignoring Jamie.

"C'mon, man, talk to me," Jamie pleaded, rushing to keep up with his friend.

"I'm fine," Tek muttered, but his voice sounded flat.

"Bullshit," Jamie scolded, pushing his way into Tek's room when he tried to close the door behind him. "You look like shit, and if you don't get it off your chest, it's only going to eat at you."

"I blew an unarmed man's brains out," Tek snarled and whipped off his bloody T-shirt, then threw it across the room. "There, it's off my chest. Now leave me alone."

"The fuck I will," Jamie countered. "I'm the reason you had to do it in the first place, so if anyone deserves the fault in this, it's me."

"You didn't pull that trigger. That was all on me." Tek sat on the bed and pulled off his shoes, tossing them in the same direction as his discarded shirt. Tek suddenly went still, the anger seeming to drain out of him as he stared at his hands. "I need a shower," he said quietly.

Jamie couldn't stand to see his friend like this, and he gave in to the urge he'd been fighting for the last two hours. He sat on the bed next to Tek and wrapped an arm around him, pulling him close.

"I would have done the same thing," Jamie told him gently. "Had he put a gun to your head, dared to threaten you, I'd have pulled that trigger without question."

"It's not supposed to be like this," Tek responded sadly. "We're... We...." Tek lifted his eyes and met Jamie's gaze. "Jesus, Jamie, it's not supposed to be like this."

"Yes, it is," Jamie reassured him. "We protect our brothers, no matter the cost. He was a threat to all of us."

"Brotherhood," Tek laughed, the sound full of bitterness, and he shook his head. "I...." Tek clamped his mouth shut and lowered his head.

Tek stared at his hands with a sad expression on his face. The emotions playing across Tek's features clawed at Jamie's heart. He understood why Tek had done it, but it was Tek who had to carry the scar of the death on his soul. It was Tek who would have to learn to live with the wound without it festering, or it would destroy him. Tek was a good man, brave and honorable, and this single act of violence didn't change that. Jamie tried to think of something to say that would make this all better. He wished there was a magic word he could utter that would take Tek's pain from him, but there were none.

Tek tried to get up, but Jamie refused to release his hold on him. "Talk to me, Tek. No secrets, remember?"

Jamie felt like a fool for uttering those words considering the secrets he was keeping from Tek, but this was different. Tek didn't need to have to deal with his best friend wanting him in ways Jamie knew were impossible. It would serve no purpose but to put a strain on their relationship.

"I need a shower. I… I need to wash my hands," Tek stammered, but he stopped trying to pull away.

Jamie tightened his hold on Tek, pulled him closer. "Not until we talk about this."

"I can't," Tek mumbled. "Not about this."

"No one is going to think less of you for pulling that trigger. You heard Rocco tonight, he was proud of you. You saved me and Sully."

"It's not just the shooting, Jamie. I mean, it is, but…." Tek wrung his hands, still staring at them.

"Is it about what he said? You know, about us being fags?" Jamie asked cautiously. "He was trying to provoke you, Tek, nothing more." *And I promise from here on out to keep my feelings for you in check.* He wouldn't put Tek at risk.

"Do you think anyone in our club thinks the same way?"

"No! They know how close we are, Tek. They know we are more than best friends, more like brothers."

Uttering the word *brother* felt offensive to Jamie considering how he felt about Tek—the things he wanted from him, the things he wanted to do to him were anything but brotherly. It made him the worst kind of sick bastard, but if he could ease Tek's mind with the lie then it would be worth it.

The same bitter-sounding laugh escaped Tek. He rested his forearms on his knees, hands clasped and whispered, "I'm so sorry, Jamie."

Jamie went to his knees in front of Tek and rubbed his hands up and down his friend's arms. "Dammit, Tek, there is nothing for you to apologize for."

"I thought I was hiding it better.... If I.... I didn't mean for.... I tried not to," Tek stammered. He lifted his eyes and met Jamie's gaze. "I'm so sorry, Jamie," he repeated.

The pain evident was so raw it stole Jamie's breath. "Hide what? Tek, what the hell are you talking about?" Jamie asked in confusion.

"It's my fault if they think you're a fag," Tek confessed, sounding defeated.

Jamie's head was swirling. No matter how he tried to understand what Tek was saying, what he was apologizing for, it just didn't make sense. How could Tek think it was his fault?

"I thought if I banged enough chicks," Tek continued, "If I showed everyone what a ladies' man I was, immersed myself in enough pussy, no one would suspect. I tried, Jamie. I swear to God I tried, but it's not going away. No matter what I do, it just won't fucking go away."

"It's my fault if they think you're a fag." Tek's declaration played over and over in Jamie's head as he continued to stare at Tek. *"No one would suspect."* Was it possible? Did Jamie dare to think? Dare to hope? Was it even fucking conceivable that they both had been keeping the same dark secret from the other?

Before he could think about the what or why of what he was doing, Jamie grabbed Tek's face in both his hands. "I should have done this six years ago," he murmured.

"What the hell, Jamie? Done what?"

"Returned your kiss." Jamie pressed his lips against Tek's.

Tek stiffened against Jamie, but Jamie had gone too far to back down now. If Tek beat the shit out of him or never spoke to him again... he was going to make damn well sure the kiss was worth it. Jamie licked at Tek's bottom lip, encouraging him to respond, praying he would. Six years of want, desire, and need rushed to the surface; the intensity of it overwhelmed Jamie, and without waiting for an invitation, he shoved his tongue past Tek's lips. A needy sound rumbled up out of Jamie as he tasted Tek's mouth, the warm wet heat consuming him.

Tek stayed stiff against him, but he wasn't pulling away, wasn't shoving or swinging, and Jamie found encouragement in Tek's nonaction. Jamie slid one hand around Tek's face, grabbed the back of his head, his fingers curling, gripping the soft strands as he smashed their mouths closer together, deepening the kiss.

Tek began to tremble. Jamie could feel his muscles coiling tighter, tighter, and tighter, and then in a rush, as if Tek could no longer hold himself back when they'd reached the breaking point, he grabbed onto Jamie and fisted Jamie's shirt to pull him closer still. To Jamie's great relief, Tek kissed him back—his tongue battling alongside Jamie's as they both fought to control the kiss.

On and on the kiss went as they explored each other's mouths. Jamie couldn't think of anything that had ever felt so perfect, so right. Tek's mouth on his, the desire and need he tasted on Tek's tongue were like little sparks of electricity that ignited every nerve ending in Jamie's body, consuming him until Tek suddenly pulled back, leaving them both breathless and staring at the other with mirrored shocked expressions on their faces.

"How?" Tek licked his lips and shuddered. "What the hell just happened, Jamie?"

Jamie started to laugh. He couldn't help it. Tek wasn't swinging, wasn't shoving Jamie away in disgust; in fact, Tek looked as relieved as Jamie felt. "I think we just proved we have both been idiots for a long, long time."

"You…. You're not…." Tek grinned and shook his head. "That would be a stupid question. Of course you're not pissed. You fucking kissed me!"

"Yes, I did," Jamie said slyly. "But may I remind you, you kissed me first."

"We were thirteen!" Tek roared.

"Yeah, so? Now we're even."

"Six years, you bastard! Six fucking years it took you to return the kiss." Tek slapped Jamie on the back. "Christ, are you slow."

A knock on the door caused them both to jerk back, Jamie nearly ending up on his ass.

"Gunner? Jimmy?" came Carla's voice through the door.

"Your mom," Jamie mouthed and jumped to his feet.

"Everything okay?" The doorknob rattled, and Jamie was grateful he'd had the good sense to lock the door when he'd followed Tek in.

"Should I let her in?" Jamie whispered.

Tek shook his head vigorously. "Tell her I'm in the shower," he replied and bolted for the bathroom.

"Umm, yeah. Everything is fine, Carla. Gunner's in the shower," Jamie called out.

"Why is this door locked?" The doorknob rattled again. "Open the door, Jimmy."

Jamie looked down at the large bulge pressing against his jeans. No way in hell was he going to let Tek's mom in, and he damn sure wasn't ready to explain why the two of them were behind a locked door while Jamie had a raging hard-on.

"He's fine, Carla. Te—Gunner just needs a few minutes. We're… umm… we're talking," Jamie told her. He grabbed Tek's bloody shirt and shoes, tossed them in the closet, and slammed the door.

"I thought you said he was in the shower," she said, sounding suspicious.

"He is. We were talking and then—" Jamie huffed out a breath. "Look, Carla, he just needs a few minutes to get his shit together. We'll be out in a bit."

"Alright, but tell him I want to talk to him. I'll be waiting at the bar."

Jamie waited until he heard Carla's footsteps move down the hall, and then he walked into the bathroom to tell Tek she was gone. Any words he might have uttered died on his tongue. Standing behind the glass-enclosed shower stall stood Tek with his one hand against the tile wall, the water pulsing against his lowered head and running down his muscular back to the swells of his tight ass. Jamie swallowed hard, but he couldn't seem to make his mouth work as he stood there staring at his friend with Tek's flavor still on his tongue and his raging hard-on taking up any blood his brain would need. Jamie squeezed his eyes shut, doing his best to block out the images of Tek's naked body, struggling to find a little control.

"Is she gone?"

Jamie opened his eyes to find Tek in the same position, only now his head was turned slightly and he was staring at Jamie. "Uh... um... yeah, she's gone," Jamie stuttered. "She wants you to meet her at the bar."

And for the second time in a matter of minutes, Jamie found himself nearly knocked on his ass when Tek stood up and turned toward him. Tek's thick cock was hard, straining out from his body. Jamie gripped the counter and locked his knees to keep himself upright as the images of him and Tek in the shower not so long ago assaulted him. Only this time in his mind's eye, there was no blonde bimbo between them.

As if Tek could read his mind, he opened the shower door. "We better not keep her waiting. Get your ass in here."

Jamie's mouth fell open, and he could only stand there like an idiot and gawk.

"You know how Carla gets if we keep her waiting," Tek reminded him. "It's not like we haven't showered together before."

Jamie swallowed hard again and found his voice. "That was different," he squeaked. But he pulled his T-shirt off, dropped it to the floor, and undid his belt. How could Tek be so calm after what had just happened between them, the new knowledge that was now out in the open? Maybe Tek was just better at hiding it than Jamie was. Jamie was a fucking mess; his shaking hands had a difficult time with button and zipper, and his legs trembled so hard he barely got his pants off without falling over.

"Dammit, Jamie, would you get in here? I'm letting out all the heat."

Jamie knew exactly where all that heat was leaking to. Right between his fucking legs. His body flushed with arousal made all the more acute now, knowing Tek felt the same way. Somewhere in the back of his mind, Jamie kept waiting to wake up from this dream, like he had every other time when he fantasized of him and Tek together. However, as Jamie stepped into the shower and closed the door, the heat and water and the hand Tek placed against Jamie's chest right over his heart felt very, very real.

"No way in hell am I going to wait six years like you did," Tek murmured, leaned in, and pressed his lips against Jamie's.

Fuck! Shouldn't they be talking about this—what it all meant and the fact that the two of them had been lying to each other for years. Only Jamie couldn't seem to get his thoughts straight, not with Tek licking at his lips. Not with his strong hand pressed against Jamie's flesh. Jamie did the only thing he could do. He opened his mouth and kissed Tek back.

The hand on Jamie's chest slid down to his hip, gripped him. Jamie stumbled forward, flailing for a second on the slick floor of the shower before he fell forward, pinned Tek's body against the tile wall with his own. Jamie gasped, ending the kiss when their hard cocks and slick chests came in contact.

"Jesus, Jamie," Tek panted. "Do you know how long I have dreamed about this... wanted this?"

Jamie shook his head. He had no idea. Never imagined that Tek had been dreaming, wanting the same things Jamie had for six long years. "So long" were the only words Jamie could force past his lips. The feeling of Tek's body against his, the look of lust in Tek's eyes short-circuited Jamie's brain—fried it.

"Why didn't you tell me?" Tek wrapped his arms around Jamie, buried his face in Jamie's neck. "How could I have not known?"

"Same reason I didn't know. Too busy trying to hide it," Jamie groaned, his hips rolling, needing... wanting... something.

Tek's head snapped up, and he met Jamie's gaze intently. "No more lies, Jamie, and no more hiding from me."

"You too," Jamie moaned, the words coming out slurred as Tek started meeting each movement of Jamie's hips with his own, creating a delicious friction in Jamie's groin. "Fuck," Jamie hissed and tipped his head back. "What are you doing to me?"

"What I should have, what *we* should have done a long time ago," Tek insisted.

Jamie jerked when teeth bit down on his shoulder and Tek snapped his hips hard against Jamie's. Jamie felt a knot forming at the base of his spine. Only Tek ever made him this horny, the only one who could send him into orgasm so easily, the only one ever. Even when he'd been with the few girls he'd let Tek talk him into banging, it was always Tek he saw behind closed eyes when he came.

"You keep that up, and I'm going to come," Jamie moaned pitifully.

He wanted to let go of the tension that coiled painfully in his gut, the sting of pain from Tek's bite pushing him closer to the edge. But it was too soon; he didn't want the pleasure to end yet. His body obviously didn't care about it being too soon, though. Jamie clutched Tek's muscular shoulders, dug his fingers into the bulging flesh, and humped hard against the man.

"Then kiss me," Tek demanded and smashed their mouths together.

"Not helping," Jamie complained against Tek's lips.

He gripped Tek harder, rutted faster, knowing Tek could handle the power within Jamie's body. It felt freeing not to have to hold back, no worries of hurting Tek like he'd had with the chicks. Tek was gripping Jamie just as hard, bruising his flesh in his iron grip, and it felt so fucking good. Better than anything he'd ever imagined—it was power against power, strength for strength.

"I don't know, from the way you're fucking yourself against me, I'd say it helped a lot." Tek chuckled, the sound deep and husky and going straight to Jamie's balls.

"Fucker," Jamie growled and shoved his tongue deep into Tek's mouth, turning that cocky sound emitting from Tek into a wanton groan and driving Jamie to deepen the kiss and thrust his hips harder.

It took forever and no time at all before an electric jolt zinging down Jamie's spine ignited a chain reaction. Jamie ripped his mouth from Tek's and threw his head back; he clenched his teeth together to stop the roar that wanted out as the first rope of spunk shot out of him. Tek obviously had lost all control as well, his body going still for a split second before his teeth sank into Jamie's shoulder again, his shout of release muffled by the mouthful of Jamie's flesh.

The first blast of Jamie's orgasm was mild compared to the way each pulse increased in intensity as pain flared in Jamie's shoulder and in his hips where Tek's nails dug in, breaking skin. Jamie had never felt anything so fucking good in his life, and as the last drop of cum pulsed from his body, he was left breathing harshly, trembling and spent—dizzy with it.

They clung to each other for long drawn-out moments as the hot water rained down over them, soothing muscles and helping them catch their breaths and slow their hearts. Neither of them seemed to be in any hurry to release the other, even long after Jamie's heart was beating a slow steady rhythm. They held each other, neither saying a word, as if the magic of the moment would be lost.

The hot water heater wasn't as content, and Tek yelped and shoved at Jamie as the water turned cold. "Son of a bitch," he snarled and fumbled with the taps, turning off the flow of cold water.

Jamie slicked back his wet hair from his face and looked down at his still semihard cock and shook his head. Christ, not even being doused with freezing cold water could dampen the effects of what Tek could do to him. He looked up at Tek with a raised brow.

"How the hell is this possible?" he asked and pointed to his dick.

Tek looked down his own body, Jamie's gaze following to Tek's flaccid dick and tight balls. Obviously, Tek didn't have the same issues. Tek looked back up with a grin. He then shook his head hard, sending water droplets flying.

"Guess you're just a freak." Tek smirked.

"Hey," Jamie protested and wiped the water from his face.

"But don't worry about it," Tek assured him and pushed himself up against Jamie, wrapping an arm around Jamie's waist and pulling him tight. "'Cause you're my freak and I like it freaky."

"I'll say," Jamie teased. "But—" He grabbed Tek's chin, leaning his head in closer until their noses were touching. "That means you're mine as well. No more fucking chicks."

"But—"

"I don't give a rat's ass what the others will think," Jamie interrupted. "We have six years to make up, and I'll be damned if I'm going to let you waste one ounce of energy on anyone but me."

"Cripes, are you a demanding fucker," Tek scolded.

Jamie tightened the hold he had on Tek's chin, his eyes boring into Tek's with complete sincerity. "You don't know the half of what I plan on demanding of you."

Jamie didn't give Tek a chance to respond. He smashed their mouths together, demanding entrance into that warm, perfect heat, and moaned loudly when Tek opened his mouth for him. He got all the response he needed when Tek shuddered against him.

Six long years Jamie had had to hide his feelings, burying them down into his gut until sometimes they made him nauseous and sick. No more. He refused to ever lie to Tek again about anything. This whole horrible misunderstanding, the six years of misery, wondering, questioning, could have all been avoided had they only been honest with each other. He'd never lie to Tek again.

And as strong in his conviction as Jamie was about the lying, it was tenfold stronger that Tek would never again share his magnificent body again with anyone but Jamie.

At an age when most kids were having shootouts at the OK Corral with wooden guns, then running home when the streetlights came on, I was given my first second-generation Glock 17 and prowled the streets at night. While other kids were dreaming of what would be inside packages Santa had put under their trees, I was packaging meth. Childhood can't be measured between the time of innocence and reason. To believe so would mean I had no childhood, and I did.

I wrestled and teased and taunted. I could play for hours with wide-eyed wonderment for new places, events, and experience. There was no reason or logic to my play. Sometimes it was silly and crazy, and sometimes the playing went too far, feelings got hurt, knees got skinned, and hearts got broken. But it was never malicious, always in good fun. The only difference was, during my childhood, I was a six foot, three inch man with broad shoulders and thick muscles, and Jamie was my playmate.

Tek Cain

Power Play

"JESUS, JAMIE. I can't do it again," Tek grumbled.

"Is that a challenge?" Jamie inquired with a wicked glint in his eyes.

Tek groaned and slapped Jamie's hand away from his dick. "No, just a fact. I've already come three times today. I'm done. I give. Uncle," he pleaded.

Jamie was going to kill him. In the three days since they'd been honest with each other about how they felt, they hadn't been able to keep their hands to themselves any time they were alone. Tek had gotten his nut once the first day, twice the second, and three times today. *Three times! In three hours!* At this rate, he'd be shriveled up and dead within a week.

They hadn't done anything beyond rubbing off on each other and mutual hand jobs—both still feeling their way along, so to speak. And as insatiable as Jamie was, Tek was almost afraid to do more. Tek looked down his body; Jamie was running his fingers through the wet cum on Tek's stomach and chest. Jamie had his head propped up on his hand near Tek's hip, that perfect mouth a mere foot from Tek's spent cock. *Almost.* The idea made him grin.

"What's that look for?" Jamie asked, sounding suspicious.

"What look?" Tek inquired, feigning innocence.

In a flash, the fingers Jamie had been painting Tek's stomach with were wrapped around Tek's overly sensitive cock, causing him to yelp.

"Ow! Ow! Let go," Tek pleaded. His back arched, and he tried to squirm away.

"Not until you tell me what you were thinking that put that wicked grin on your face," Jamie countered.

Tek grabbed Jamie's wrist and tried to pull his hand away, but the bastard tightened his grip and made Tek yelp again. "I am so going to kick your ass," Tek warned, digging his fingers into Jamie's wrist.

"What was that? You want to kiss my ass? Yes, please," Jamie said with a mischievous grin curling his lip.

"Beat your ass," Tek amended, still squirming.

"You already beat me off once today, but if you insist," Jamie taunted. "I wouldn't say no to another round."

Tek went still, eyes going wide as he gawked at Jamie. The painful prickling sensation along his shaft diminished into a pleasant tingle. "For fuck's sakes, Jamie. You already got off three times, how in the hell can you possibly want to go again already?"

Jamie shrugged, his grin growing. "I don't know. I guess you are just irresistible."

"And you're insatiable."

"And the problem is?" Jamie inquired.

Tek glared at Jamie. "Would you turn my dick loose before it falls off? All those damn calluses are rubbing me raw."

"Shall I use something else other than my hands?" Jamie waggled his brows, the smile on his face turning downright lewd.

"What? You gonna suck my dick?" Tek asked crudely. Their couplings up to this point had been raw and quick. Both enjoyed the power they could exert over the other. The idea of Jamie submitting to Tek's need, putting himself in a less than lead role intrigued Tek. In fact, he liked the idea a lot, and his dick twitched, making a gallant effort to rise to the occasion the more he tossed it around in his mind.

Jamie's cheeks turned a light shade of pink, and he shrugged.

"Seriously? You'd suck me off?" Tek asked in surprise.

"I've thought about it," Jamie admitted. "Haven't you?"

"Hell yeah, I've thought about you sucking my dick."

Jamie gave him an irritated look. "No, you ass," Jamie grumbled. "I meant, haven't you thought about sucking me off? What it would feel like to have my cock shoved down your throat?"

"Yeah, it would feel like I'm fucking choking," Tek sniffed.

Tek tried biting back the laughter that wanted to boil up out of him when Jamie let out a huff, but it was impossible to hold it back. When Jamie scowled, his bottom lip turned down into what looked like a pout.

"Ugh. You can be such an asshole sometimes," Jamie complained, then released his hold on Tek's cock and flopped onto his back.

"Aww, poor Jamie," Tek taunted. "Are you going to start pouting now? That is so adorable."

"Go to hell," Jamie grumbled and covered his eyes with his forearm. "See if I ever offer to suck your dick again."

"I was teasing, you big lug."

Jamie flipped him off.

Tek ran his hand across his stomach, his nose wrinkling at the sticky mess from the cum drying on his torso. "I need a shower."

"Don't let me stop you."

"You're not going to come with?" Tek ran his hand over the drying remains of Jamie's orgasm on his belly. "You could use one too."

"I'll take mine when you're done," he grumped.

"Aww c'mon, Jamie. Don't get all pissy on me. I was teasing."

"Well, I'm not."

Tek stared at Jamie, looking for any signs he was joking, but he didn't see any telltale hint in his familiar features—no outward proof that he was trying to hold back his laughter. Tek tried to pry the arm away from Jamie's face. Jamie never could hide emotions from his eyes, but Jamie flexed his beefy arm and refused to let Tek pull it away.

He and Jamie were well matched in size and strength, and Tek had no doubt he could force Jamie's arm away—if he used the strength of both his arms. "Jamie, goddammit, look at me."

"No!"

"I'm warning you."

The stubborn shit clenched his jaw and refused to lower his arm. Tek straddled Jamie's waist and was about to snatch Jamie's arm away when it hit him. What if he really had hurt Jamie's feelings? Tek knew how hard it had to be to admit for the first time you wanted to suck dick. Hell, Tek had been thinking about it—a lot. It had been on the tip of his tongue to bring the subject up, and he'd had plenty of fantasies of both giving and receiving, but he hadn't had the balls to do it yet. He shouldn't want to be on his knees for anyone, not even Jamie, and yet....

Tek's shoulders slumped. "Okay, I'm sorry I made the joke. It was stupid of me," he conceded.

Silence.

"Jamie?"

No response.

Shit! Guilt rolled Tek's gut at the thought of hurting Jamie's feelings. Damn, he could be such an insensitive ass sometimes. "Jamie, I'm really sorry, okay? I know how hard that was for you to admit," Tek said gently and rubbed his hand soothingly over Jamie's chest. "I've been thinking about it a lot too but didn't have the balls to bring up the subject or.... Oomph!"

Tek's head spun with the sudden shift in position, and he found himself on his back, blinking up at a grinning Jamie who was now straddling Tek's waist. Jamie grabbed Tek's arms while he was still somewhat dazed and stretched them up over his head, effectively pinning him.

"What the—"

"I knew you wanted to be a cocksucker," Jamie laughed. "I just wanted to hear you admit it."

"You are such a jerk! Get off me," Tek demanded and tried to throw Jamie off.

The strong bastard pressed down his full weight on Tek and locked his legs around Tek's thighs. They were stretched out, pressed against each other from chest to toe; the only parts of their bodies not touching were their heads and necks, but only by a few inches.

"Make me." Jamie snorted. "In fact, I'll make you a little bet."

"A bet, huh?" Tek asked suspiciously.

"Yup."

Tek opened and closed his fists a couple of times, testing the hold Jamie had on his wrists. He also flexed his legs but again found that

Jamie's hold was pretty secure. With a well-timed head butt along with a shift in his weight, Tek might just be able to throw Jamie off.

"Alright, let's hear this bet," Tek urged.

"You throw me off, and I'll suck your dick. If you can't, well then…" Jamie waggled his brows again. "You know."

"You'll still suck mine?" Tek asked hopefully.

Jamie made an annoyed sound and rolled his eyes.

"Fine, fine," Tek conceded. "If I can't, I suck yours. Deal."

"Don't you want to hear the rules first? Every *fair* match has ground rules."

"Seriously?"

"Yes. Rule one, no biting. Rule two, no drawing blood, and rule three, no head butting." Jamie winked knowingly. "This is a nice friendly match of strength against strength."

"How is this a fair wager with you already having the upper hand by being on top, hmm?"

"Because the last time we wrestled, you started out on top. And if I remember correctly, I won," Jamie beamed.

"That's because you cheated," Tek mumbled.

"What was that?"

"Nothing," Tek demurred. "Okay, deal. On three."

"And no throwing the match just so you can suck my dick," Jamie snorted.

"Three," Tek burst out and arched his back while at the same time clenching his hands into tight fists and pulling downward.

"Fucking cheat," Jamie growled.

Tek matched grunt for grunt and curse for curse as he struggled against the hold Jamie had on him. A quick change in position had him gaining an inch, only to have Jamie shift and the hard-fought inch was lost. Muscles strained and bulged, sweat beaded on his brow, and Tek battled hard, but no matter how hard he struggled, Jamie kept the upper hand—never giving more than an inch. The bed creaked and groaned with the weight, threatening to give way, but Tek ignored the danger and pushed himself hard, thrashing, pulling, and pushing.

"Do you give?" Jamie taunted.

"Never!" Tek roared.

Tek snapped his hips, ignoring the pain in his surprisingly hard cock as it slammed against Jamie's. When the hell had that happened? Just moments before he'd have sworn he wouldn't have been able to achieve an erection. Yet the slip and slide of sweat-slick bodies, the power, strength, and Jamie's breath against Tek's lips was one hell of a powerful aphrodisiac. He was cocked and loaded, and not just for a fight.

Jamie's eyes darkened, the lust evident in them and in the hardness of his cock against Tek's. If Tek couldn't overpower Jamie with brute force, maybe he could…. Tek grinned, relaxed his arms and legs, and rolled his hips. Then he did it again and again and again.

"Bastard," Jamie groaned.

"Not that I'm aware of," Tek sniffed and started thrusting his hips, setting a quick, gentle rhythm.

Jamie hissed through gritted teeth and increased the hold he had on Tek's legs, no doubt trying to stop the movement of Tek's hips, but it only succeeded in grinding their cocks even harder together.

Another idea popped into Tek's head, and he hid his smirk by pressing his mouth against Jamie's and teasing Jamie's bottom lip with the tip of his tongue. Tek then sucked it into his mouth, scraped his teeth against it softly, never slowing the rhythm of his thrusts.

"Da…. Damn you," Jamie groaned and squeezed his eyes closed.

Tek continued to lick and nip until Jamie was trembling against him and the grip on Tek's wrists began to slacken ever so slightly. *Almost.* Jamie groaned and turned his head, but Tek wasn't about to be deterred.

"God, I want to suck you off so bad," he murmured seductively. He licked a path from Jamie's jaw up his cheek to the sensitive spot just below Jamie's ear. "Wrap my lips around your cock, suck and taste."

Jamie's trembling increased. *Gotcha, big guy.*

"Junior, Tek," Jamie's dad bellowed, followed by hard raps against the door. "Rocco has called a meeting."

Jamie jerked sideways at the same time Tek rolled, and then they were flying, only to land with a hard thump on the floor, Tek landing on top of Jamie.

Tek instantly sat back on Jamie's thighs and threw his hands in the air. "I won!" he hooted victoriously. "I win! I win! I win!"

"Boys! Stop fucking around, and let's go!" Smokey demanded.

Jamie's gaze landed on Tek's straining cock. "Yeah, stop fucking around," he grunted, shoving hard against Tek's chest—sending him flailing backward. Jamie slid out from under Tek and jumped to his feet. "Fucking cheater!"

Tek could only stare up at Jamie's scowling face and laugh. The deeper the scowl, the harder Tek laughed until he was clutching his stomach and tears streamed from his eyes.

Jamie put his hands on his hips and puffed up a little, obviously in an attempt to look intimidating. "Yuk it up, dickweed. I will have my revenge."

"How…. Oh shit…. How can I take you seriously?" he squeaked out between snorts of laughter. The giggles took hold of him, robbing him of any more words, and he could only point and laugh at Jamie's erection.

"Such a child," Jamie chastised, but he barely got the words out before he fell into a laughing fit of his own.

THE EASY and jubilant feelings of the morning were washed away, leaving behind a somber disposition and angry knot churning in Tek's belly as he sat in the club meeting room and listened to Rocco speak.

"The Bangers are pissed, and we can be damn sure they will attempt retribution. We need intel," Rocco mused aloud. He turned to Cole. "What have you got on their recent movements?"

"Not much," Cole admitted. "We lost our inside guy. Jester got ninety in county on a parole violation."

"Shit," Rocco cursed. He ran a hand over the gray scruff on his chin.

Rocco looked tired. Ever since the shit went down in the warehouse, Tek's mom had been riding Rocco's ass hard for putting her boy in danger like that. It seemed ridiculous to Tek since Carla had been helping to cultivate him into a leader of the MC. She'd been part of Crimson VIII since she was eighteen, knew the dark and ugly side of it. But in her own twisted way was still a mom, and in her eyes, any threat to her son was a direct threat to her—something Carla Cain-Lundy didn't take lightly. She was one tough chick and didn't take shit from anyone, including her husband.

"I don't know why we don't just go in and take the dopers out," Sully put in. "We have the manpower."

"That would be a clusterfuck of stupid," Smokey retorted. "Feds are all over our asses. They know we had something to do with the warehouse explosion and are just looking for an excuse to bring us down."

Jamie shot a questioning look at Tek, who just shrugged. Tek had nothing to add, no plan, and he just wanted to forget the whole ugliness of what happened in that warehouse. The only time he could do that was when he was alone with Jamie; the rest of the time, what he did, what he'd been forced to do haunted him.

Tek pulled his pack of smokes from his pocket and tapped one out. He slid one between his teeth and lit it, pulling a deep drag into his lungs and letting it out slowly. The nicotine helped to calm his nervousness, but not much.

He'd never questioned the dealings of the club before, blindly following every order without hesitation, but something shifted inside him in that warehouse. The dark place he could go to, the coldness, scared him. The fact that he could put a gun to an unarmed man's head and squeeze the trigger so easily, without thought or an ounce of care for another human being, not only scared Tek, but horrified him.

"Gunner!" Rocco yelled, snapping Tek out of his musings.

"Huh...." He scanned the faces around the table, all eyes on him. "What?"

"I said you need to hook up with that little blonde you were with the other night," Rocco informed him. "What was her name?" Rocco snapped his fingers repeatedly as if it would help him remember.

"Donna," Cole reminded him.

"That's it! Donna. She used to run with one of the Bangers. See what you can get from her. Fuck it out of her if you have to," Rocco ordered.

Tek felt Jamie stiffen next to him, and he stole a glance to see Jamie scowl. Tek placed the cigarette back between his teeth and nodded at Rocco, knowing full well he wouldn't break his promise to Jamie. But Tek could tell from the way Jamie stayed tense at his side, he had his doubts. The idea that Jamie didn't trust his word both hurt Tek's heart and pissed him off in equal measures. They would need to talk about that later.

"Buck, Junior, I want you two to scope out the Bangers clubhouse. I need numbers, see if they have hooked up with another club, pulled in rogue members."

Buck—whose real name was Eugene Buckler, one of the best hog mechanics in the club—and Jamie both nodded.

"You think that's a good idea?" Tek questioned. "The guy you sent back with the knife in his nuts will be able to recognize Junior here," he said, stabbing a thumb in Jamie's direction. "Why not send one of the new prospects?"

"Boy, are you questioning me?" Rocco challenged and slammed his hand down on the table.

"I just thought—"

"You don't think the Bangers already know what each and every one of us look like, including the new prospects? They may be dopers, but you're a fucking idiot if you underestimate an opponent, especially a greedy one. I guaran-fucking-tee you they are scoping us out."

Tek bristled at being chastised like a child in front of the other members, but he clenched his jaw shut, keeping the protest from escaping.

"Alright, let's get this shit done," Rocco added and brought his gavel down on the table, effectively ending the meeting.

As they shuffled out of the room, Jamie pushed up close to Tek and whispered, "You need to stop trying to protect me in front of the others."

"And you need to learn to trust me," Tek countered and walked away.

I was so eager to please, to fit in. I wanted to be like the others, accepted. I was ignorant in my youth. Fitting in meant becoming cold-blooded. The cold is unforgiving. It wraps itself around a man, penetrates his very core, freezes the very blood within his veins.

Heat is required to forge anything. Without it, life cannot exist.

Tek Cain

The Calm Before the Storm

JAMIE ROLLED his shoulders and tried to do his best to stretch his aching legs in the confines of the VW bug. He'd been sitting inside the cramped space for the last two hours staring at the front door of the Lucky Strike Saloon that the Westside Bangers used as a clubhouse, watching doper after hooker after junkie going in and out. A man his size was not made to be in such a small vehicle.

Jamie turned and frowned at Buck. "Did you have to borrow the smallest car you could find?"

"Borrow? Hell, this is my car," Buck sniffed.

"Seriously, dude? You bought a yellow bug on purpose?" Jamie shook his head. "Where are your balls, my man?"

"I have to keep them in the trunk," Buck chuckled.

Jamie glanced toward the back of the car and arched a brow.

"No, dumbass, up there," Buck corrected him and nodded toward the front of the car.

Jamie shifted in his seat, wincing at the pain in his ass, and resumed watching the front door of the bar. "Another reason to hate this car. Not only is it small, it's bassackward," he huffed.

"It's cute," Buck defended.

Jamie snapped his head around and gaped at Buck. Buck wasn't as big as Jamie—standing around five ten—but he was stocky, well built. His long scraggly hair hung to his waist when he didn't have it braided, which he often did along with the beard that hung halfway down his gut. His arms were covered in tattoos: skulls, pinup girls, devils, weapons, manly shit. All that, plus the fact the man could tear down a car engine and put it back together in record time, and he drove a goddamn bug?

Jamie gave up on trying to puzzle it out and slumped down in the seat. "You are seriously one weird dude," Jamie stated and turned once again to his target.

"I can live with that."

Figures. But Jamie didn't say it out loud, his attention suddenly on a man dressed in a long leather trench coat who rounded the corner heading toward the bar. Jamie sat up straighter and studied the guy. He didn't recognize the middle-aged man with short salt and pepper hair, but whatever he was up to, it was nothing good. No one wore a heavy coat like that when it was eighty degrees out.

"Heads up," Jamie informed Buck and nodded toward the stranger. "You know him?"

Buck studied the man for a second and then gasped. "Oh fuck, that's Jimmy Saunders."

"Who?" Jamie asked, not taking his eyes off the newcomer.

"Jimmy Saunders," Buck repeated. "He was a big-time defense attorney about fifteen years ago. He's a crooked son of a bitch. Went down for a shitload of shady dealings including witness intimidation, tampering with evidence, and attempted murder."

"Okay, so he's a crooked attorney, not like that's a rarity. But why would he be hanging with the Bangers?" Jamie inquired. "Better question is, why in the hell is he wearing a trench in this weather?"

"I don't know," Buck admitted as he fired up the car. "But Rocco has some meets to set up."

"Why? Maybe he's just looking to score some dope," Jamie surmised.

"Yeah 'cause everyone wears a fucking trench coat in summer to buy dope," Buck remarked and threw the car in drive. "Before Jimmy went down, he worked for the Mongols."

"Shit!"

"Exactly," Buck agreed.

TWO QUICK raps followed by a pause and then two more raps had Jamie opening the door to the hotel room.

"Hey," he greeted Tek and stepped back to allow him in.

"Hey."

The scent of sickly sweet perfume followed Tek in, causing Jamie to choke down a gag in response, the aroma even worse than the mold and stale smoke of the shithole room. He shut the door and flipped the lock bar into place, doing his best to keep the disgust from showing on his face. Jamie ran a critical eye over Tek. His hair was mussed, the expression on his face unreadable, but his body was tense.

"How'd it go?" Jamie asked cautiously.

Tek pulled off his T-shirt, threw it on the chair near the bed, and then sat down on the mattress. "I need a shower," he grumbled and unlaced his boots.

"Okay."

"Go ahead and ask," Tek snapped and yanked his boot off before letting it drop to the floor with a resounding thud.

"Learn anything about the Bangers?"

Tek took off his other boot and slammed it down on the floor. "Goddammit, Jamie, you know that's not what you want to ask. So just ask the fucking question so I can take a fucking shower!"

"I know you didn't fuck her," Jamie reassured him. And yet Jamie's gut clenched with doubt.

"Bullshit!" Tek spat and jumped to his feet. "I saw the look in your eyes and the way you tensed when Rocco ordered me to fuck it out of her if I had to, and I can see the doubt written all over your face."

Anger flared in Jamie, anger at himself for not believing Tek, for questioning his promise, but he turned it on Tek instead of directing it to where it should be. "Don't get all sanctimonious on me," he accused. "You keep trying to protect me! You make me look like a goddamn pansy in front of the guys."

"And what the hell does that have to do with you not trusting me?" Tek countered. "So what! I want to protect someone I care about. That's a long goddamn way from you not believing in me enough to keep a motherfucking promise!"

"Oh so it shouldn't bother me about some chick rubbing her pussy all over you, but I shouldn't be upset that you think I am one. Is that it?"

"I never said that!"

"And I never said you *would* fuck some chick, just that I hate the fact that she'd rub all over you!" Jamie roared.

"Then why are we fighting?"

Jamie stared at Tek. They were both posturing and breathing harshly. Tek's face was red with anger, and from the heat in Jamie's cheeks, he was sure he looked the same way.

"I have no fucking idea," Jamie snorted and grabbed Tek's belt loop, pulling him close.

"Ass." Tek grinned and rolled his eyes.

"Jerk," Jamie retorted, then smashed their mouths together and kissed the infuriating man until they were both breathless. Jamie leaned his forehead against Tek's. "You stink," he complained.

"I told you I needed a shower. I smell like a French whorehouse."

"A cheap one at that." Jamie sniffed and grabbed Tek's hand. "Let's go get you de-Frenched."

While Tek set the taps on the shower, Jamie pulled off his T-shirt and threw it haphazardly over his shoulder. He then undid his jeans and pushed them down and stepped out of them while he ran an appreciative eye over the smooth skin of Tek's back and ass as he removed his pants.

"Mmm-mmm," Jamie hummed and patted Tek on the ass as he followed him into the shower. "Very, very nice."

"Yeah, well, don't get any ideas about my ass," Tek warned.

Jamie laughed and then moaned loudly. He'd been agitated and tense all day, and the flow of hot water beating down on his flesh instantly began to ease some of the tightness. "Okay, I won't," Jamie assured him. "If you'll wash my back."

"I'll do you if you do me," Tek countered.

"Deal," Jamie groaned, closed his eyes, and stuck his head beneath the streaming water.

"God, you're easy," Tek teased.

"Only for you, baby."

A sharp sting to Jamie's right butt cheek made him yelp. "Hey!" he protested and rubbed the abused flesh.

"That's what you get for calling me baby," Tek grumbled.

Jamie was about to ask Tek if he'd rather be called sweetheart, but the words died in his throat when blunt fingers began kneading his shoulders. He'd ask later. Maybe. *Who cares?* Jamie hung his head as those talented fingers began working out the knots in his shoulders, down his spine, and back up.

"Christ, you're tight."

"I was stuck in a tiny little car all afternoon. Did you know Buck bought a bug?"

"Yeah, for his sister," Tek informed him. "He's been doing some detailing on it so he loaned her his truck."

"Well, it's real cute," Jamie grumped, echoing what Buck had said earlier.

"And I bet you were cute in it."

"Shut up," Jamie mumbled and then moaned again when Tek started lathering up his back. Jamie widened his stance and let Tek's fingers and the pulsing water do their magic.

His shoulders, back, arms, legs, and ass were massaged, lathered, and rinsed, leaving Jamie loose and feeling better than he had all day.

"Turn around," Tek murmured.

Jamie did as he was told and met Tek's gaze. "So really, how did it go with the bimbo?" he asked and took the bar of soap from Tek after he finished lathering his hands.

"She gives blondes a bad name," Tek chuckled. "She smells like shit but don't know shit. What about you and Buck?"

Jamie ran the soap over Tek's torso, washing away said stink from his body, his neck, and face. "Do you know a guy named Jimmy Saunders?"

"Sure," Tek admitted with a shrug. "He was the attorney who was in the Mongols' back pocket until he went down years ago. Why?"

"Well, he's out. Buck and I saw him walking into the Bangers' club today."

Tek's hands stilled on Jamie's stomach, and his eyes went wide. "What the hell would that scumbag be doing with the Bangers? That piss-poor club can't afford his services."

"I don't know. Buck went to inform Rocco. I'm sure they'll figure it out. All I do know is, if the Bangers are getting support from the Mongols, the retribution for the warehouse is going to get bloody." The shocked look in Tek's eyes turned haunted. "Hey," Jamie said gently and stroked his hand across Tek's cheek. "You did what you had to do."

"I didn't have to," Tek disagreed. "I killed an unarmed man, Jamie."

"An unarmed man who was a threat to the club, to you and to me," he corrected. "He would have made good on his threat, Tek. You did the right thing."

"I held that man's life in my hands, and this dark ugly thing took over me. I could feel its coldness seep into me, and I sold my soul to it," Tek confessed. He pushed into Jamie's touch, the remorse radiating off the man palpable. "What I did, what I'm becoming scares me, Jamie."

"What you are is Tek Cain, future president of Crimson VIII and my best friend, and on top of all that, you are a damn good man," Jamie said adamantly.

"I don't feel like a good man, Jamie." Tek shook his head vigorously. "I don't want to talk about it right now, okay? I just...." He wrapped his arms around Jamie's waist and leaned his head on Jamie's shoulder. "I just want to not think about anything and be warm for a while."

Jamie let the soap drop to the floor, pulled Tek closer, and ran his hand up and down Tek's back. "Okay," he whispered and kissed the top of Tek's head. "No thinking about anything but you and me." Tek nodded and clung to Jamie. Jamie slid his fingers through Tek's hair and pulled his head back until their eyes met. "Nothing but good and happy thoughts, okay?"

Jamie didn't give Tek a chance to respond. He pressed his lips against Tek's, tongue demanding entrance. Tek opened to him, invited him into his warm, wet mouth, his tongue sliding along Jamie's. Jamie moaned, deepened the kiss until it was all-consuming, demanding

Tek's full attention. Hands kneading flesh, bodies pressed hard against each other beneath the hot flow. Surrounded by thick steam, they continued to devour each other's mouths, biting, licking, exploring until the world outside disappeared.

The need for oxygen forced Jamie to break the kiss, but he continued to slide his lips across Tek's cheek, along his jaw, nuzzled the side of his neck. He felt Tek harden against his belly, his own cock responding in kind to the pleasurable stimulation. Without words—there were no need for them—they slowly began to sway against one another inside their steam cocoon, touching, tasting, exploring.

Jamie scraped his teeth across Tek's collarbone. Tek tipped his head back, a deep rumbling moan echoing off the glass enclosure. Jamie drew the sound out by kissing his way down Tek's breastbone, lapping at the water rivulets, tasting soap and sweat and Tek. Tek gripped Jamie's shoulders as he began to tremble when Jamie moved down to lick and tease Tek's belly button.

Grasping Tek's hips, Jamie went to his knees and ran his bearded jaw against Tek's straining erection. He was rewarded with another deep and husky groan. Encouraged, Jamie turned his head and placed a soft kiss to the flared cockhead, tentatively licked at the small slit.

Tek gasped and clutched Jamie's shoulders harder. "God, Jamie, that feels so good," he praised, one of his hands sliding through Jamie's wet hair.

"Then I better keep doing it." Jamie smirked. He wrapped a fist around the base of Tek's cock and ran his tongue around the tip before he sucked it into his mouth. Mindful of his teeth, Jamie sucked gently, swirling his tongue around and dipping it in and out of the small opening.

Jamie took Tek a little deeper, sucked a little harder, and began bobbing his head. He could taste the precum oozing from the slit, the flavor musky, slightly bitter, but not at all unpleasant.

The hand in Jamie's hair tightened, and Tek thrust his hips, pushed his cock deeper, which caused Jamie to gag and pull off.

"Shit! I'm sorry," Tek apologized and loosened his hold on Jamie's hair.

"It's okay, just wasn't expecting it, is all." Jamie sat back on his calves and worked his jaw from side to side. "Just go slow, okay?"

"Kind of hard not to get overly excited when you're sucking me," Tek chuckled. "But I'll try."

"Just till I get used to it," Jamie reassured him and took Tek's cock back into his mouth. Jamie grabbed the back of Tek's muscular thighs, pushed and pulled in a slow rhythmic pattern, taking a couple inches into his mouth and then back out.

The sounds Tek was making, the way his fingers tightened and released Jamie's hair, and Tek's fat cock against his tongue were a powerful punch of sexy. Jamie's cock was throbbing and hard. Each thrust, Jamie took a little more, sucked a little harder, loving the way he could make Tek tremble, curse, and moan. Jamie sucked greedily, wanting more of Tek's delicious flavor in his mouth, and he encouraged Tek to thrust harder, deeper.

"Fuck!" Tek cursed. "You keep that up, and I'm going to come."

Do it. But Jamie didn't stop bobbing his head, too greedy and hungry for Tek's cock to stop now.

"Jamie," Tek hissed and pulled Jamie's hair hard at the same time he pulled back, his cock slipping from Jamie's mouth. "Damn that was close," he panted.

"Hey, I was enjoying that," Jamie complained. "Give it back."

"Yeah?" he panted with a grin, petting Jamie's hair. "You sure you can handle it?"

Jamie licked his lips and smirked. "Try me," he challenged. "And don't be gentle. I can handle it."

"I know you can," Tek said sincerely. "But I don't want to hurt you."

"You won't. Now shut up and do it," he demanded.

"Pushy bastard," Tek grumbled, but he was grinning as he swiped his cockhead over Jamie's lips. "Open up and say ah."

Jamie opened his mouth wide and fell on Tek's cock, sucking it down deep.

"Holy shit!" Tek howled and snapped his hips.

Jamie dug his fingers into the flesh of Tek's thighs, making damn good and sure Tek couldn't take his treat again. If Tek's experiences were anything like Jamie's, he'd never been allowed to release the full power of his body with a girl. They were too small, too soft to handle someone like Tek. Jamie was damn sure going to prove he was neither of those things.

Jamie knew the moment Tek let go the reins of control; he gripped both sides of Jamie's hair in his hands and started fucking Jamie's mouth with hard, brutal snaps of his hips, cursing, babbling, and moaning. And Jamie loved every fucking second of it—the rawness in his throat, the stinging pain in his scalp.

Tek's thrusts became erratic, the sounds he made getting louder and louder. Jamie knew the man was close. Christ, Jamie was too. He released his hold on Tek's thigh with his right hand and wrapped it around Tek's cock, gripping it hard and stroking it in time with Tek's hips.

"Almost... I'm...." Tek's muscles went impossibly tighter, and Jamie jerked himself harder, wanting to blow his load at the same time Tek did.

"Here.... Oh... Oh fuck, here it comes," Tek roared and shoved his cock deep into Jamie's throat, holding it there for a long drawn-out moment, cutting off Jamie's air supply.

Jamie's eyes watered, but before he could start to panic, he forced himself to swallow. He'd never had his cock that deep into someone's throat before, but it must have felt really fucking good, because Tek roared again and went nuts, jerking and twitching as he emptied his load down Jamie's throat.

Jamie struggled to keep up with the flow of Tek's release but took it down hungrily, and it was enough to push him over the edge. His cock pulsed hard in his fist, and he came just as the last drop of Tek's seed slid down his throat.

"Holy motherfucking Hell," Tek groaned and stumbled back, catching himself with the safety bar before he could fall on his ass. "I think you sucked my strength out through my dick," he snorted.

Jamie ran his tongue over his top lip and then sucked his bottom lip into his mouth. He was disappointed they only tasted like soap and water and not Tek, but they tingled, felt raw from being stretched in a really good way.

He pushed out his chest and smirked up at Tek. "You're welcome." He beamed.

"Give me a minute," Tek panted, "and I'll return the flavor, I mean favor."

Jamie carefully went to his feet. Tek wasn't the only one whose strength was a little drained. "No need," he assured Tek. Legs shaking, he wrapped an arm around Tek's waist and used him for support. "That was the hottest fucking thing I've ever done."

"You came?" Tek asked, sounding incredulous.

"Like a fucking fountain," Jamie chuckled against Tek's lips.

"Uh… well, then you're welcome too," Tek snorted. "Now can we get dried off and sit down for a minute before I fall down?"

"Pansy," Jamie joked. But it was a damn good idea.

Clinging to each other, still wet, Tek and Jamie fell onto the bed. They laid face to face, Jamie's hand on the warm flushed skin of Tek's hip, Tek's arm around him, rubbing his back. Neither of them said a word, just stared at each other with matching goofy grins on their faces. The sun going down cast the room in dusky shadows, and once again Jamie was struck at how it felt as if he and Tek were the only two people in the world—hidden and safe from everything and everyone.

"Thank you," Tek whispered.

"You're welcome," Jamie replied. "Not bad for my first time, huh?"

"Hell, you were amazing, but I wasn't talking about the blow job."

"No?"

Tek shook his head. "I'm warm," he said gently. "Not just from the shower or the sex, but being with you makes me feel…." Tek stared at him in the diminishing light, a gentle smile on his handsome face that caused Jamie's chest to tighten. "I don't know, Jamie. I'm never cold when I'm with you."

A swell of emotion welled up in Jamie, forming a lump in his throat. He didn't know how to respond to that, even if he could get the words out past his constricted throat. So instead, he wrapped his arms around Tek, held him, and kept him warm.

Funny thing about the calm before a storm, it gives one a false sense of security—hope. Maybe the storm will shift with the winds, move toward another town of unsuspecting folks? Perhaps it will lose some of its power before it reaches you. Or if you're real lucky, it will just fizzle out and you'll end up with nothing more than a warm summer rain.

I wasn't so lucky.

However, in the midst of the mangled wreckage of a life destroyed by ravaging winds of change and floods of blood, I found hope.

Tek Cain

Brewing Storm

"WE ARE so fucked," Tek hissed.

He'd been lying on his belly for the last hour, binoculars to his eyes, as he watched about twenty members of the Mongols gather at the home of the Bangers' president, Freddy Knox. Tek did his best not to move, but it was getting more and more difficult with rocks stabbing into his legs and gut and the hot summer sun cooking his flesh.

To hell with it, he had what he'd come for—proof the two gangs were now working together. Tek slid backward from the brush he'd been using as cover until he was far enough down the slight incline where he wouldn't be seen, then went to a crouch. Without being detected, he made it back to the tree line and groaned as he stood tall. His muscles protested the long hour of inactivity. Tek pulled his cell from his jeans pocket and flipped it open, pulling up his contacts as he made his way through the woods.

"We got twenty or so Mongols at Knox's place," Tek informed Rocco when he answered.

"Shit! Alright, get your ass to the club," Rocco ordered.

"Want me to swing by and grab Jamie?"

"He's already here." The line went dead.

Tek flipped his cell shut and returned it to his pocket. Why the hell was Jamie at the club? They were supposed to hook up at the hotel when Tek got done with his surveillance. He checked his watch—it was nearly the time they'd planned to meet. They'd been hooking up at the hotel every chance they could—not wanting to take any more risks of getting caught. And as loud as Jamie was when he came, the chances were great. Something important must have happened for Jamie not to be at the hotel. It had been three days, and for his insatiable lover, it would be three days of torture. The thought caused Tek to smirk as he slid behind the wheel of his truck. Jamie wasn't the only one jonesing for some alone time. First, he needed to find out what the hell was going on.

When Tek walked into the meeting room, all eyes turned on him, the only empty chair, his. He slid into it and gave Jamie a questioning look. Jamie just shrugged.

"Good, now we can get down to business," Rocco announced. "Tek here spotted twenty-plus Mongols at Knox's crib. Which means there isn't any doubt the Bangers found some help. I say we hit them now, but I'm open to hearing suggestions."

"That would be a bloodbath," Cole countered. "The Mongols have nearly twice the members we have."

"Not if we call down a couple other chapters," Sully put in. "I know Corona del Mar has been itching for some action."

Tek pulled a smoke from his pack and lit up as he listened intently while the others tossed around ideas. He didn't like the idea of going after the Bangers and Mongols with guns blazing. Even with the jump on them, there would be casualties on both sides, and the odds just weren't those he was willing to gamble with. However, doing nothing was like sitting around with their thumbs up their asses waiting for the attack. Yet taking the offensive, fortifying their position, maybe they wouldn't take as many losses. *Shit!* Any loss of life was one too many. They needed a better plan.

Leaning a little closer to Jamie, Tek whispered, "Going postal on two clubs is suicide."

"Agreed."

"You got anything?" Tek asked.

Jamie frowned, looking thoughtful for a second. "Maybe," he finally admitted. "I mean I don't know if it would work, but it might be better than anything we've heard so far."

A beer cap hit Jamie in the chest, and they both snapped their heads toward Rocco.

"Are we boring you two?" Rocco asked, the irritation evident in the tone of his voice.

"No, not at all." Tek grinned widely and then took another pull from his cigarette, blowing it out casually.

"So then I take it you have the answer to our problem all figured out?" Rocco growled. "Please share with the class. Or better yet, maybe you'd like to take my chair and lead the class."

The other members snickered and laughed, but Tek ignored them. "Go ahead, Jamie, solve all our problems."

"Tek," Jamie hissed. "I told you—"

"Yes, Junior, please enlighten us."

"Ow!" Tek grunted when a boot made contact with his calf. He glared at Jamie who glared back.

"Serves you right, you fucker," Jamie said for Tek's ears only; to Rocco, he said, "I don't know how much I can enlighten you, but I was just thinking. Why not pit the Mongols against the Bangers, let them kill each other rather than getting our hands dirty or, worse, shot."

"Go on," Rocco encouraged. He leaned his elbows on the table and rested his chin on his fists. The expression on his face said he was taking Jamie seriously.

"Well, the Mongols are running guns for the Irish Wolfhounds. Why not disrupt one of the shipments and make it look like the Bangers pulled it off. We could do the same to the Bangers with their dope runs."

Tek stared at Jamie with pride. It was a great fucking idea. He wanted to kiss the man senseless.

"The kid may have something there," Cole said thoughtfully.

"Of course he does," Smokey interjected. "He's my kid."

Tek settled on giving Jamie a manly slap on the back. He'd congratulate him properly later. "Hell of a plan, dude."

"Thanks," Jamie responded, his cheeks going pink with the praise.

So fucking cute!

"Cole, contact the Wolfhounds, set up a meet," Rocco ordered. "And Sully get on the dope. Anyone have anything else to add?" Rocco paused, looking around the room. When no one added anything, he brought the gavel down on the table. "Let's get this done."

Tek stubbed out his cigarette and went to his feet. "C'mon, Jamie, this calls for a beer. I'm buying."

"Damn right you will," Jamie snorted.

They began to head out when Rocco called out, "Tek, see you for a minute?"

Tek patted Jamie on the back. "Meet you out there in a bit." Jamie nodded, and Tek turned his attention to Rocco. "Sure, what's up?"

Rocco waited until the last of the guys exited the room before speaking. "I've heard some shit about you and Junior that has me a little concerned."

Tek's blood froze in his veins. No way could anyone know about him and Jamie. They'd been careful, dammit. *Fuck!* He wished he hadn't put out his smoke. Tek swallowed down his panic and, as casually as he could, asked, "What bullshit rumors have you heard now?"

"Staying out all night, going missing for long hours at a time." Rocco arched a brow. "Tell me it's pussy that's keeping you two out all night and not drugs, and I'll keep your mom off your back."

Tek nearly choked on his relieved laughter. "No dope," he assured his stepdad. "And you can tell Mom to stop worrying. I'll be damn sure to wrap it before I slap it."

"Good man," Rocco smirked. "Now let's go get that beer," he said and slung an arm over Tek's shoulder.

Tek rolled his eyes as Rocco led him out of the room. What a fucked-up family he had. *Fight, steal, kill, run guns, drink, and random pussy, but no smoking the bong.*

JAMIE LEANED back against the bar, his teeth about ready to shatter he was clenching his jaw so tightly. Not the festive mood of the club, the alcohol warming his gut, or the kickass jams were enough to cut through the irritation—no, steaming, raging jealousy was a better description for what he was feeling.

Jamie got it. He did. But having to watch girl after girl rub themselves all over Tek was going to drive Jamie to murder. The way they ran their hands through Tek's long hair, across his chest, kissed his neck, his cheeks… *ugh!* His ass!

Jamie spun around and snatched his beer up and downed it. "Hey, you," he snarled at the barmaid. "Another beer."

"I told you, my name is Amber," she informed Jamie and set another beer in front of him.

"Yeah, yeah, yeah," Jamie retorted with a dismissive wave and drank half the beer in one gulp.

"Damn, you really need to get laid. Maybe it would help with that rosy disposition of yours."

"You're fucking right I do," Jamie snapped. But Tek was having a damn good time, running the table, playing with the bitches, and drinking without any signs he wanted to stop any time soon.

"Well?"

Jamie looked down at the dark-haired girl behind the bar. She was looking at him with a suggestive grin on her overly painted red lips and batting her long fake lashes at him. She had big blue eyes that would actually be kind of pretty if she hadn't surrounded them with so much black eyeliner and a ton of shadow on the lids. She reminded Jamie of a painted raccoon. And she was small. Maybe five foot two in height, couldn't be more than a hundred pounds, even if her tits were huge and practically falling out of her halter top. *I'd break you in half.*

He drank the rest of his beer and slammed it onto the bar. "Yeah, I'll take another one." He turned back to the club, ignoring the loud dramatic huff from behind him, just in time to see yet another chick groping Tek's ass. *I'm done!* Jesus. A man could only take so much.

Jamie stomped over to the pool table, not quite steady on his feet, and snapped, "I'm outta here," as he walked by.

"Hey," Tek called out. "Where ya going?"

"Home," Jamie shot back.

"Hold up, I'll give you a ride."

Jamie shoved the door open and stepped out into the night air. The cool wind felt good on his heated skin, and he took a deep breath, holding it for a few seconds before blowing it out slowly. He was truly losing his mind. But it just pissed him off that everyone was so free and open in their displays of sexual conquest. Dudes felt chicks up at the bar, groped and kneaded tits and ass on the dance floor. Hell, a lot of the guys banged them right in front of everyone. It was nothing to see

Sully and Buck sitting on the couch next to each other while they were getting head. But could he kiss Tek? No! *Fuck!* He couldn't even touch Tek. In the clubhouse you could be as nasty and freaky as you wanted. Just don't be fags. Jamie leaned back against the wall and closed his eyes. His head spun with the combination of anger, jealousy, and sorrow. It wasn't fair.

He heard the door open, and Jamie turned his head and opened his eyes to see Tek step out, scanning the parking lot. "I'm right here," he told him.

The light from within the club was enough that Jamie could see the concern in Tek's eyes when he looked at him. "What's going on?" Tek asked as he leaned his shoulder against the wall next to Jamie.

"I just needed to get the hell out of there."

"Did something happen?" Tek asked in confusion.

"Yeah, I got sick and fucking tired of watching you play," Jamie muttered.

"Oh, stop being a poor sport. I was kicking ass and taking names. Yours included." Tek snorted. "Won seven in a row."

"I wasn't talking about pool, Tek," Jamie snapped.

"Huh?"

"Never mind," Jamie muttered and pushed off the wall.

"Bullshit," Tek growled. He grabbed Jamie's arm and spun him around. "If you have an issue with me or something I did, then you tell me. Don't play these silly fucking games."

The door opened again, and Sully stumbled out with his arms slung over two chicks. "Hey, guys," he slurred. "Want to come to my orgy?"

"The more the merrier," one of the girls giggled.

Tek released Jamie and waved Sully off. "Nah, I'm good. I'm sure they have enough to handle with you."

"Probably," Sully snorted. "Junior? Want to come watch the master in action? Bet I could teach you a thing or two."

"I'm sure you could," Jamie deadpanned. He'd seen some of the shit Sully was into, and he'd already learned all he'd ever wanted to know from Sully about sex. Most importantly, that he never wanted to witness it again. "But I think I'll pass tonight."

"Your loss," Sully declared.

They watched silently as Sully and the girls rounded the corner. Once they disappeared, Tek turned to Jamie. "C'mon, I'll give you a lift home."

"Nah, I'd rather walk and so should you," Jamie informed him.

"I had one drink three hours ago." He grabbed Jamie's arm and yanked him toward his truck. "Now stop being a dick and c'mon."

Jamie tried to shrug Tek's arm off, but he held fast, pulling him along. Tek opened the passenger side door and shoved Jamie. "Now you can either get in the truck on your own or I'll put you in. Either way, you're getting in this fucking truck, and we're going to talk about what has your panties all in a bunch."

Jamie thought briefly about refusing. A good fight might just make him feel better. But he was suddenly too tired and too buzzed to put up much of a fight. He slid into the truck.

"Good choice," Tek said and slammed the door. He ran around the front of the truck and got in. "Buckle up," he ordered and fired up the engine.

Tek peeled out of the parking lot in the opposite way of Jamie's house. "Hey, where the hell are you going? I thought you said you weren't drunk?" he asked and hooked his seatbelt.

"In the mood you're in, I figured there would be screaming and cursing. I'm sure you don't want your daddy to hear."

"I'm not—"

"Bullshit! You're drunk and you're pissed off. The two are a deadly combination when you have secrets like we have. As soon as we get to the hotel, you can be as drunk and as pissed as you want."

Jamie clamped his mouth shut. Tek was right. The secret they carried could get them killed. He'd heard the other members talking about fags before. He'd seen the disgust and loathing in their expressions. Rocco spoke for the mentality of the club when he'd said, *The only good fag is a dead fag.* Jamie crossed his arms over his chest and leaned his head against the window, staring at the darkness beyond. He'd wait to say anything until they were behind closed doors.

Only, he doubted there would be much screaming and cussing. He didn't feel all that angry anymore, the sadness of what the future held for him and Tek taking over his head and heart.

"All right, let's hear it," Tek demanded as soon as the hotel room door was shut and locked.

Jamie flopped down in the chair and ran his hands over his face. "I drank too much and got stupid is all," Jamie explained. "It won't happen again."

"Well, something set you off. Talk to me, Jamie," Tek coaxed. "I can't fix it if you don't tell me what I did."

"Nothing for you to fix," Jamie assured him. "I got jealous of the chicks rubbing all over you, and it pissed me off. It's my issue to deal with, not yours." Jamie rested his forearms on his knees and lowered his head, feeling stupid for his earlier outburst. "You didn't do anything wrong," he added dejectedly.

"You think I like to be groped and rubbed on by those bitches? Think I like smelling like a two-dollar whore? C'mon, Jamie. You know me better than that."

"I know," Jamie admitted.

Tek went to his knees in front of Jamie. He put a finger to Jamie's chin, encouraging him to look up. "You're the only one I want groping me. You do know that, right?"

Jamie nodded. He did know Tek wasn't into chicks. Jamie had believed him when Tek said he'd never wanted to be with them but used them as a cover for his true desires as Jamie had done. And he understood all too well why they had to do it. Still, it hurt like hell to have to witness it.

"Then tell me what's going on inside your head," Tek pleaded as he rubbed Jamie's arms.

"I'm being an idiot," he admitted. "I know better than to drink this much. I turn into an emotional sap, and I don't know how to handle it."

"You always have been the softer one," Tek chuckled.

Jamie shot him a glare.

"Okay, okay," Tek sniffed, holding out his hands in a defensive gesture. "I meant the more sensitive one of us. And before you go getting all pissy about it, I like that about you. On the outside you're like this big burly kickass dude who is so fucking strong and powerful, but on the inside you're thoughtful and kind." Tek went back to rubbing Jamie's arms soothingly and shrugged one shoulder. "I like it."

Jamie's belly fluttered pleasantly with the praise. He wanted to be both strong and powerful for Tek. Prove that he could rule next to him and was an asset to Tek's future position in the club. Yet, the emotional shit was wreaking havoc on his heart.

"I wish I wasn't all squishy on the inside sometimes," he finally admitted. "Take tonight, for instance. I realized how unfair everything is and that we don't really have a future, Tek."

"Of course we do, Jamie," Tek interjected. "Hell, we haven't been apart barely a day since we were born, and I can't see that changing anytime soon. Cradle to grave, Jamie."

"And it might be sooner than we think if anyone finds out we're fags. Our future is lying and hiding and waiting for fucking stolen moments," Jamie spat as the anger bubbled up again at the injustice of it.

"I know it sucks and I'm sorry," Tek said sincerely. "If I could change it right now, I would, but maybe one day, it won't have to be like this. Be patient with me a little longer, okay?"

"It's not you, Tek. It's the club and…." Jamie leaned his forehead against Tek's shoulder and wrapped an arm around his waist, instantly feeling a little better with Tek close. "There I go being all stupid again," he muttered.

"You're not stupid, Jamie," Tek said fiercely, hugging him back. "It's not right we have to hide, and I hate it as much as you do. But let's get this shit done with the Mongols and Bangers, and then I will figure something out, I promise."

Jamie lifted his head and met Tek's gaze. "No, *we* will figure something out."

"Damn right, we will," Tek agreed with a sly grin, then took Jamie's hand in his and went to his feet. "Now c'mon, let's go enjoy our stolen moment. I could use some warmth."

Anger, rage, fear, sadness, they were turning my soul into nothing but blackness. But it was the rage that burned brightest within me—killing me. I had no idea how to control it, couldn't have known what it would do to me if left to fester. A good family teaches us love, caring, and generosity. Mine taught me hate, rage, and shame.

I wish they would have also taught me how to control them.

Tek Cain

Hate, Rage, and Shame

THE DOOR splintered from the weight of Tek's boot and flew open. Black ski mask over his face, weapon drawn, he rushed in and swept the room. When he found no one in the front room, he ushered in Jamie and Buck, who were dressed in all black as Tek was with matching masks concealing their faces. With a wave of his hand, Tek cautiously made his way down the hall.

A man rushed out of a side door, shotgun aimed at Tek, and snarled, "Who the fuck—"

Tek cut off the man's words and his life with a bullet to the head. He felt no remorse. Nothing. Empty. He'd been able to conjure up that cold place in him as they prepared for the hit, and he easily ignored the dead man at his feet. No fear, his pulse normal, his breathing slow and even, only coldness. Tek peered into the room—a bathroom—found it empty, and moved on farther down the hall.

They had been staking out their target for days and knew that at the moment there would be two more Bangers somewhere within the dilapidated old house. Metal music from the basement vibrated the floor as Tek made his way through the structure. He found no one else in any of the rooms. The other two Bangers had to be in the basement, and as he stopped with his hand on the doorknob to check that Jamie and Buck were ready, Tek hoped the music was enough to have drowned out the noise of their entry and the bullet. If not, they were about to descend into an ambush.

Tek met Jamie's gaze and saw he was nervous but focused. Tek nodded to him in silent question, and when Jamie gave a curt nod in response, Tek yanked the door open. The sounds of Anthrax thumped loudly in Tek's ears, and the heavy scent of dope filled his nostrils. A light burned brightly from the bottom of the stairs. Luckily, there were no bullets whizzing past his head nor a gun pointed at it as he stepped through the door.

Keeping close to the wall, Tek made his way slowly down the stairs, finger resting on the trigger of his Glock. On the last rung, he held a fist up, signaling the others to halt. Gun leading the way, Tek peeked around the corner. The entire basement was lit up with several sun lamps hanging from the ceiling, shining down on row upon row of plants in various stages of growth. Against the far right wall, two men with their backs to Tek were weighing and bagging up dope. On the table in front of them was the source of the blaring music. A large stereo, with the volume apparently cranked, left the two Bangers clueless of what had occurred, better yet, unaware of what was about to happen.

Tek turned around to face Buck and Jamie and pulled the mask down from his mouth. "Two, far right wall with their backs turned. Stay low and quiet. Buck, you take the one on the right, I'll take the one on the left. Jamie, you got our backs. Ready?" Both men nodded, and Tek held out his fist. "All eight."

Buck bumped his fist against Tek's and repeated the vow in a low voice. Jamie did the same. Tek held Jamie's gaze for a second longer until warmth started to spread through his gut, and he turned away. He covered his mouth once again and searched for the coldness. He knew the moment he found it, his mind pushing out everything but the job at hand, and he stepped around the corner.

Gun aimed at the back of his target's head, Tek moved quickly and quietly, acutely aware of Buck and Jamie behind him. Neither doper realized anyone else was in the room until it was too late and Tek had his gun pressed to a temple.

"So much as flinch and I will end your miserable fucking life," Tek growled into the man's ear.

The unsuspecting man let the bag drop from his fingers, but he didn't move.

Tek stole a glance to the side; the other doper was in the same position with Buck's gun pressed to his head. He then looked back at Jamie briefly who was in a shooter's stance, gun moving back and forth between the two Bangers.

"Turn down that fucking music!" Tek shouted.

Jamie reached around Buck and hit the power button, sending the room into an eerie silence.

Tek pressed the barrel of the gun harder against the Banger's head, ensuring there would be a deep impression and bruise as a reminder. That was, if the doper didn't try to play hero and end up with a hole in his head instead. Jamie pocketed his gun and pulled out heavy-duty zip ties, restraining the wrists of the man Tek was holding and then doing the same to the other. Even with both men's hands bound, Tek didn't release the pressure of the gun. Only when their ankles were also efficiently secure and duct tape was over their eyes and mouths did Tek lower his weapon.

Stuffing his gun in the waistband of his jeans against his lower back, Tek turned his prisoner over to Jamie and pulled off his backpack. This was the fourth hit in the past month they'd worked on together; each knew their jobs. Silently, they worked, Buck and Jamie tying the Bangers together in a corner as Tek filled his pack with the numerous bags of dope that littered the table.

Once the bags were collected and prisoners dealt with, the three of them began destroying every plant. Tek felt a rush of glee surge through him as he ripped plants from the dirt, crushed them in his hands, and threw them to the ground. He fucking hated illegal drugs. Hated what a man would do for his next fix and had a special loathing for those who dealt in them. There were a lot of things his club had done that Tek wasn't proud of, but the drugs had always bothered him the most. A man would sell his soul for the next fix; women sold their bodies, abandoned children; babies were born addicted. He snatched another plant from its dirt bed, threw it to the floor, and ground it under his boot. He then took out his frustration on the sun lamps.

Tek ripped the leg from one of the tables, sending dirt and pottery crashing to the floor. Glass and sparks rained down as he swung the wooden leg like a bat. Tek let the anger wash through him as he swung over and over and over, destroying every light, ignoring the way the glass shards stung the area around his eyes, each connection of wood to glass satisfying. When every light was extinguished—except a single bulb hanging from the ceiling near the bottom of the stairs—Tek turned his rage on the tables. Sweat ran down his spine, his pulse thundering in his ears as he flipped tables over, kicked and stomped planters, shredded aluminum foil.

Arms wrapped around Tek from behind, restraining. Panic flared up in Tek, and he fought to throw off the tight embrace, clawing at forearms, twisting and struggling. His heart pounded so hard it felt as if it were bursting out of his chest, glass and sweat burned his eyes, making him disoriented.

"Tek," Jamie hissed, barely above a whisper. The low, familiar voice was enough to cut through the haze of rage, and Tek stilled. "That's it," Jamie coaxed. "Deep breaths."

Tek trembled as the fury seeped from his body with Jamie's soothing voice, his strong arms holding Tek firmly, supporting and grounding him once again in reality.

"Better?"

"Yeah," he responded huskily, throat raw. His head was throbbing, eyes burning and muscles screaming; he was dizzy and very, very far from okay. But he was better than he was before Jamie brought him back from wherever the hell the anger had taken him.

Tek took a deep, calming breath and let it out slowly. He then reached into his front jeans pocket—Jamie's arms fell away—and pulled out the swatch of material with a patch on it. He let it fall from his fingers.

"I'm okay," he muttered, more to convince himself than Jamie, and headed up the stairs. Tek didn't stop until he was sitting in the truck.

"What the fuck was that?" Buck demanded as he slid in behind the wheel and slammed the door.

Jamie yanked off his mask as he climbed into the back seat, Tek watching him intently. "You okay?" Jamie asked cautiously.

Tek threw his backpack at his feet and fastened his seatbelt. "I'm fine," he told them both.

"You sure as fuck didn't look fine a few minutes ago," Buck snapped as he fired up the truck and stomped on the gas.

"The job got done," Tek countered defensively. He pulled the mask from his face and shoved it into his pocket, wincing as the glass shards stung his face. A painful jab to Tek's lower back reminded him he'd stored his gun in his waistband, and he retrieved it and checked the clip.

"That's beside the point," Buck countered. "What the hell happened to you, man?"

"I got pissed, now let it go," Tek grunted. He laid the weapon in his lap and leaned his head against the window. Fuck, he was drained. He just wanted a shower, some ice for his burning eyes, and sleep, hours and hours of uninterrupted sleep. However, he knew if the nightmares didn't keep him from achieving what he wanted, Jamie would. It was a conversation he wasn't looking forward to. He had no answers to give, only shame.

HOW JAMIE knew Tek needed some time to process what had happened, Tek didn't know, but Jamie barely said two words to him while they informed Rocco about the hit. He didn't jump to Tek's defense while Buck ranted and cursed about what he'd seen Tek do, nor during the reaming he'd taken from Rocco for being a loose cannon. But really, how could he? Even on the ride to the hotel, Jamie had sat quietly in the passenger seat of Tek's truck. There had been no worry or disgust marring his features, only a quiet thoughtfulness in his friend's expressions.

Tek shrugged out of his coat and laid it on the chair as Jamie closed and locked the door. He started to speak, but Jamie's lips against his cut off his words. When Jamie wrapped his arms around him, pulled him tight, and shoved his tongue down Tek's throat, what he intended to say was forgotten. The kiss, hard and deep, was a clash of lips and teeth that demanded Tek's focus as did the powerful hands pulling at his clothes.

Jamie broke the kiss and started pulling at Tek's shirt. "Off," he growled.

"Pushy bastard," Tek snorted and yanked it off over his head.

"We have one hour," Jamie reminded him. He fumbled with the belt on Tek's jeans. "I don't want to waste it with needless conversation."

Tek agreed and, without a word, pushed Jamie's hands away and undid his jeans before letting them fall to the floor. They were both breathing hard, the room otherwise quiet. Impatient, Tek toed off his shoes as he worked at Jamie's belt, getting it open and his jeans pushed down his hips as Jamie removed his coat and pulled off his T-shirt.

The minute Jamie was free of his shirt, Tek shoved him back on the bed. Shoes, socks, and jeans discarded haphazardly around the room, Tek placed a hand on either side of Jamie's head, supporting himself with his arms, and pressed his hard cock against Jamie's, smirking at the hiss it produced from his lover.

Jamie responded by grabbing Tek's hips and grinding their groins even harder together, forcing an echoing hiss from Tek. Jamie held on to Tek as he pushed higher up on the bed. In perfect sync they moved together, driven by need, arms and legs wrapped around each other.

Tek ran his tongue down the length of Jamie's neck, biting down on the bulging muscle of Jamie's shoulders. Jamie jerked and then shuddered when Tek soothed away the sting with his tongue and sucked gently on the abused flesh.

The rhythm of their bodies increased in tempo to an almost frenzied pace, hard cock sliding along hard cock, a steady stream of precum slicking the way. Tek pushed back and looked down at his lover. He needed to see Jamie's face, see the pleasure and ground himself in the present.

Jamie's eyes were dark with lust beneath heavy lids. He gasped and moaned as they humped and rutted hard against each other, his fingers digging into the meaty flesh of Tek's ass. Tek took it all and gave it back, never taking his gaze from Jamie's handsome face. The anger, frustration, and coldness from earlier were forgotten as he basked in the heat of Jamie.

When Jamie came it was more of a sigh, a whisper of Tek's name as he tensed and jerked. The sight of Jamie giving in to pleasure, hearing his name spoken like a prayer was enough to send Tek over the edge, painting Jamie's belly and chest.

They collapsed into a heap of tangled limbs, fingers still kneading, holding, neither wanting to lose the connection. They lay together, silent and touching, until their breaths were slow and even.

Jamie kissed him. "You feel better?" he asked softly.

"Yeah, a lot," Tek admitted. "Even if I am a sticky mess."

"The sticky mess is just a bonus," Jamie snorted.

Tek sighed and buried his face in the side of Jamie's neck. "I don't want to go back out. I'm so tired of it, Jamie. I just wish the whole fucking world would disappear, and I could stay just like this for a week."

"You'd starve," Jamie teased and then kissed him again. "But I know what you mean. This shit with the Bangers and Mongols is going to get out of control."

"It's more than just that. I was talking more about the frustration of wanting to be with you. You're not the only one feeling the stress of it. It's fucking me up emotionally."

"Is that what happened today?" Jamie asked gently.

"At first, it was anger for the dope, the Bangers, that I was once again put in a position I had to take a life, all this shit with the club, ya know," he admitted. "But as I was swinging that piece of wood, I started thinking about you and what you said about how unfair it all was, and I just fucking lost it."

Jamie didn't say anything, but he tightened his hold on Tek, let him know through his embrace and touch that he understood. Tek's head resting on Jamie's chest, he could hear the steady rhythm of Jamie's heart, feel the slow, even rise and fall of his breath. Tek's body was like a sponge as it drew in Jamie's heat, and it was enough to burn off the cold that had settled into his soul.

Times like this, these stolen moments of peace, were the only time Tek could escape the evilness that was taking over him. He had no illusions of ever finding forgiveness for his sins. But when he was in Jamie's arms, he felt like a decent man, a good man, someone worthy of love.

But like all good things in Tek's life, it came to an end too soon. Time was the enemy, and once again he was forced to leave the peace of Jamie's arms and return to reality. Reluctantly, Tek left the bed, washed the remnants of their time together from his stomach and chest, and splashed cold water onto his face. He avoided his reflection in the mirror, no longer able to stand what he saw.

When he stepped out of the bathroom, he tossed a wet rag to Jamie, gathered up his scattered clothing, and got dressed. As he sat on the edge of the bed to put on his shoes and socks, he looked up at Jamie, who was pulling his shirt on. "You ready for this next hit?"

"As ready as I'll ever be," Jamie responded. "Hit 'em hard and fast."

"That's the plan." And the sooner this shit was over, the better in Tek's book.

One last shared kiss and they stepped out of the hotel room. Tek rolled his shoulders as he headed to his truck; he could already feel the tension seeping back into his muscles. As they approached Tek's truck, two men stepped out of the black sedan that was parked next to them.

"Mr. Cain," the driver said and pulled out a badge from inside his jacket and flashed it. "Federal agents. We'd like to have a word with you and Mr. Ryan."

Tek's pulse sped, and he eyed them suspiciously, his feet rooted to concrete.

"What's this about?" Jamie asked, moving to put himself slightly between the officers and Tek, Jamie obviously mistrustful of the strangers.

They had every right to be apprehensive. One of their members, John Boy, had been picked up by two men claiming to be feds who showed up at his house one night. His remains were found a week later in the desert by a couple of hikers. He'd been shot execution style.

"You mind if I see that badge?" Tek nodded to the driver. "Yours too," he grunted to the other man.

"Sure," the driver said easily and handed Tek his badge, as did the other officer.

Tek studied the badges: Agent Mark Sheppard and Agent Michael Regan. The badges looked authentic, but as he handed them back, Tek was still wary, his gut clenching in warning.

"What's this about?" Tek echoed Jamie's question.

"We'd like to offer you gentleman a deal," Agent Sheppard remarked, slipping his badge back into his pocket. His grin caused the hair at the nape of Tek's neck to stand on end.

"We don't deal with the feds," Tek said adamantly.

"Oh, I think you'll be most interested in this deal," Agent Regan put in. He reached into his pocket, and Tek tensed. Tek only relaxed slightly when Agent Regan pulled out an envelope instead of a gun and held it out to Tek.

Tek shot a questioning glance at Jamie, who looked unnerved, his eyes wary. "What's this?" Tek asked, taking the offered envelope.

The air rushed out of Tek's lungs and his heart stopped dead in his chest when he opened the envelope to find a photo of him and Jamie in the shower, Jamie on his knees with his mouth wrapped around Tek's cock. Tek couldn't breathe, his head spinning as he continued to stare at the photo. They'd obviously been watching them for months. Tek expected to feel rage that they had spied on his and Jamie's intimate moments, but he felt dead. Because that's exactly what he was, a dead man walking.

A car door slammed shut, and Tek looked up, dazed, unsteady as he captured the dual grins on the agents' faces.

"From the look on your face, I can see you understand what the terms of our deal are." Agent Sheppard slid a business card next to the photo. "I'll give you two some time to think this through. You have twenty-four hours to make your decision."

"Good evening, gentleman," Agent Regan smirked.

Tek watched the agents get into their car and drive off as his world crumbled around him.

Eye for an eye, tooth for a tooth, blood for blood, you're going to die.

We're all going to die.

Tek Cain

Death

TEK TAPPED the steering wheel of his truck impatiently and checked his watch again. It was one minute later than the last time he'd checked. It hadn't taken him and Jamie long to come to a decision. Going witpro meant going rat, and while neither of them could do that to the club, neither could they stay. To do so would be risking certain death if those pictures were turned over. They had to run, disappear—put a continent between the two of them and their old lives. They planned to leave the West Coast behind and start anew in one of the biggest, most anonymous cities in the world. New York. Tek glanced up at Jamie's house and then back down at his watch again. Now if the bastard would just hurry up, they could start this journey.

He'd dropped Jamie off an hour ago, ran home, showered, threw his shit in a bag, loaded his truck, and hurried back. How long did it take to grab some fucking clothes and your weapons? Tek blew out a frustrated huff and checked the house again; it was as still and silent as it had been for the last fifteen minutes he'd been sitting watching it. A bad feeling began to roil Tek's gut. *Fuck it!* Tek stepped out of his truck and jogged up to the front door. He turned the knob. Finding it unlocked, he entered the house.

"Hey, Jamie! What's taking you so long?" Tek called out. He expected Jamie to come bounding down the stairs, still wet from a too-long shower—the man did love to run a hot water heater dry—but the house remained quiet. Tek headed up the stairs.

The queasy feeling in his gut intensified when he noticed what appeared to be blood on the carpet, and he broke into a dead run, heart hammering as he raced to Jamie's room. The room was in disarray. Clothes thrown around, furniture overturned; evidently a hell of a struggle had taken place.

"Jamie!" Tek bellowed, but the only reply was his own voice reverberating off the walls of the small room. Sheer terror began to seep into every fiber of Tek's being, and he began to shake violently, weakening his legs and threatening to drive him to his knees. "Jamie! Where are you?"

He started scanning the area, trying to make some sense of what had happened, looking for some kind of clue that would help him find his best friend. A large handprint in blood by the door was enough to nearly send Tek over the edge into insanity, but he forced himself to stay on his feet, to keep searching for... something... anything.

Somebody had taken Jamie, forced him from this room, and when he found the son of a bitch who dared to take what was his, Tek would kill them. He had no doubt it would be one killing he wouldn't regret. The thought of revenge and torture spurring him on, Tek narrowed his focus, forced himself to still and take in the room again with intent.

"Who got the jump on you, Jamie?" Tek mused. They had apparently caught him coming out of the shower; a wet towel lay on the floor near the door. Tek spun slowly. They'd been waiting in here. There! He pointed to either side of the door. They hit Jamie with something hard enough to disorient him and rip flesh, and then he steadied himself against the wall after touching the wound. Tek turned again. A bag was packed, the clothes strewn around the room clean, but no signs of the clothes Jamie had been wearing. Tek rushed to the bathroom. He found evidence of Jamie's recent shower, his shaving kit on the counter, another wet towel on the floor, but no discarded clothing, which meant they had at least allowed Jamie to dress. That meant....

Tek snatched his cell phone from his pocket and fired it up. He and Jamie had a shared app that allowed the other to know where they were. "C'mon, c'mon, c'mon," he complained when the app was slow to open. "Got ya!" he hooted in victory when Jamie's location appeared as a blinking red light. "Sit tight, I'm on my way!"

Tek rushed out of the house and jumped into his truck. Before firing up the engine, he fished around in his bag and pulled out his sheathed knife and attached it to his belt. He checked the clip of his Glock and hid it in the pocket of his coat. Then he pulled out his Tec-

9—the very gun Jamie had gifted Tek with would be the one to save his life—and laid it across his lap.

Tek stomped on the gas, pushing the engine into a determined vengeful roar. His cell felt leaden in his hand, the flashing beacon his only hope. It wouldn't take him directly to Jamie, but it would narrow his location down to within a square mile. Tek had no doubt he'd find him. There was no other option. Fear and the need for vengeance kicked up his adrenaline, each heartbeat and growling vibration of the powerful engine lighting his every nerve as he flew down the highway, gas pedal pushed to the floor.

Tek left the city of Chatom behind, heading north as the sun began to set. For long painful miles, he had no idea where the hell he was going or where he would end up. He was unsure of just how bad off Jamie was, but feeling, knowing, that Jamie wasn't okay, Tek let the pain and anger take him over and blacken his vision into dangerously honed focus. Each mile that passed beneath his tires felt like an eternity, causing Tek's muscles to thrum with tension and his head to throb. Truck pushed to the max, "Highway to Hell" aptly blaring from the speakers, Tek's thoughts were consumed with pain. The pain he would inflict upon those who dared to touch Jamie.

The tiny flashing light led Tek to familiar territory, and within the mile range, he shut down his phone and shoved it into his pocket. He knew exactly where Jamie was and knew exactly who would die by his hands tonight. A satisfied sneer curled Tek's lips as he drove farther into Mongol territory.

Tek pulled to a stop and cut the engine a good distance from his target, thankful for the cover of darkness. Stepping out of the truck, he set his Tec-9 aside, removed his leather coat, and retrieved a black hoodie from his bag. He slipped it on, pulled the hood down low over his face, and slid the Glock into the waistband of his jeans.

He made his way through the trees surrounding the cabin, the strong wind rustling the branches, the creatures of the night going silent with his presence—a lone bark ahead the only thing to announce his arrival. The closer he got, the louder, more ferocious the barking became. Tek stopped behind a wide oak tree and caught sight of the large dog chained near the side of the cabin. The animal was straining against his chains, his glowing eyes focused on Tek, jaws snapping.

Tek had a split second to form a plan. Going with the first thing that came to mind as he ran toward the door, he hoped like hell the shadows and his dark clothing were enough to keep him out of sight from anyone looking out from within the cabin. He also said a little prayer the dog's chain would hold, since he valued the flesh on his ass.

Pressing his back against the wall next to the door, Tek pocketed his gun, picked up a rock from the ground, and pulled out his blade. His heart was hammering in his chest, the rush of blood in his ears nearly enough to block out all other sounds, but he forced himself to take slow, even breaths, refusing to allow the fear and excitement to overwhelm him.

After what felt like forever, the door opened and the barrel of a gun pointed out as the man holding it swept the area without showing himself. Tek tossed the rock sideways, hitting his mark. The ding of stone against the tin garbage can did its trick, and the gunman rushed out the door, weapon aimed toward the direction the sound came from, exposing his back to Tek. What an idiot, he deserved to die. Tek didn't hesitate, he sprang.

"Call out 'fucking raccoons'," Tek ordered the man, his blade pressed against the man's windpipe. When the man hesitated, Tek pushed the knife harder, enough to break skin, to show how serious he was.

"Fucking raccoons!" the man shouted, and Tek severed his windpipe in one quick slash, ensuring he'd never utter another word.

Tek held the man until the gurgling sounds and twitching ceased, then carefully eased the dead Mongol to the ground. As happened far too often of late, the coldness took him over again. Each time he called on it, he'd found it was easier to reach it, pull it to the surface. He knew if he continued, he would no longer have to summon it, search it out, he would become it. But that was a worry for another time, another place; at the moment the only thing was saving Jamie, coldness and soul selling be damned. First, he had to do something about the barking before someone else came out to investigate. Strangely enough, the thought of hurting or killing a dog bothered him more than the human life he'd just taken.

Tek hesitated, eyeing the vicious animal as he scrambled to come up with a way to stop the insistent snapping and snarling without killing the dog.

"Goddammit, Tao," someone yelled from inside the house. "Shut that dog up, or I'll shoot you both."

Time's up. Tek approached the dog, forearm up, distracting it, demanding its focus. He could smell the dog's warm breath as it snapped, feel its spittle on his face. "Sorry, pooch," he mouthed with true regret and lifted his forearm higher, tightening his grip around the blade in his other hand. When the dog lunged upward and exposed its vulnerable neck, Tek silenced the animal.

Tek wiped his blade on his jeans, returning it to his sheath as he edged close to the window. He could hear at least two men talking, neither the familiar voice of his lover. Tek needed to be silent but quick in his recon of the house. He only had moments before they came searching for Tao.

Thankfully, the gods of vengeance must have been smiling down on him, because when he peered into the cabin, he found it to be a one-room structure. Both men he'd heard talking were sitting at a table. One was drinking from a fifth of whiskey, the other cleaning a large blade as he rambled on about something that had his face animated. In the center of the room, tied to a chair, head bowed, was Jamie. Tek's heart skipped a beat, and he held his breath as he fought against the red haze of anger that threatened to rob him of sight. Blood matted Jamie's hair from a large gash over his right eye, which was swollen and turning an ugly shade of purple. Tek let out the breath he was holding when he saw the big chest rise and fall. *Alive.* Jamie was beaten, but still alive.

Dropping to a crouched position, Tek pulled out his Tec-9, checked the ammo, and flipped off the safety. He was far from a religious man, doubted God had a whole lot of care for him and his actions, but Tek prayed just the same. He prayed that his bullets hit their mark. Which was really a messed-up thing to ask God to help him with, but fuck it, he asked for it anyway.

After one last long breath out, Tek jerked to an upright position, bared his teeth, and pointed the weapon toward the table. Tek had caught them both by surprise. The moment he saw one man open his mouth, Tek pulled the trigger, firing round after round into the two men. He smiled with maniacal glee at the screams of pain as the bullets tore flesh, mangled limbs, and ended pathetic lives.

The noise was deafening, Tek's ears ringing, and he kept his finger pressed against the trigger, firing in a sweeping motion between the macabre dance of the two Mongols until his weapon was empty and the world fell silent.

Breathing harshly, Tek turned his head, expecting stunning blue eyes to be staring back at him, but his heart sank. All the noise and commotion and Jamie hadn't moved. He had to get to Jamie now! Tek threw his empty weapon aside and gripped the windowsill.

A single shot rang out as pain exploded in Tek's left arm; fingers numb, bone shattered, his arm became dead weight. He stumbled back, his feet hitting an obstacle, and he landed on his back. His chest seized, he couldn't breathe. It took him a second to understand the impact that had knocked the wind out of him was not a bullet to his lungs. He rolled on autopilot and pulled the Glock from his waistband as he moved. Where had the gunman come from? How had he missed one? No time to think about movement, pain, fear, Tek fired in the direction of the hulking shadow.

He rolled, fired, and rolled again until something stopped his movements. Silence.

Tek lay there for long drawn-out moments, listening to nothing but his own pulse roaring in his ears. Cautiously, gun raised, he pulled himself to a sitting position and spotted the man who had shot him, lying still, dead from a single shot to the head. *Fucker!*

Tek laid his gun down and pulled off his hoodie, wincing as the material scraped across his wound. He could feel the warm wetness oozing down his arm with each beat of his heart. Stop the bleeding. Get to Jamie. Tek pulled his knife and cut a strip of material from his hoodie. Using his good hand and his teeth, he secured the makeshift bandage around his bicep, pulled it tight. He squeezed his eyes shut as the world spun and exploded into pain.

Fucker! He cursed again when the dizziness subsided and he opened his eyes. He fought down the bile that rose up in his throat as he went to his feet. He was nauseated, his arm throbbing, and unsteady on his feet, but he had to get to Jamie.

As he made his way into the house, Jamie still hadn't moved. Panic once again overwhelmed Tek, spurring him to act; ignoring his own pain, he rushed to Jamie and lifted his head.

"Jamie! Wake up." Jamie's head lolled back; his eyes twitched beneath the lids, but he didn't open them. "C'mon, man, you gotta talk to me. Open those eyes!"

Tek patted Jamie's cheek. Nothing. "Jamie!" he roared and grabbed a handful of hair, forcing Jamie's head up. "Open your fucking eyes right fucking now! We have got to go!"

Jamie grunted but he still didn't open his eyes.

Tek tightened his grip on Jamie's hair. "Open your goddamn eyes, or so help me God, I will kick your ass!" he screamed into Jamie's face.

Relief rushed through Tek when Jamie's right eye fluttered open, the left too swollen to open. The pupil was blown, the normally white globe bloodshot, but it was the most beautiful thing he'd ever seen.

"Jesus! Don't scare me like that," Tek complained and pressed a relieved kiss to Jamie's lips.

"Te.... Hi, Tek," Jamie slurred. His mouth turned into a half smile as his good eye fluttered closed once again.

Great! Tek didn't know whether to be pissed or relieved when it hit him they had drugged Jamie to subdue him. No way would Jamie have stopped fighting unless he was beaten nearly to death or drugged. The only wound Tek could see was the one over his eye so it had to be the latter.

Tek scanned the room. How in the hell was he going to get Jamie out of here with only one arm? No fucking way could he carry the heavy bastard. Jamie was just going to have to man up. Tek retrieved a glass of cold water from the sink and poured it over Jamie's head.

Jamie spit and sputtered and shook his head, sending water droplets flying. "Hey!" he complained and shook his head again.

"Wakey, wakey," Tek insisted and started cutting through the ropes that held Jamie to the chair. "No time for a nap, big guy. We got to go."

"Go where?" Jamie asked in apparent confusion. "Can I jus' have nap?" he slurred, his head lolling on his shoulders as he spoke.

"Nope, time to hit the road, bud." Tek sheathed his knife and slid his arm under Jamie's shoulder. "C'mon," he encouraged.

"I tired," Jamie complained. "Sleep."

Tek gritted his teeth as he pulled Jamie to his feet. Jamie was nearly dead weight, leaning on Tek hard and causing the pain in his arm to scream. But Jamie was on his feet. He'd take the small victory even if he did want to puke or cry or both.

It was slow going, but he finally half dragged Jamie out the door of the cabin. He briefly thought about leaving Jamie behind and getting his truck, but he shoved the idea away immediately. No way in hell was he leaving Jamie alone. It was his turn to man up.

Minutes felt like hours as they struggled through the darkened woods. Tek constantly had to force Jamie to keep moving all the while refusing to give in to his own pain and exhaustion. The adrenaline high of the fear and battle was gone, and he was spent. One agonizing footfall at a time, they finally made it back to Tek's truck. He could now allow Jamie to sleep; he'd earned his reward for fighting through the fog of drugs for this long.

Tek helped the exhausted man into the truck, Jamie snoring before Tek could get him all the way in his seat. He placed a kiss to the top of Jamie's head. "I've got your back. Sleep well," he murmured and kissed him again before hitting the lock and shutting the door.

Tek wanted more than anything to crawl in beside Jamie and sleep, but he had hours before he could enjoy that luxury. He had a scene to stage and miles to put between them and this life. He didn't dare sleep until they were far enough away that he could keep Jamie safe.

Storm winds blew straight into the face of time, the hands stopped momentarily, only time can never truly be stopped. A life-shattering event, merely a blip in history, and yet for those involved, it can feel like a hellish eternity.

For me, the winds of change destroyed my life, but in death, I found freedom.

Tek Cain

Breaking Free

JAMIE CLUTCHED the bag full of medical supplies in his hand as he tromped up the stairs toward their hotel room. It really couldn't be called a proper medical kit, just some disinfectant, bandages, gauze, and tape, but it would have to do. He'd prefer to take Tek to the hospital, but it was too dangerous. Bullet holes meant police, a lot of questions, and fingerprints. Still, it would be better than if.... No, Tek would be fine. Jamie refused to think anything else.

Tek was lying on the large king-sized bed, asleep. He was naked, a white sheet draped across his waist, his chest rising and falling erratically, and the muscles of his arms and legs were tense, twitching, evidence of the pain Tek was experiencing from his wound even in slumber.

Jamie closed the door softly and moved closer to the bed. He laid out his supplies on the bedside table and then went into the bathroom to retrieve towels and the bucket of ice. He brought them back into the room, adding them to his other supplies, and kneeled down next to the bed. He placed his hand against Tek's forehead and felt the heat of a slight fever. He hoped it was a result of the pain and not early infection setting in. Tek barely responded, only a slight twitch in his cheek as Jamie touched him. The poor man had been up for over forty-eight hours. Tek had cared for Jamie until the drugs were out of his system. Drive, coffee, drive, more coffee. Tek had ignored his own wound and refused to stop, insisting they weren't safe, until Jamie had forced him to stop. It was now Jamie's turn to repay the favor.

"Tek," he whispered, running his fingers along Tek's cheek. Tek stirred, his brow creasing, but he didn't wake. "Hey, I have to clean your wound. You need to wake up for me," Jamie said a little louder.

"I don't want to," Tek muttered without opening his eyes. "It's gonna hurt."

Jamie grinned with relief at the pout on Tek's lips. "Yes, it is," he told him and unwrapped Tek's wound.

"You could have lied, you bastard," Tek grumbled.

"I'll get you a lollipop if you'll be a good boy," Jamie teased.

Jamie inspected Tek's wound. The skin around the gunshot was red and angry-looking, but it was no longer bleeding. Tek had worried the bullet had broken the bone since he'd lost the use of it during the battle, but it must have been the trauma of the blast. The bone was intact, and the bullet had passed through the meaty flesh of his bicep. The possibility of infection was Jamie's biggest concern.

Jamie laid the towels beneath Tek's arm to keep the bed from getting wet and bloody, then grabbed the bottle of disinfectant and opened it. "Ready?"

"No," he complained tightly. "But go ahead."

Tek squeezed his eyes shut, his teeth digging into his bottom lip as Jamie poured the disinfectant around the wound. Tek stayed tense as Jamie wiped away the excess fluid and blood. It was only going to get worse. Jamie hated the thought of hurting Tek, but he had to.

Tek watched him with a questioning look as Jamie donned a pair of surgical gloves and pulled out the packing strips of Iodoform gauze. "Tek," he said softly. "You might want to bite down on your pillow."

"Why?" Tek squeaked in alarm. "What are you going to do?"

"I have to pack the wound." Tek started to reach for his arm, protect it, but Jamie slapped it away with his forearm. "Don't touch it. Your hands are dirty," he scolded lightly.

Tek arched a single brow and pursed his lips. "No!"

"Sorry, bud. But you're just gonna have to man up."

"No," Tek repeated and glared at him.

"You can either let me pack it or I take you to the emergency room and let them do it," Jamie told him adamantly. "It's your choice, but either way, it's getting packed. It has to drain. If the wound closes with all that crap from the bullet in there, it will get infected."

"And how do you know this shit?" Tek asked suspiciously.

"Because I'm smart," Jamie sniffed. "Now bite down on your pillow and be a good boy."

Jamie had helped with more than one injured member of the club over the years. He wasn't a doctor, far from it, couldn't even call himself an adequate assistant, but he knew enough about wounds and the healing process. He just hoped it was enough.

"Goddamn!" Tek howled when Jamie shoved the first bit of gauze into the wound, and then bit down on his pillow to muffle the sounds of his screams as he'd been instructed.

Jamie's chest tightened as pitiful sounds continued to pour from Tek, but he clenched his jaw and packed the wound and bandaged it. Tek was sweating profusely and the color had drained from his face by the time Jamie was done doctoring him up.

"All set," Jamie informed him, placing the last strip of tape.

"Where the fuck is my lollipop?" Tek growled and pulled the pillow over his face.

Jamie pulled his gloves off and tossed them into the bag with the other garbage. He pushed up off the floor and went to his jacket and pulled out a pint of whiskey. "Sorry, this will have to do," he said, holding up the bottle.

Tek peeked out from under the pillow. "Where the hell did you get that from?"

"Five-finger discount," Jamie chuckled.

"Dumbass," Tek snapped and sat up. "You shouldn't be taking chances like that." His brows dropped into a frown. "But since you did, why the hell didn't you give it to me before you tortured me? That's cruel, man. Gimme," he demanded, beckoning Jamie by wiggling his fingers.

Jamie grabbed a cup, opened the bottle, and poured a generous amount. He brought it to Tek and handed it to him as he sat down on the edge of the bed. "I figured you'd need it," he said with a shrug.

"Well, no more chances," Tek warned him and downed half the booze. He winced at the flavor and wrinkled his nose. "The last thing we need is for you to get caught shoplifting."

"I won't," he promised. He reached over to the table and grabbed the bottle of ibuprofen and poured two into his palm. "Here, take these. They'll help with the inflammation."

Tek popped them in his mouth and swallowed them with the rest of the whiskey. "We should probably get back on the road soon. And I'd like to ditch the truck."

Jamie's brows lifted as he stared at Tek incredulously. "And do what? Walk? You're in no shape."

Tek waved him off. "I'm fine, but I wasn't talking about walking."

"And you complained about me stealing a bottle of booze," Jamie snorted and rolled his eyes.

"This is different," Tek insisted. "I'm sure the Feds have an APB out on the truck."

Jamie was silent as he thought about their options. There were too many risks involved in stealing a car, too many variables that could go wrong. "I thought you covered our tracks?" Tek had told him how he had set the scene at the cabin, making sure there was plenty of his and Jamie's blood smeared around and then sending a cryptic text to Rocco before destroying both their prepaid phones. He assured Jamie that no one would ever find any of the bodies, including theirs. Yet Jamie was still full of doubt, things that didn't make sense. "You never did tell me how you managed to hide the dead Mongols with only one good arm?"

"You don't need to worry about that, Jamie. All you need to know is that they will never be found," Tek informed him, a haunted look in his hazel eyes.

"No secrets, remember?"

Tek shook his head. "It's not a secret—just some details won't do you any good to know."

"But—"

"Look, Jamie," Tek interrupted, looking at Jamie with a pleading gaze. "Just let it go. It's over and done with. That life, that shit, the stuff we've done, it's behind us. From now on we're looking toward the future and letting our fucked-up past stay where it belongs. In the past. The men we were, the club, all of it, it's dead, okay?"

Jamie crawled up farther onto the bed to sit next to Tek, slung an arm around his shoulder, and pulled him close. "Yeah, okay," he agreed and kissed Tek's temple. He knew Tek wouldn't be able to leave it all in the past, the horrors of some of the things he'd done were etched in the lines around his eyes and seared into his brain. He knew Tek had nightmares at times; he'd heard him talking in his sleep, but he'd let it go for now, try and help him forget. "I still don't think it's a good idea to steal a car to drive us into our future. I say we get a good night's rest, and tomorrow we just drive. I bet it won't be too hard to ditch the truck in New York. Make sure it's never found again."

Tek turned in Jamie's arms and rested his head on Jamie's chest. He grunted in pain when he moved his arm. Jamie grabbed the pillow and wedged it beneath Tek's arm, keeping it propped up.

"Thanks," Tek murmured and then settled against Jamie. "I wasn't suggesting we steal a car. I have money, you know?"

"Yeah, I know," Jamie assured him. "But we're going to need that money to disappear. It's not cheap to live in New York City, and I'm so not living with the crackheads and hookers," he chuckled. "Besides, buying vehicles leaves a paper trail. Let's just get there, and then we will figure out what to do with the truck, okay?"

"Yeah, okay," Tek agreed sleepily. It only took a few minutes before Tek was snoring lightly.

Jamie spent the rest of the night holding Tek, dozing in and out, worrying. His mind refused to shut off and let him sleep. He worried about their past catching up, their future, but mostly, he worried about Tek: his wound, his exhaustion, and especially the haunted look he'd seen in his best friend's eyes.

"ON THE road again, just can't wait to get on the road again," Tek sung at the top of his lungs and then burst out laughing when Jamie glared at him and turned up the radio. The sound of Mötley Crüe's "Shout at the Devil" filled the cab of the truck.

Tek lowered the volume. "What's the matter? Don't you like my singing?" Tek sniffed.

"You have been singing it for two days. Enough already," Jamie grumbled.

"Aww, are you getting cranky, baby?" Tek asked mockingly.

"I passed cranky back in Chicago," Jamie grumbled. He ran his fingers through his hair and let out a big sigh. "I'm sorry. I'm just getting edgy," he admitted. "Ready to be there, ya know?"

"I know," Tek assured him and turned the radio off. "Everything is going to be okay."

"Why, because you said so?" Jamie asked, sounding weary.

Tek knew part of Jamie's problem was he wasn't sleeping. Every time Tek opened his eyes, he'd find Jamie staring at him, looking deep in thought. When he wasn't watching over Tek, Jamie was fiddling with Tek's bandages, probing at his wound, cleaning it, fussing over him like a mother hen.

"Yes. Because you take damn good care of me, and I know you won't let anything happen to me. That's how I know," Tek told him sincerely. "No one can sneak up on us 'cause we've always got the other at our back."

Jamie laid his hand on Tek's thigh, a tired smile pulling at his lips as he rested his cheek against the back of the seat. "Damn right, we do," Jamie agreed.

"We have a brand new life ahead of us, Jamie. Just you and me against the whole goddamn world. It's going to be fucking amazing, I promise," Tek said confidently. "Lay your head right here," he told him and patted his lap. "I'll tell you all about it."

Jamie laughed, but he did as Tek asked and laid his head in Tek's lap. With the hand of his bum arm, he ran his fingers through Jamie's hair as he maneuvered down the highway. He needed Jamie to rest before he ended up sick. Tek was confident they could lose themselves in New York, but that didn't mean he was as confident about staying lost. They were going to have to be smart, keep their heads down, and neither of them could do that if they were falling down from exhaustion.

Keeping his voice low and massaging Jamie's scalp, Tek told Jamie a tale of what living together in New York City would be like. Come hell or high water, he would make it happen. He'd promised.

Tek never broke a promise to Jamie.

I had been a caged animal, poked at, mistreated, starved, only I hadn't realized it until I broke free. Years of anger, hate, mistrust, had cultivated paranoia, left me panic stricken, disturbed, scared. I ran aimlessly from one town to the next. Never safe. Never trust. Never stop.

Run!

Run!

Run!

Fear fueled my lunacy.

I was sick with worry. Sick in my mind. Sick in my heart. Sick in my soul. The need to protect Jamie was the source of my insanity, and yet it was also my salvation. On an isolated patch of land, deep in the woods, far away from humanity, I finally stopped running. And as winter set in, the snow surrounding us, protecting us, we found our haven.

I cast aside my demons, found strength, courage as Jamie eased my troubled mind, kept me warm.

Tek Cain

A Slice of Heaven

IT TOOK months of zigzagging around the country before Jamie's paranoid lover finally allowed them to stay in any one place for more than a few days. When they did finally stop, it wasn't in the city as they'd originally planned, but in upstate New York. Tek reasoned they'd need a safe house if things got hot in the city. With a large chunk of the cash Tek had taken from the club, they'd bought a hunting cabin in the middle of the woods. It was the reason Jamie found himself in a fort of ice and snow preparing for his attack.

Stealthily, Jamie lifted his head up over the ice wall trying to get a visual on Tek. Jamie could plainly see Tek's fort. He'd built it between two large snow-covered pine trees, said he'd worried about being attacked from the side. Well, the crafty shit hadn't thought about aerial attacks. Jamie eased up out of his crouch and lobbed the snowball over the wall of Tek's fortress.

"Take that," he hollered and threw another one.

Jamie jerked when something hit the back of his head, white exploding around him. He turned and was hit in the forehead with another perfectly aimed snowball, blinding him in a flash of snow. Jamie dropped down, wiping the wetness from his face, but he miscalculated where the assault had come from. Worse, he'd underestimated his opponent. Jamie flailed helplessly as Tek barreled into him and they crashed through the wall of Jamie's fort.

"Surrender," Tek demanded. "I have you surrounded."

Jamie clutched at Tek's coat and rolled them. "Never!"

They rolled and fought for the upper hand. Jamie momentarily got the advantage and pushed Tek's face into a snow pile, but before he could savor his small victory, Tek arched his back and shoved hard with his arms. Jamie hit the ground, Tek's back against his chest, and Jamie wrapped him in a tight bear hug, pinning Tek's arms at his sides.

"Infidel!" Tek roared and struggled against Jamie's tight hold.

Jamie hid his face behind Tek's head, laughing at the crazy man's antics. Tek continued to call out ridiculous insults of treachery and chicanery while he kicked up a blizzard in his attempt to free himself. Even the freezing ground against Jamie's exposed lower back couldn't dampen his amusement. Jamie got a handful of snow and rubbed it into Tek's face.

Tek spit and sputtered as he batted away the arctic facial. "Uncle!" Tek cried out.

"Ha! I win!" Jamie hooted, released his hold on Tek, and gave him a shove. He should have known better than to trust someone as competitive as Tek. The next thing Jamie knew he was spun onto his belly and Tek sat on his back. Jamie had to turn his head to keep his face from being pressed into the snow.

"Uncle Victorious, bitch!" Tek threw his hands in the air and bounced as he did a little happy dance while straddling Jamie.

Jamie thought briefly about throwing Tek off, but the utter joy in Tek's voice had Jamie folding his arms beneath his head and smiling up at his jubilant lover. The emotion was so rare these days, Jamie basked in seeing Tek so carefree and happy.

"Fine, fine. You win," Jamie grumbled with mock irritation. "Now do you mind getting your lard ass off me before my boy bits get hypothermia?"

Tek went to his feet and held out his hand for Jamie. "Nothing boy about you," Tek said and waggled his brows. "But I'd be sad if your man bits froze off."

Jamie rolled and allowed Tek to pull him to his feet. "Then I suggest you take me in and get me out of these clothes," Jamie informed him as he tried to wipe as much of the snow from his wet coat and jeans as he could.

"Be my pleasure," Tek responded with a sly grin.

Jamie followed Tek to the cabin, the thick snow making it difficult to walk and made all the worse by the cold that was seeping into Jamie's bones and making him shiver. "And a fire. A big-ass roaring fire," he insisted.

Tek held the door open and ushered Jamie in. Jamie shrugged out of his coat, hung it on the hook near the door, and then removed his boots and wet socks. Jamie hissed when he stepped in a pile of melting snow.

"I don't know if I'll ever get used to how cold it is here," he grumbled and wiped his feet on the rug.

"Probably not," Tek agreed. "But snowball fights are kind of fun, and the warming up part is really, really fun."

"That remains to be seen," Jamie deadpanned. He tromped to the fireplace, rubbing his arms vigorously. He stoked the fire and then added another log. Water dripped from his hair and beard as the heat began to thaw him.

"Oh, I'll show you all right," Tek assured him as he stepped up behind Jamie.

Tek grabbed the bottom of Jamie's T-shirt and pulled it off, and then removed his own. Tek pressed his cool chest to Jamie's back, causing Jamie to shiver again. "I don't know how people live in these inhuman conditions," Jamie griped. "Hell, I don't know how I'm going to survive another two months of it."

"We have plenty of supplies and lots of wood," Tek told him and then kissed the side of Jamie's neck. "And more than enough body heat to keep you from freezing your man bits off."

It didn't take long before the heat generated from Tek's body rivaled that coming from the fireplace. When Tek unbuttoned Jamie's pants and slid them down his legs, the warmth only increased, especially in his groin as he hardened.

"Body heat is a good thing," Jamie murmured and stepped out of his jeans, kicking them to the side.

"Oh yeah," Tek agreed and ran his hands over Jamie's chest and stomach.

Jamie turned in Tek's arms and reached for the button on his jeans. "Get these off," he murmured against Tek's lips. "Everyone knows the best way to share body heat is to be naked."

"Mmm-hmm." Tek shoved his jeans down and off, then pressed up closer and grabbed Jamie's hips.

Jamie hissed when Tek's wet and cold groin came in contact with his, but with a little friction from their swaying hips, the coldness was quickly chased away. Tek hardened against him. They shared gentle, unhurried kisses while hands roamed over cool flesh as the fire crackled and popped, heating the room as their hands heated each other's flesh.

Jamie eased them down onto the rug until Tek was beneath him and they were stretched out from chest to toe as they continued to explore each other's mouths with lips and tongue. It wasn't always easy being locked away in an isolated cabin. Some days the monotony and boredom were hard to deal with. But after spending so many years hiding his feelings and then their relationship, Jamie would never take these moments for granted. If isolation was the price he had to pay to touch and kiss Tek whenever he wanted to, then he would gladly pay it.

Tek moaned into the kiss, his hands roaming Jamie's back as his hips rolled and thrust. Jamie shifted, lying between Tek's legs, encouraging him to spread them wider to accommodate Jamie's size. Jamie's lower body propped up slightly on his knees, and he began to meet each one of Tek's thrusts with one of his own. Their hard cocks rubbed against the other, pushing Jamie's need and want higher and higher. Kisses became deeper, hands frantic as they rubbed and dug fingers into flesh.

Jamie pulled his hips back and snapped them hard, the head of his cock sliding along the soft skin of Tek's balls and pressing against Tek's ass. Jamie was about to pull away when Tek gasped and arched, so Jamie did it again. He pressed against Tek's opening with short, soft thrusts, nudging, pushing over and over until Tek was moaning.

"You like that," Jamie murmured into the kiss.

"Yeah," Tek groaned, his voice deep and husky with arousal. "A little harder."

Jamie propped himself up on his elbows so he could watch Tek's face as he teased the tight hole with the head of his cock, pushing just hard enough to tease the tight ring of muscles, then pulling back. Tek's eyes were closed, his front teeth gripping his bottom lip as he moaned. Fuck his man was gorgeous when he was lost in pleasure.

Jamie had teased Tek's ass plenty of times with fingers when he'd been blowing him or jerking him off. It always made Tek nuts and shoot like a fountain. But he'd never fucked him. He'd dreamed about it, stroked himself to orgasm to fantasies of bending Tek over and ramming deep inside him, but he hadn't acted on his desires. Holy shit, how he wanted to act now. It took every bit of his restraint not to slam into that perfect tight heat.

Jamie's skin tingled, muscles thrumming and his dick so fucking hard it hurt as he fought not to give in to his need while he rubbed, rubbed, rubbed against Tek's hole. Tek arched his back again just as Jamie pressed forward, and the head breached the tight ring of muscles.

Tek's eyes snapped open and went wide with shock. "Ow. Wait," he panted.

Jamie pulled back, slipped from Tek's body. "Shit. I'm sorry. Got carried away."

"'S'all right," Tek assured him. "Just wasn't…. I want you to."

"I don't know if I could be gentle," Jamie panted. Jesus, he wanted to, but he honestly didn't know if he could do it without hurting his man.

"Then don't…." Tek shook his head and licked his lips. "Just…. Fuck, Jamie, just get the lube and condom. Don't make me beg."

Jamie scrambled to the sofa and grabbed the lube from beneath the cushion and huffed out a frustrated breath. No condom.

"Dammit, Jamie, would you hurry up? There, next to the bed," Tek pleaded.

Jamie looked over his shoulder to see Tek, knees bent, feet planted on the floor as he thrust up into the hand wrapped around his straining cock.

Jamie's legs were a little weak, his erection bobbing painfully as he dashed to the bedside table. He jerked the drawer open so hard the contents spilt on the floor, but he ignored the mess and snatched up a condom, opened it, and fumbled to roll it down his shaft. Jamie dropped to his knees between Tek's legs and popped the cap on the lube. Jamie poured a small amount into his palm, slicked up his sheathed cock, and smeared the rest along Tek's ass.

Tek slid his hands beneath his knees, spreading himself open, offering himself to Jamie. Jamie couldn't stand it another second, and he moved closer and guided his cock until the head was pressed against Tek's opening.

"You sure," Jamie asked through gritted teeth.

Tek's response was to bear down on Jamie's cock. The head popped into him, and they both hissed. Jamie held perfectly still, even held his breath as he searched Tek's face for signs of distress.

"Hurt?"

Tek swallowed hard and shook his head. "Just give me a minute," he said harshly. "Jesus, your dick is a lot bigger than your fingers."

Jamie chuckled, the movement causing him to push a little deeper into Tek, and he groaned as the tight hole contracted around the head of his dick. Jamie struggled not to push in any farther, but it was hard, so fucking hard not to bury himself deep inside Tek.

Tek stared up at him with wide eyes as his body adjusted to the invasion. Jamie began to worry he was hurting Tek and started to pull out. "No," Tek protested, and Jamie froze. "I... I want it. Just go slow, okay?"

Tek was rolling his hips, rocking his ass side to side trying to work Jamie's cock deeper. Jamie clenched his jaw, his pulse thundering as he held himself perfectly still. Sweat ran down Jamie's spine, and he shuddered, pushing his dick another fraction of an inch into Tek's body.

"Okay, move," Tek groaned.

Jamie hesitated, afraid to release the tight hold he had on his lust, but also afraid not to. He was held suspended as the two needs battled against one another.

"Dammit, Jamie," Tek growled and wrapped his legs around Jamie's waist, pulling him down as Tek thrust upward, taking Jamie to the hilt in one swift movement.

They both gasped, still and silent for a second, and then Jamie pulled back ever so slightly and pushed in again. Tek's panting mouth curled into a slight grin with the movement. "Feel good?" Jamie asked then pulled back again.

Tek shook his head and then nodded. "I don't know," he chuckled. "Fucking burns." He rolled his hips. "Ah... I... yeah. Do it again."

With painstakingly slow thrusts, Jamie began to move in and out. His body trembled with the effort to go slow as Tek's ass gripped his cock like a tight fist, but somehow he managed. After long moments, Tek's body began to relax around his erection.

"Oh fuck," Tek moaned, then dug his fingers into Jamie's shoulders and lifted his head to press his mouth against Jamie's. "Harder," he demanded.

Jamie's arms shook from holding both his own body and Tek's up, but there was no way he'd miss the pleasure shining in those hazel eyes or the blissed-out expression on Tek's face.

"You feel so goddamn good. Your ass is so.... Damn," Jamie groaned, his thoughts jumbling as he picked up the pace, sliding in and out of Tek's ass with ease.

"Wait till you try it from my end," Tek grinned dreamily. He released his hold on Jamie and fell back against the rug, then lifted one hand to caress Jamie's cheek. "It's like... it's like you're warming me from the inside out."

"I'll always keep you warm," Jamie promised.

"Always," Tek echoed, his eyes fluttering closed.

Jamie shifted, going up on his knees. He grabbed Tek's thighs, pushed them to his chest, and bent him nearly in half when Jamie pressed their mouths together as he began fucking Tek in long hard stokes, going balls-deep before pulling out and slamming back in. Over and over he fucked Tek as they breathed each other in, becoming one breath, one body of heat and passion.

Tek's erection rubbed along Jamie's belly with each thrust, leaving wet trails of arousal. Jamie dropped one of Tek's legs, leaned to prop himself up on one forearm, and wrapped his hand around Tek cock, giving him more heat, more friction as Tek began to go nuts beneath him, thrusting and rutting hard, a string of naughty curses and incoherent pleas pouring from him.

"I... so close... harder," Tek demanded, his voice harsh and strained between gasps.

Jamie couldn't take his eyes from Tek. His eyes were closed, head tilted back, exposing the straining muscles in his neck as he chased his orgasm. Jamie had never seen anything so beautiful or felt anything more fucking perfect than the way Tek's body gripped him, holding him deep inside. It was on the tip of Jamie's tongue to say... what? *I love you?* The words just didn't seem enough, not big enough, special enough for what Jamie felt for Tek. There were no words to use for the indescribable. Instead, Jamie showed Tek with his body what he felt, gave him every bit of his strength and power, his very breath as he rammed into Tek over and over.

"Uh... I'm.... Fuck, Jamie, I'm gonna...." Eyes closed, mouth open as if in a silent scream, Tek's body went impossibly tight and his channel clamped down on Jamie's cock, holding him balls-deep for a few heartbeats before Tek exploded. Wet heat fountained over Jamie's fist as Tek cried out his pleasure so loud Jamie's ears rang.

Jamie drove himself in and out of that perfect heat through each contraction of Tek's orgasm. A jolt raced down Jamie's spine. His balls drew up tight. He knew he was going to come; there was no way to stop the inevitable. Tek's ass milked it, demanding it. *Not yet. Hold on just a little longer.*

Tek slumped back against the rug, his sweat-dampened hair matted to his forehead, his swollen lips open as he panted. And then his eyes blinked open. Those gorgeous hazel eyes were dark with satisfied lust, and he smiled.

Jamie lost it.

He slammed into Tek one last time, tried to crawl inside Tek's body as he pushed in deep, and threw his head back and roared as he came so hard his head spun in a dizzying array of lights behind his tightly closed eyes. Jamie hung in that magical place that only Tek could take him, not wanting to land, not wanting the pleasure to end.

When he couldn't draw it out for a second longer, Jamie slumped against Tek, their combined sweat and Tek's cum hot between them. Jamie gasped for breath, taking in huge gulps of air as his heart pounded.

So gorged on pleasure, Jamie could only lie against Tek, listen to him breathe, and soak in the heat of Tek's body. He groaned when Tek rolled them and then hissed when his softening cock slipped from Tek's body. But then Tek was pressing up close, laying his head on Jamie's shoulder, and it was exactly where Jamie wanted to be. He wrapped one shaking arm around Tek and ran his fingers along Tek's bicep.

"You okay?" Jamie whispered. Even talking seemed like too great an effort.

Tek splayed his fingers out against Jamie's chest, right over his thumping heart. "Never better," he slurred sleepily and then patted Jamie weakly.

"You've been thinking about this, huh?"

"Hmm?"

"The stashed condoms in the drawer," Jamie pointed out.

"Oh, those," Tek chuckled. "A good Boy Scout is always prepared."

"You were never a Boy Scout." Jamie snorted.

"Yeah, well, I obviously would have been a kickass one."

"True dat," Jamie conceded and kissed the top of Tek's head.

As they came down from their high, Jamie's right side was warm from the roaring fire and Tek's body pressed tight against him. But from the other side, cold air blew against his heated flesh. With the last of his strength, Jamie grabbed his T-shirt and cleaned them up as best he could and then stretched and snatched the blanket from the couch. He covered them both, trapping in the heat, shielding Tek from the cold.

As they snuggled together, Jamie had a new admiration for winter and never wanted to leave their little slice of snow-bound heaven.

New York City, with its bustling metropolis and millions of people, is one of the loneliest cities. It was easy to get lost. We shaved our beards, cut our hair, and wore nondescript clothing, became one of the locals. Anonymous. However, it wouldn't have mattered how we dressed or wore our hair, no one noticed us. Not once in two years did a single person meet my gaze. No one said good morning, waved, or acknowledge either of us in any way.

However, Jamie and I didn't need anyone else. We had each other. We worked, lived, and loved side by side. The city can be lonely and violent, yet for Jamie and me, it was the safest place in the world. We found ourselves, new friends, and a whole hell of a lot of fun. Even then, I knew our past would eventually catch up with us, but at the time, we were having the time of our lives.

Tek Cain

Stepping out of Anonymity

"HEY, YOU about ready?" Tek yelled at Jamie who was taking his dear sweet time in the bathroom.

Jamie stuck his head out the door, toothbrush in hand and toothpaste dribbling down his chin. "Would you stop already? Jesus."

Jamie disappeared, and then the water came on briefly followed by loud gurgling sounds. Tek stood near the door, arms across his chest, and tapped his foot impatiently. "I have a job interview, and I can't be late," he reminded his pokey partner.

After a few minutes, Jamie stepped out of the bathroom, wiping a hand across his mouth. "It's not for another hour, would you relax? We have plenty of time."

Tek's gaze was drawn to Jamie's back as he moved toward the dresser. Water rivulets still ran down his flushed skin, the thick muscles flexing as he moved. For someone Jamie's size, now standing an inch taller than Tek at six foot six inches, he moved with the grace of a lion—even if he was built like a brick shithouse. Tek licked his lips as Jamie let the towel around his waist fall to the floor and he got a good look at Jamie's tight, perfect ass.

"You know," Tek said seductively, moving up behind Jamie as he pulled briefs from the drawer. "We could leave at seven and still make it in plenty of time if we spring for a cab." Tek licked a water droplet from Jamie's spine, causing the man to shudder.

"No, we won't," Jamie said with what sounded like regret in his voice. "You and I don't know the meaning of quickie."

"Sure we do," Tek said and then licked another water droplet. "It means an hour rather than our normal two-hour session." Tek took a step back. "Oh right." He pushed his palm to his hardening erection. "You're right. We don't have time, dammit."

Jamie stepped into his briefs and then turned around, a mischievous grin on his handsome face. "We could always skip the foreplay, and I could just bend you over the bed and try for a new record."

Tek spun away before Jamie could grab him. "Hell, no. It's your fucking turn to bottom. My ass is still sore," he complained. He stomped back across the room, tossing over his shoulder, "Now get dressed before I say screw the interview and bend your ass over."

Tek leaned against the front door and crossed his arms over his chest, steadfastly refusing to look at the laughing bastard while he dressed. He and Jamie were compatible in almost everything. If Tek cooked, Jamie did dishes and vice versa. They shared the chores around their small studio apartment fifty-fifty. They liked the same foods, the same sports teams, even shared the same clothes. However, when it came to sex, they had one difference. Tek cocked his head and thought about it for a second. Actually, they were the same in that aspect as well. Both loved to give and receive blow jobs, hand jobs. Both were big into heavy petting, kissing, and lots and lots and lots of foreplay and teasing. They were also both tops, and hence fucking had become a power exchange and all about compromise.

Tek began to tap his foot again as he waited. He checked his pockets for his keys and patted the back of his waistband to make sure his Glock was in place. For two years he and Jamie hadn't had any problems living in the big city, but Tek was still wary, always looking over his shoulder, waiting and always packing. He couldn't ever afford to let his guard down.

"C'mon already before I leave you here," Tek complained.

Jamie finished tying his shoes and tucked in his blue T-shirt as he made his way to the front door. "Would you knock it off? You'll get the job, but not if you go in there scowling and snapping."

"I'm not snapping," he snapped and then realized how he sounded. "Okay, maybe a little bit," he sniffed. "I fucking hate job interviews. They always ask too many personal questions, want too many stupid documents."

Jamie wrapped an arm around Tek's waist and pulled him close, pressing a soft kiss to Tek's lips. "It will be fine," Jamie said against his mouth. "No one has questioned our IDs before, and you need this job."

"I know," Tek conceded and hugged Jamie back, feeling some of his ire drain as he held his lover. Jamie always had a calming effect on Tek—his rock.

The money Tek had taken from Rocco's safe was running out, and with winter coming, Tek wouldn't be able to work as much as a day laborer, if at all. No way could they make it on Jamie's salary from his delivery job until spring. Tek clung to Jamie for a few more moments, letting Jamie's heat soak into him, ground him, before he lifted his head and kissed Jamie back.

"Alright, let's go get me a job."

Jamie winked at him and released his hold. "After you."

"You just want to stare at my ass," Tek teased as he turned and opened the door.

"Your point?" Jamie asked drolly and followed Tek out into the hall.

"Yeah, well, you're still not tapping it later, so you might as well get your fill of it now," Tek said. He locked the dead bolt and then pocketed his keys.

"Aww, c'mon. I was gonna give you a celebratory fuck in honor of your new job," Jamie teased and bumped Tek's shoulder.

"Oh, we'll be celebrating all right," Tek agreed, grinning widely. He slapped Jamie on the butt and added, "You can bet your sweet ass on it." Tek's grin grew impossibly wider at the indecipherable curse Jamie mumbled, but Tek got the gist of the complaint.

The subway cooperated for once, and they arrived at the club twenty minutes early. "Better early than late I always say," Tek announced and opened the door for Jamie.

"Since when have you said that?" Jamie countered. "I swear you're going to be late for your own funeral."

"Damn right, I am," Tek sniffed. "By about fifty years if I can help it."

The club was a mix of modern sleek and dark gothic, not exactly what Tek had expected. Come to think of it, he really didn't know what he'd expected. He'd never been in a leather daddy club, but this was nothing like he'd imagined. High-gloss black tables and chrome mingled with old, heavy, leather couches and wrought-iron hanging lanterns. The few men in the club weren't what Tek had expected either. Not a single piece of leather. The couple of men at the bar were dressed in sports coats and those sitting at the tables were sporting a preppy college-kid look.

"Nice place," Jamie commented.

"Yeah, it is," Tek responded. *Real nice*, Tek mused with a frown. *Maybe too nice for a dumbass ex-biker like me.*

Tek nodded to the men at the bar when he approached, then held out his hand to the bartender. "Hi, I'm looking for Ty."

The bartender shook his hand and smiled warmly. "You found him. You must be Tek?"

"Yes, nice to meet you. I hope you don't mind I brought my partner along," Tek said, stabbing a thumb over his shoulder at Jamie, who was flanking him. "This is Jamie. He's just gonna sit in the corner and wait for me."

"Don't mind at all," Ty said and held out his hand to Jamie. "Nice to meet you. And you're more than welcome to sit in on the interview."

"Nice to meet you too," Jamie replied, accepting Ty's handshake. "But I don't want to impose. I'm just here to take Tek out to celebrate his new job," Jamie teased.

"I like your confidence," Ty chuckled. "But really, it's no imposition. Trust me, if Tek here takes the job, my partner will be sitting in on the final interview," he said with a wink.

Tek instantly liked Ty. He had a warm smile and a laid-back attitude. Tek could picture the short, stocky man with his longish blond hair and clean-cut look catching a wave.

"Have a seat. Can I get either of you a drink?" Ty offered.

"No, I'm good, but thank you," Tek said and took a seat at the bar. Jamie declined as well and took the stool next to Tek.

"Hope you don't mind, but I have to work the bar while we chat. My bartender is running a little late."

"Not at all," Tek assured him.

"Okay, cool. So Tek, you have any experience bouncing?" Ty raised a brow. "Not that you would need any with your size."

"I did a little a couple years ago." He glanced around the room. "Doesn't look like you have much need for a bouncer," he noted. Damn sure nothing like the rowdy crowd they had at the MC every night.

"Doesn't get busy until later, but it's the weekends that can get insane. Do you have a problem with working weekends?" Ty asked him.

"Nope, prefer it actually," Tek commented. And so would Jamie. Jamie didn't work weekends, and knowing his lover like he did, Jamie would want to be somewhere in the crowd when Tek was working.

They spent the next half hour talking and laughing, nothing too serious or personal, more about how crazy drunks can get than anything else. Tek's initial impression of Ty as being a nice, friendly man only intensified over the course of their chat, and by the time the late bartender showed up, Tek was feeling pretty confident he had the job.

"About time you got here," Ty said as a dark curly-haired man joined him behind the bar.

"Don't be bustin' my ass, boss," the bartender sniffed. "Tackett already did that." He giggled as he tied an apron around his waist. "Whoa," he exclaimed when he took in Tek and Jamie. "If I didn't already have a man, I'd be crawling all over those mountains," he commented to Ty with a flirty smile on his full lips.

Tek felt Jamie stiffen next to him, so he placed a reassuring hand on Jamie's thigh and squeezed.

"Oh please, Micah," Ty told him drolly; then an evil glint ignited in his eyes. "Why don't you hit on that one?" he suggested, pointing to Tek. "'Cause I'd really, really love to see your scrawny ass tied into a pretzel by that one," he said, pointing to Jamie.

"Jesus H. Christ!" Micah barked. "You two are a couple?" he asked, mouth agape and eyes wide as he looked back and forth between Jamie and Tek. "Which one of you is the boy?"

"The what?" Tek asked in confusion.

"You know, the submissive. I'd really like to know, because...." Micah whistled and brought his hand to his chest dramatically. "That would make the other one one badass mega-Dom." He poked Ty with an elbow. "Not to mention a scary son of a bitch, huh, Ty?"

Ty grunted and shoved at Micah. "Would you behave," Ty chastised. "Tek, Jamie, this is Micah Slade, soon-to-be ex-bartender. Tek is thinking about coming to work for us."

Micah stuck his tongue out at Ty and then turned his attentions back to Tek. "You sure you want to work here? The boss can be a real

Debbie downer sometimes." Micah leaned in and whispered conspiratorially, "And a bit of a drama queen."

"Micah," Ty warned.

"I mean, he's the best boss ever," Micah said with a wink. "Better get to work. Welcome aboard, Tek. Nice to meet you, Jamie," he tossed over his shoulder and wiggled his way down to the customers at the end of the bar.

Ty sighed heavily, but the twitch of his lip was evidence he was used to the small man's antics. "You have to excuse Micah," he said to Tek and Jamie. "He's a bit of a fruit cup, but he's a lovable one. He flirts like the dickens. Makes him popular with the clientele, but don't let him fool you. He's head over heels in love with his man and loyal to a fault."

"I think he's adorable," Jamie chuckled as he continued to watch Micah.

"And taken," Tek grunted. "And so are you," he reminded Jamie. But Tek could easily admit the little shit was adorable.

Ty and Jamie both laughed.

"So, Tek," Ty asked, still chuckling. "Interested in the job?"

"Yes," Tek said with a nod. "I'm very interested."

"Good! You'll have to pass the scrutiny of Blake, but I'm sure you'll do just fine. And I'll put in a good word for you. Can you start Friday?"

"I'll be here, and thank you, I really appreciate it," Tek said sincerely.

"So do I," Ty said, holding out his hand out again. "Welcome to the Guards of Folsom."

"I told you you would get the job," Jamie said proudly as they walked out.

Feeling damn good about the interview, Tek slung his arm over Jamie's shoulder. "I think it's going to be great working there. I really like Ty."

"Me too," Jamie agreed. "And that Micah guy would be fun to work with. He's cute."

"Are you trying to make me jealous?" Tek grumped.

"Maybe," Jamie teased. "But you are cuter, especially when you get all possessive," Jamie chuckled.

"Wait till we get home, I'll show you how possessive I can be of your ass." Tek smirked.

"Well, you do deserve a celebration."

"Damn right, I do," Tek said happily. He was really looking forward to working at the club and relieved they wouldn't be homeless come winter.

As they made their way to the subway, Jamie suddenly asked, "What did Micah mean about one of us being a boy and a mega-Dom?"

"He probably assumed we were members of the club," Tek informed him.

Jamie was silent for a moment and then admitted. "I don't get it."

"It's a BDSM club, Jamie. You know, Dominants, submissives, leather, bondage, spankings, that kind of stuff."

Jamie stopped dead in his tracks. "You're shittin' me."

"Nope, dead serious."

"Wow," Jamie said, sounding shocked.

Jamie started walking again but kept glancing at Tek with a strange look on his face. "What?" Tek asked.

"Bondage, huh?"

"Yeah, you got a problem with that?" Tek inquired.

"Kinky."

"Yeah, so? I'm just going to be working the door, Jamie, not tying anyone up and spanking them."

"I know."

"So what the hell is that weird look for?" Tek demanded.

Jamie ignored his question and raised his brows, lip twitching. "I think I should be the mega-Dom."

"Oh hell no," Tek snorted. "You are definitely the boy tonight. This is my damn celebration."

Jamie's smile turned into a roughish leer. "For tonight."

Jamie took the stairs down to the subway, and it was Tek's turn to stop dead in his tracks when he heard Jamie mutter something about "I'm gonna need a really thick rope."

Life has a strange way of steering you directly down the path you were meant to travel, ending up at a place you were meant to be. I don't know if I ever believed in the whole destiny, fate, mumbo jumbo or if it was simply a coincidence. All I know is that behind the door of a BDSM club in New York City, I found a job, amazing friends, and discovered a whole new side of me. Damnedest things, those coincidences.

Tek Cain

Hello Kink

LEANING BACK in his chair, legs stretched out, Jamie tapped his finger against the tabletop in time to the techno beat blaring from the speakers. He had a perfect view of the crowded club, the bar, dance floor, seating areas, and most importantly, he had a clear view of the door where Tek stood arms across his chest, looking imposing as hell. And fucking hot. Tek's hair had grown back out, curling up against the collar of his black dress shirt. He'd also allowed his goatee to grow back in, although he now kept it closely trimmed after Jamie discovered what that prickly stubble felt like against the insides of his thighs and against his stomach. Tek was also wearing black dress pants; the soft material clung to him like a second skin, highlighting his thin waist, muscular thighs, and perfectly sculpted ass. Jamie had never been big into fashion, but after seeing Tek dressed up, he had a new appreciation for tailored clothing.

Jamie's admiration of dress clothes wasn't the only new discovery he'd made within the walls of the Guards of Folsom. He also found he was very, very appreciative of a man in leather. The way leather clung to a masculine form, the way it smelt, the feel of it, and thick strips of it across a broad chest was a major fucking turn-on. Another thing he'd discovered was that after years of hiding his affections for Tek, being in a place where men touched, kissed, and danced openly was a freeing experience. He no longer felt like a freak, no longer angry. He was finally at peace.

"Please forgive my forwardness, but are you Jamie?"

Jamie stiffened and turned toward the voice. He frowned at the older man with salt and pepper hair at the next table. He was dressed in black leather pants and his black T-shirt was tight against his broad chest. He was smaller than Jamie but still an imposing figure. Jamie wasn't used to anyone but Tek calling him that, and it also unnerved him a stranger would know him.

"Who wants to know?" he asked warily.

"Tackett Austin," the stranger said and held out his hand.

Jamie's frown deepened. He didn't know this man, and he hated being at a disadvantage. He slid his left hand into the pocket of his jacket, fingers wrapping around the butt of his gun, and shook the man's hand with his right.

"Can't say as I ever heard of you."

"We've never met," Tackett said with a smile. "But I couldn't help but notice the way you were watching Tek."

Jamie tensed and slid his finger against the trigger. How the fuck did this man know Tek?

"My boy came home all in a flutter of excitement telling me about the two mountain-size men he'd met. I put two and two together." Tackett's grin turned smug. "I think I should thank you for that," he chuckled. "Micah can be... a challenge when he's wound up."

Jamie relaxed and pulled his hand from his pocket. "I can imagine," Jamie snorted. "I met him when Tek was interviewing for the job. He's a spitfire."

"You have no idea. Do you mind if I join you," Tackett asked, pointing to the empty chair next to Jamie.

"Be my guest."

Tackett brought his bottle of water and slid into the chair. "Enjoying the club so far?"

Jamie nodded. "It's a lot different than the clubs back home." *Fuck!* That was the understatement of the century, although there was almost as much leather.

"Really? Where are you from?" Tackett asked.

Shit! "Out west," he responded vaguely and changed the subject quickly. "I meant, I'd never been in a BDSM club before."

"Really? How long have you been in the lifestyle?"

Jamie felt his cheeks heat, and he hid it behind his bottle of water, tipping it up and drinking half of it down. "I'm... we're not in... we're not...." Jamie waved his hand weakly, trying to find the right words. He'd never discussed his sex life with anyone but Tek, and even they hadn't discussed kinks. "This is a new experience for both of us," he finally settled on. "I didn't even know what a mega-Dom was."

"There's no such thing," Tackett laughed. "My pup likes putting a flare on things."

"Pup?"

"It's what I call my Micah. He can be a very naughty one at times."

"Micah doesn't mind being called a pup and a boy?" Jamie asked in confusion.

"Not at all," Tackett responded. "I'm not calling him a dog or a small child, Jamie," Tackett explained. "They are more terms of endearment of his standing, much like he calls me sir, master, or mega-Dom." Tackett smirked.

Jamie picked at the label on his water bottle as he tried to wrap his mind around the whole thing. No way would he ever be able to call Tek either pup or boy. It didn't fit him. Yet the idea of dominating Tek was something he'd been thinking about a lot lately. His favorite fantasy of late involved Tek naked and tied to their bed with thick ropes around his wrists and ankles. His thoughts were preoccupied by it; he wanted to try it but had no idea how to approach Tek.

"I can tell you have some questions," Tackett said, interrupting Jamie's musings. "Trust me; nothing you can say will shock me. I've pretty much seen and heard it all. Hell, I've been a Dom for over twenty years so I can assure you I've done most of it too."

"Wow!" Jamie exclaimed. "That's a long time. How did you get into it? I mean, how did you know you were a Dom?"

"I've had a propensity for kink since I was a teenager," Tackett said easily. "I've also always been a demanding lover. I like being in charge, so I guess you could say I've always been a Dom. What about you, Jamie? Have you always been a Dominant?"

Jamie had to think about that for a moment. On one hand he supposed he'd always been kind of dominant, but he'd also been less than confident when it came to his desires and sometimes looked to Tek for guidance.

"I don't know," he admitted truthfully. "What makes you think I am?"

"I'm very good at reading people. The way you're taking in the club and by the way you respond and react to what you see, you're trying to fit yourself into those roles. You're more comfortable when seeing yourself as the Dominant, and yet, your man there is also a Dominant so you're trying to figure out how that's going to work." Tackett leaned back in his chair and tipped his water bottle at Jamie. "How am I doing?"

"Impressive," Jamie said, astonished at how much Tackett had figured out just from observing him. "Any advice?"

"The way I see it you have two choices."

"Which are?" Jamie encouraged, leaning forward and listening intently.

"One, you could bring in a submissive. I can introduce you to Rig and Bobby. They used to own this club before Ty and Blake bought it and have been in the lifestyle longer than I have. They are a wealth of information and are also both Doms who share a boy."

Jamie shook his head vigorously. "No way!" he said adamantly. "Not that I wouldn't want to meet them, but I don't share Tek."

"If you're serious about exploring kink that involves dominance, then your only other option is to switch."

Jamie ran a hand over his chin and then propped his head on his hand. "Switch what?"

"Roles. You'll have to learn to be both submissive and dominant. Oops, I'm being summoned," Tackett announced, looking to the bar where Micah was motioning him with a hand, and stood.

Jamie had been listening so closely he hadn't even been paying attention to his surroundings. Tackett was obviously better at it than he was. Jamie imagined Tackett Austin could teach him a lot, and not just about kink.

Tackett fished in his pocket and pulled out a business card, then handed it to Jamie. "Here's my card. It has my cell number on it. Call me if you'd like to discuss the lifestyle further. It was very nice meeting you, Jamie."

"Thanks, I will," Jamie assured him and took the card. "It was nice meeting you too," he said sincerely.

"I'll look forward to our next conversation, then," Tackett said and, with a wave, walked to the bar.

Jamie watched him go. Tackett walked with a confident stride, head held high, each step deliberate. Jamie might not be as good at reading people as Tackett was, but he knew enough to know an alpha male when he saw one. And Tackett Austin was one. Jamie glanced at Tek who was scrutinizing a patron as he entered the club. *And there is another one.* One Jamie couldn't wait to dominate.

"YOU WERE awful quiet on the way home," Tek said, tossing his keys on the coffee table. "Everything okay?"

"Everything's fine," Jamie responded, his voice muffled as he dug around in the fridge.

Tek flopped down on the couch and propped his legs up on the table. "You didn't get too bored, did you?" he asked as he rolled his neck.

"Nah," Jamie said as he handed Tek a bottle of beer and sat down next to him with his own. "I met Tackett Austin. We sat and talked for a while. He's kind of cool."

"Micah's Dom, right?" Jamie nodded. "He introduced himself to me when he came in the club. What did y'all talk about?"

Tek took a long pull from his brew and relaxed farther into the couch. His feet were a little achy from being on them so long, but for the first night on the job, he'd done all right.

"This and that," Jamie said with a shrug.

"This and that?"

"Yup," Jamie answered concisely as he sipped on his beer.

Tek knew there was more to the story than what Jamie was telling him by the way he was avoiding Tek's gaze. Tek stared at him with an eyebrow raised knowingly and waited.

"What?" Jamie finally asked after the silence became too much for him.

"I want to know what you and Tackett talked about that's got you so damn quiet and avoiding my eyes."

"I'm not avoiding them," Jamie denied and gave Tek a sidelong glance.

"Mmm-hmm," Tek murmured disbelievingly.

The longer Jamie stayed quiet, the more curious Tek became, but he waited patiently. It did little good to nag Jamie into telling him what he and Tackett had talked about. The silent staring thing, that got Jamie every time.

"Knock it off," Jamie grumped and snatched the remote from the side table. "You're being a pest." He clicked on the TV and started going through the channels.

Tek didn't respond, rather he shifted on the couch a little so his head was turned directly toward Jamie and waited. Jamie continued to zip through the channels, but Tek was getting to him. He could see the flush of color move up Jamie's neck as he got flustered.

Jamie turned his head and glared at him, his lip curling into a sneer. "You are the most annoying fucker I've ever met. Did you know that?"

"Yes, I'm aware of it." Tek smiled sweetly at him. "It's part of my charm," he teased and batted his lashes at Jamie.

"Fine!" Jamie switched off the TV and tossed the remote aside. "We talked about how he could tell I was a Dom and you must be my boy."

Tek's eyes went wide in shock and then narrowed as the color increased in Jamie's cheeks, a sure sign he was lying. "I call bullshit. I'd wager he called it the other way around after he saw the size of my guns." Tek flexed his bicep.

Jamie rolled his eyes. "Yeah, that's it."

Tek downed the rest of his beer and set the bottle on the table. "So really, what did he say?"

Jamie licked his lips nervously and shrugged. "It was weird. The guy could tell what I was thinking from just watching me. He'd make one scary fucking Fed."

Tek blinked at him and stiffened automatically. Anytime he was reminded of his previous life, he had the same reaction. He was getting better at pushing the thoughts of what he'd done out of his head, rarely ever had nightmares anymore, but the past still weighed heavily on him.

Jamie must have noticed his reaction because he quickly added, "Sorry," and laid his hand against Tek's thigh.

"'S'alright," Tek assured him and entwined their fingers. "So what was it you were thinking about that Tackett figured out?"

"He said he could tell by the way I was checking out the club, from my reactions or some shit, I was trying to imagine myself in the different roles, which I was. And then he said I was more comfortable imagining I was a Dom, which was right. Freak, huh?"

"Both," Tek confirmed.

Jamie stared at him and pursed his lip. "What do you mean both?"

"The fact that you were thinking about yourself in the role of a Dom and that Tackett knew it. What'd he say about me?" Tek asked curiously.

"He said you're also a Dominant."

"Pfft, that's obvious," Tek snorted.

Jamie ignored Tek's jest. His expression stayed thoughtful. "Then he gave me some advice…. You know," he muttered with a shrug. "If we ever decided to do that stuff."

"Which is?"

"Well, on the first one, I told him no fucking way," Jamie said adamantly, shaking his head. "He said we could get a third, you know, a submissive to share. I told him we don't play like that."

Tek nodded. He and Jamie were still figuring out their roles, what they liked and disliked and always trying new things. But they were both powerfully possessive and would never invite anyone else to join in. Hell, neither of them wanted the other to go without a shirt around others, and it was only partially due to the tats on their backs that would expose them as Crimson VIII members.

"So if we did want to play," Tek said noncommittally. "What advice did he give?"

"Tackett said we should switch."

"Switch?"

"That was my response too," Jamie chuckled. "Take turns being the Dominant." Jamie reached into his pocket and pulled out a card and handed it to Tek. "He said he would be more than happy to answer any questions. He'd even introduce us to a couple of Doms who are a couple. They used to own the club."

Tek took the card and studied it. Tackett was the CEO and President of some software company Tek had never heard of. Rich business owners were definitely the kind of friends he and Jamie needed to be associating with rather than the lowlifes they'd grown up around. And if they happened to be part of the BDSM lifestyle, all the better. Tek was learning quickly that discretion and keeping an open mind without judgment were a must for anyone working in or a patron of the Guards of Folsom. It was the perfect environment for him and Jamie.

Tek handed the card back. "So are you going to call him?"

Jamie stared at the card for a long drawn-out moment. From the thoughtful expression on his face, he was carefully choosing his words. Tek thought about telling him he thought they should. The idea had definitely piqued his interest, but he waited to see what Jamie thought.

"I'd like to," Jamie said quietly. "That is, if you want to?"

Tek took the bottle out of Jamie's hand and set it on the table, then shoved him back on the couch. "I think it would be fucking hot," he said, leering down at Jamie and waggling his brow. Tek pressed his groin to Jamie's and rolled his hips seductively. "Wanna try now?"

The clank of bottles hitting the floor sounded seconds before Tek wrapped his arm around Jamie's neck and flailed ineffectively as he was rolled. The next thing he knew he was on his back where the table had been, a ripe curse on his lips.

"Yeah, I do," Jamie growled and grabbed Tek's wrists, pinning them over his head.

Tek blinked up at him, stunned momentarily until the dizziness passed. "Bastard," he finally grumbled.

"You asked," Jamie chuckled and then nipped Tek's bottom lip.

Tek was about to roll them again when Jamie brushed his lips against Tek's. The soft brush of their mouths and Jamie's warm breath caused Tek to shiver, and he parted his lips. Jamie teased and lapped gently at Tek's mouth as he positioned Tek's arms so he could grasp both Tek's wrists in one hand. He brought the other to rest against Tek's cheek. Tek went passive, allowing Jamie to do what he wanted, and was rewarded with a seductive moan. Jamie deepened the kiss, exploring Tek's mouth with a gentle sweep of tongue, and Tek forgot all about trying to get the upper hand as the need heated inside him when the tender kiss increased in strength and passion.

Breathing in heavily through his nose as jolts of electricity zinged through him, Tek encouraged his lover by rolling his hips, increasing the friction against his hard cock. Jamie gasped, responding in kind by pressing his full weight down on Tek, grinding his equally hard shaft against Tek's.

Tek's hands curled into fists as he fought the urge to break free from Jamie's solid grip. He wanted to rip Jamie's clothes away, dig his fingers into the thick muscles of Jamie's back, and take control. The dueling desires were maddening. He loved dominating Jamie, taking charge over such a powerful creature, and yet being on the receiving end of such a powerhouse of brute strength was a major fucking rush. He shook all over as the battle between the two opposing desires raged.

Tek groaned as Jamie grabbed Tek's pec and squeezed hard, curling his fingers into the thick muscle. The heavy caress was almost too much, painful and yet not nearly enough.

"Fuck," Jamie grunted against Tek's mouth and suddenly grasped the material of Tek's dress shirt and yanked, buttons popping, material tearing.

"Asshole," Tek growled and started to struggle.

Jamie tightened his hold on Tek's wrists with one hand and tore at Tek's shirt with the other, ignoring Tek's complaints. "Keep fighting me and I'll be forced to tie you down."

"I'd like to see you try," Tek dared. The muscles in his arms strained as he pulled against Jamie's hold. Fuck the bastard was strong.

Jamie raised his head, his blue eyes dark with lust, and leered at Tek. "Is that a challenge?" he asked thickly.

"Good luck with that," he said wryly.

With lightning quick speed, Jamie had Tek's biceps pinned to the floor with his knees, Jamie's groin against Tek's chin. Before Tek could even utter a complaint, Jamie whipped off his belt and secured it around Tek's wrists.

"Want to challenge me again?" Jamie laughed and nudged the bulge in his jeans against Tek's chin.

"Yeah," Tek snarled. "I dare you to whip out your dick and see if you can avoid my fucking teeth."

"Challenge accepted," Jamie said dubiously and popped the button on his jeans and eased down the zipper.

"Jamie," Tek warned.

Jamie ignored the threat in Tek's voice and pulled his cock out and tapped it against Tek's jaw. "Yes, Tek?" he questioned with a grin on his smug face.

Tek snapped at it in a halfhearted attempt to sink his teeth into the delicate flesh. "You wouldn't dare," Jamie snorted and jerked back.

"Try me," Tek grumbled and snapped his teeth again.

"Nah, that's not the wet, warm hole I had in mind," Jamie taunted and worked his way backward until he was straddling Tek's thighs and unbuckled his belt. "You have other"—he popped the button on Tek's pants—"less dangerous ones," he murmured and slid down Tek's zipper.

Tek's body thrummed with arousal, the predatory look on Jamie's face fueling Tek's desire even more, but he wasn't going to make it easy for him. "Figures you'd take the easy way," Tek grunted and made an attempt to shove Jamie off him.

"Ah, ah, ah," Jamie tsked and grabbed Tek's bound wrists. He pulled Tek's belt from his waistband, and looping it around the other belt, he leaned over Tek, pushing his chest into Tek's face as he secured his hands to the leg of the couch.

Tek was a little more than curious as to what Jamie would do. Heat raced through him, and his cock throbbed in anticipation. Tek was more than curious; he was fucking excited to find out. Still, as Jamie finished hooking up the belt, Tek sank his teeth into the hard muscle of Jamie's chest.

"Ow!" Jamie howled and jerked upright. He pulled up his shirt and looked down at his chest and frowned at the teeth impressions. Jamie raised his head slowly and smirked at Tek. "You're going to pay for that," he said huskily.

Tek shuddered. He watched Jamie appreciatively while he pulled off his shirt, tossed it aside, and then stood over him. Tek licked his lips and swallowed hard as Jamie shoved his pants and briefs down and off. Jamie had an impressive physique, but when his skin was flushed with arousal and his fat cock hard and straining upward, he was beyond stunning.

Jamie went to his knees next to Tek and struggled to pull down the tight pants. Tek laughed as Jamie huffed out a frustrated breath when the garment refused to cooperate.

"Should have thought about that before you tied my hands," Tek sniffed. Jamie's eyes narrowed and his grip tightened. "Don't you fucking dare rip these," Tek demanded.

"Then lift your damn hips," Jamie scoffed.

Tek lifted his hips and allowed Jamie to pull them down. He shuddered again when his ass made contact with the cold hardwood floor. "Wouldn't this be better on the bed?" It sure as hell would be for Tek's ass and back.

"No headboard," Jamie said curtly and reached beneath the cushion of the couch. "Plus we have everything we need right here," he informed him as he pulled out some lube and a condom.

Tek raised a brow at him. "How long have you been planning this?" he asked suspiciously.

Jamie just shrugged, his lip twitching as he situated himself between Tek's legs and leaned down until their chests were barely touching, propping himself up on his forearm next to Tek's head. "Always good to be prepared," he said against Tek's lips.

Tek closed his eyes as Jamie's other hand began to roam across his shoulder, up his bicep and forearm, then back down to his side as he pressed his groin against Tek's. They both hissed with the contact, their hips moving in a familiar dance.

"Ropes," Jamie murmured against Tek's cheek.

"Huh?" Tek asked, not really caring since his focus was on the way Jamie's cock was sliding against his, the friction and heat so damn good.

"I think you would look even hotter bound in ropes," Jamie informed him, licking a path to Tek's ear and nipping at the lobe.

Yeah, sure, whatever. As long as Jamie kept his hips moving and those warm lips and tongue against his skin, he could do whatever. Jamie must have known he had Tek right where he wanted him too, because the click of a top opening sounded seconds before slick fingers traced over Tek's thigh as Jamie sat back, a knowing grin curling his lips.

"Thick ones," Jamie commented and shoved Tek's right leg up and out, holding it up with his hand as the fingers of the other teased at the sensitive skin behind Tek's balls. "Thick black ropes around your wrists."

Tek could only nod when Jamie's slick finger pressed against his opening, breaching the tight ring of muscles. Tek nodded again; hell, he didn't even know what he was agreeing to, but anything Jamie wanted in that moment he'd give him if he kept pushing that lubed finger deeper.

"Bind you to the ceiling, more black ropes around your ankles," Jamie murmured as he began sliding that finger in and out of Tek.

Tek squirmed and groaned, it sounding more like a whimper when Jamie added another finger alongside the first. "Jamie," he pleaded, for what he didn't know.

Tek had never bottomed well; it felt good, but he'd always liked to control the actions, Jamie's orgasms, and movements. But for some reason he couldn't quite explain, he liked the way the binds on his wrists affected him, made him feel submissive. It was as if he knew he couldn't fight, couldn't rule, and his body certainly liked the effects being bound was having. He was achingly hard, wanted Jamie buried deep inside him.

Jamie obviously knew what Tek was pleading for. He let his fingers slip from Tek's body, and in a matter of moments, his sheathed cock pressed into Tek. "Is this what you need?" Jamie asked, voice tight as he pushed in slowly.

Tek gasped as the burning sensation flared as his body tried to adjust to the invasion. But he wanted it, wanted it badly, and he lifted his hips, begging with his body for more. Jamie read him perfectly and lifted Tek's other thigh and then planted his hands on the floor near Tek's chest. Tek's legs were draped over Jamie's biceps as he began to move. Each stroke was long and deliberate, burying himself balls-deep in Tek before pulling out slowly. Over and over, oh so fucking achingly slowly, Jamie moved, never taking his gaze from Tek's. It felt so fucking good, but he wanted more, the gentle rocking not nearly enough.

"Is it?" Jamie asked again.

Tek clenched his teeth, instinctively tried to reach for Jamie's hips to force him to go faster, but the leather belts bit into his wrists. "No," he responded pleadingly. "Harder. Please, Jamie."

Jamie pulled halfway out and thrust in hard with a grunt, rolled his hips, and then did it again with more force. Tek cried out as pleasure and pain shot through him. Jamie bit his lip, his arms trembling under the weight, and truly fucked Tek. Just fucking losing it, he was like a wild man as he slammed in and out of Tek, giving him exactly what he'd begged for. Jamie seemed to find his own pleasure with each moan, whimper, or curse Tek made.

Tek's sweat-dampened back stuttered along the wood painfully, each thrust of Jamie's hips driving Tek's spine into the floor, and still Tek begged for more. "Harder," he rasped out, voice hoarse.

Jamie went up on his knees, lifting Tek's lower body off the floor. Jamie dug his fingers into Tek's thighs, gripping hard. He grunted with each thrust and pulled Tek forward at the same time, going impossibly deeper.

He and Jamie hadn't ever been what one would call gentle with the other. Both knew the powerful body of the other could take it. But this…. This was raw and visceral and carnal, and Tek loved every fucking painfully pleasurable second of it.

"Tek…." Jamie growled, his entire body shaking. It was the only warning Tek got before Jamie's back bowed, hips thrusting erratically as he came.

Tek strained against his bonds, the look of his lover lost in pleasure nearly pushing him over the edge, but he didn't want to miss a second of the sight above him. Tek clamped down on the reins on the orgasm racing through him as Jamie rode his out, whispering Tek's name like a prayer.

Jamie slumped forward, struggling for breath as he pressed his lips against Tek's cheek. "Damn, you made my fucking toes curl," he panted.

Still buried deep in Tek's body, Jamie wrapped his fist around Tek's aching cock. Two firm pulls along his dick was all it took, and Tek was coming, shouting out Jamie's name as wave after wave of pleasure coursed through him.

The scent of sweat and sex hung thickly in the air, and Tek inhaled the pleasing aroma, nostrils flaring like a winded racehorse. The analogy was fitting. Tek felt as if he'd been ridden hard and fast, chest heaving, muscles shaking from exertion. He was too exhausted to move, and white dots swam behind his closed lids. The wood floor wasn't the most comfortable thing he'd ever been on, but he thought maybe he could just sleep for a little while, body mellow and sated. It barely registered when Jamie slipped from his body, other than the loss of heat, and he sighed.

Tek could feel Jamie standing over him, and he blinked his eyes and looked up at him sleepily. "What?"

"That's a good look on you," Jamie commented with a smug smile, then looked down at his cum-covered hand and wrinkled his nose. He pulled off the used condom, grabbed his shirt, and padded to the bathroom.

Tek, too blissed out to care about messes, closed his eyes again and tried to roll onto his side. He'd forgotten all about the belts, but as the euphoric high of his orgasm began to wane, he became painfully aware of the raw and irritated skin around his wrists.

"Hey," Tek croaked. "Forget something?"

Jamie stepped out the bathroom with a towel in his hand. "Oh right, sorry," he muttered and ran the towel over Tek's chest.

"I meant the belts," Tek grumbled.

"I don't know. I was thinking I'd leave you tied up. Might want to take advantage of you again," Jamie said wryly.

"Yeah, like you'd be able to get it up again anytime soon," he remarked flippantly. "Now get these off, my fingers are going numb."

JAMIE'S SMILE fell as he stared at Tek's wrists. "Shit!" he cursed and rushed to free him.

Tek winced as the leather strap was loosened and wiggled his fingers to get the blood flowing. His muscles screamed as he brought his arms down and examined the angry red marks on his flesh.

"Are you okay?" Jamie asked with concern as he ran his finger over one of the marks.

Tek's lip twitched as an idea popped into his head. He studied the marks on his flesh. His smile turned into a mischievous grin as he met Jamie's concerned-filled eyes. "You're gonna pay for that." Thick black ropes sounded like a damn good idea.

I thought I had learned all I'd ever need to know growing up in Chatom, California. I had been taught by the hardest, meanest sons of bitches—the streets. I could read a man by the way he carried himself, could defend myself and those I cared about. Knew how to make a dollar, provide and survive. But I missed one very important lesson, pleasure. Sure, I had received it, given it, but I'd never truly experienced it until I learned to listen to my body, explored it, and controlled it. Oh, and holy hell, what a lesson I learned.

And taught Jamie.

Tek Cain

Explorations

THIS HAD been his idea, he'd brought up the subject, had been the one to make the call and set up the meeting with Tackett, Bobby, and Rig. Now standing in a darkened club amongst sawdust, scraps of lumber, and various saws, hammers, and drills, Jamie felt like a fool. It was as if his and Tek's sex life was being discussed, analyzed, and judged.

Jamie leaned back on the workbench, felt the grit and dirt beneath his palms, and sighed. He glanced at Tek who was listening raptly to Rig and nodding. Jamie wanted to slap him for being so calm and so fucking eager.

"So it's not that you don't find pleasure in bottoming, it's letting go of your need to be in control that's the issue here, am I correct?" Rig asked he looked back and forth between Tek and Jamie.

Jesus, does he have to say it like that? Jamie supposed it could have been worse. Rig could have said, *"Since you like dick up your ass."* Jamie cringed. He glanced again at Tek, who was still nodding.

"Jamie?" Rig asked.

"Oh sorry, umm, yeah, that's it," he responded, his cheeks heating. He was so going to beat the shit out of Tek later.

"Are you okay?" Bobby asked Jamie with a concerned look on his face.

Jamie scrubbed his hand over his week-old beard. He was finally letting it grow back in, but it was driving him nuts. His pants were too tight, his hands dirty, and he was fucking embarrassed. No, he wasn't all right.

Tek nudged him with an elbow. "This was your idea," Tek reminded him.

"I know, but I didn't think it would be this hard," he muttered for Tek's ears only.

"Ah, thank you, Vincent," Tackett said as the waiter set down a tray full of glasses and a bottle of scotch.

"You're welcome, sir. Anything else I can get for you? Anything?" Vincent asked, his voice low and seductive.

Vincent was small, his features pale under bright auburn hair, his posture and aura, from what Jamie had learned, spoke of his submissiveness. The glint of mischief and the flirty smile he was giving Tackett as Vincent ran his fingers along Tackett's arm was evidence of the double meaning in his question.

"That'll be all," Tackett said evenly without looking at the man and dismissed him with a wave of his hand.

Jamie watched curiously as the man's expression darkened dangerously before he spun on his heels and stomped out of the room. There was definitely some history there.

"Come have a drink," Tackett called to Jamie as he began filling glasses with the amber fluid. "Perhaps it will help you relax."

"Yeah, Jamie, relax," Tek muttered.

Jamie made an affronted sound that was basically a fuck you. He wasn't sure the drink would help, but he accepted the offer and plopped down in the chair next to Tackett, Tek following and taking the empty seat to Jamie's right.

"Thanks," Jamie mumbled and took a sip, the scotch smooth and warm all the way to his belly.

"Damn, that boy doesn't give up," Rig laughed and slapped Tackett on the back. "What the hell did you do to him?"

"I gave him the spanking he so very much needed. Didn't even fuck him," Tackett said defensively.

"Ah, then this is young Vincent's problem," Bobby said with a slight grin. "He won't give up until he's savored your beast."

"Not going to happen," Tackett responded curtly. He brought his glass to his lips and, before taking a sip, murmured, "I value my beast attached, thank you very much."

Rig hooted and slapped the table hard enough the bottle nearly toppled. "I'm sure your naughty pup likes it attached as well. But if I were Vincent, I wouldn't go about showing his nuts when Micah was around."

"Perhaps you and Bobby can take him on, keep him busy," Tackett suggested. "You'd be doing him a great service. You know, saving his nuts and all," he chuckled.

"Not our type," Bobby said with a sniff. "Way too prissy."

Jamie sipped his drink slowly, listening as the three older men discussed the various submissive men in the club. Jamie found himself relaxing now that the focus was no longer on him. The same easy feeling settled over Jamie that he'd experienced his first night in the Guards of Folsom, one of peace. Hearing these men talk about their sexual exploits with other men as they laughed and good-naturedly teased the other produced a feeling of camaraderie in Jamie. He didn't have a clue as to what some of the shit they were talking about was, but it didn't matter.

Jamie tilted his head and looked at Tek who was laughing along with the others and realization hit Jamie right in the chest. For the first time in his life, he felt like he belonged. As odd as it was, while sitting in a club in New York City, he had the sense of being home. Jamie set his glass on the table, laid his hand on Tek's thigh, and squeezed gently. Tek looked over at him and winked and then laced their fingers together.

"What about you, Jamie? Interested in any of the subs in the club?" Rig inquired.

Jamie shook his head. "I like mine big and beefy," he said easily.

"Submission isn't about the size of your body," Bobby informed him. "It's a state of mind. Remember that one sub?" Bobby asked, looking at Tackett and snapping his fingers several times. "The one nearly as big as Tek and Jamie here."

"Mario," Rig piped in.

"That's it! Son of a bitch was huge!" Bobby exclaimed. "To look at him, you'd think he was a Dom, but he was a complete, and damn well-trained, I might add, submissive."

"Really?" Tek asked. "I'd think someone that big and powerful wouldn't want everyone knowing he was weak."

"Ah, but that's the thing, Tek. Subs are far from weak. In fact, they have all the power in a Dom/sub relationship."

"No way," Jamie said disbelievingly. "How in the hell does someone who is being tied up and beat on have all the power? That makes no fucking sense."

"So you're saying Micah has all the power over you?" Tek added in the same skeptical tone.

"In more ways than one," Bobby snickered.

Tackett flipped Bobby off. "To answer your question, Tek, yes, Micah wields all the power when we're doing a scene. It takes a very strong man to have such control over his body. Micah also has the power to stop the scene at any time by using his safeword. I can only do to Micah what he allows me."

"Wow," Jamie mused and ran his hand across his itchy jaw. "I never thought of it that way before."

"I can give you an idea of how difficult it is to submit. If you're up for it, I'd like to do a little experiment," Tackett offered.

Jamie and Tek stared at each other for a moment in silent questioning.

"It's nothing kinky, and I won't ask you to take your clothes off or spank the other," Tackett added with a knowing grin.

Tek shrugged. "Okay," Jamie told Tackett. "What do you want me to do?"

Tackett gulped the last of his scotch before standing. "If you gentleman will follow me," he said and moved to the center of the room.

They both followed Tackett, still holding hands.

"Jamie, if you'll stand right here," Tackett said, pointing to the spot just in front of him. "Hands at your sides. Yes, just like that," he said approvingly when Jamie moved into position.

"Your only job is to stand there. You're to keep your eyes open, and you're not allowed to move or speak. Easy enough, right?"

"Sure," Jamie answered.

"Good, now, Tek, I just want you to touch him. You can touch him anywhere you wish. Jamie's body is yours to do as you please.

However, for now, you may only use your hands, lips, or tongue. And, you cannot move him out of position nor can you cause him any pain. Got it?"

"Oh this is going to be fun." Tek smirked. "Got it."

Jamie gave a small nervous laugh at the mischievous tone of Tek's voice but forced himself to relax. All he had to do was stand there and not talk. No biggie.

"Jamie, try to clear your mind as you submit your body to Tek and obey the rules. You may begin," Tackett informed them and returned to his chair.

"I feel like a kid in a candy store," Tek murmured against Jamie's ear. "Where shall I start? What delights shall I sample first?"

Jamie pulled away from the tickling sensation as Tek blew against his ear.

"That's one, Jamie," Tackett announced.

Jamie shot a look at Tackett, who was pouring more scotch in his glass, and started to protest, but he clamped his mouth shut. *Don't move, right.*

"Yeah, don't move, baby. I promise this won't hurt a bit." Tek's lip twitched as the bastard tried to hold back his laughter.

Jamie bristled at being called baby, but he tightened down on his muscles and his reaction and stood stone still.

Tek ran his hand across Jamie's chest, his palm brushing over Jamie's nipples causing them to harden, and then slowly made his way down Jamie's stomach, his fingers hovering over the button on Jamie's jeans.

"If we were home," Tek whispered for Jamie's ears only. "I'd have you undressed so fucking fast and be on my knees." Tek's hand cupped Jamie's growing erection. "Would you like that? Want me to suck your dick?"

Jamie's eyes closed as heat infused his groin, and he hardened further in Tek's strong grip. "Yes," he affirmed breathlessly.

"That's two."

Jamie's eyes flashed open, and he turned his head to glare at Tackett. Before he could think better of it, he complained, "But he asked me a question."

Bobby covered his mouth and turned away, but Jamie could see the man was trying to hold back his laughter by the way his shoulders shook. Tackett and Rig, however, were both staring at Jamie with raised brows. *Fuck!* This was harder than he'd thought. Jamie shook his head and found a spot on the wall to focus on. *No talking, no moving, clear my mind.* He could do this.

"As a submissive, you must learn to suppress your urges and desires," Tackett drawled. "Your Dom's pleasure must become more important than your own."

How the hell was that even possible, Jamie mused. The way his dick was twitching, his skin tingling, all Jamie wanted to do was to grab Tek and kiss that cocky grin off his face. That and push into the firm grip on his cock, but he refused to move. He was hell-bent on showing them he was strong enough to do this.

Tek moved to stand behind Jamie, pressed his chest against Jamie's back, and nuzzled the side of his neck. When Tek's tongue left a wet trail along his flesh, Jamie clenched his jaw and stared unblinkingly at the wall.

Teeth came next, nipping at the large juncture of neck and shoulder. Jamie curled his fingers into fists and clamped down on the shudder that threatened. The room was silent except for the muffled sounds of the music playing out in the main club and Jamie's harsh breath as he breathed heavily through his nose.

Tek began worrying a spot on Jamie's shoulder with teeth and lips as his hands slid around Jamie's waist and pulled him hard against him. An involuntary moan escaped him as Tek's hard cock pressed against the crease of Jamie's ass, and he pushed back against it.

"Jamie," Tackett called out sharply.

Jamie's eyes snapped open, and he jerked upright. He hadn't been aware of his eyes closing or that he was leaning heavily against Tek as his lover rubbed against his ass.

"You have broken the simple rules I've set for you numerous times in a matter of minutes," Tackett chastised lightly, coming to stand once again in front of Jamie, drink in hand. "Is it really that difficult to follow a few simple rules?"

"It's a lot harder than I thought it would be," Jamie admitted, chagrined.

"You see, true submission takes an inner strength very few possess," Tackett said softly. "They must, in a sense, have complete control over their minds and bodies and willingly hand both over to their Dom. A good Dom can teach him, push his bounds, and take him places he never thought he could. But ultimately, it is the sub who holds the real power."

Tek tightened his hold on Jamie and rested his chin on Jamie's shoulder. "Those are some badass little dudes," Tek surmised.

"And big dudes," Tackett reminded him with a grin. "But yes, I suppose they are. Damn sure nothing weak about them."

"I'll say," Jamie agreed. "I think I need a drink."

"And more practice," Tek chuckled and released Jamie.

They all returned to their seats, and Jamie accepted a fresh drink from Bobby.

"Tonight was just for fun," Bobby informed them. "But when you're truly doing a scene, both of you should be completely sober. I have a list of rules and some literature on safe play I'll make sure to get to you," Bobby offered.

"That would be great," Jamie responded. "But I think for tonight I'm gonna go home, enjoy my buzz, and have a little vanilla fun." The experiment had left him more than a little turned on, and he had a bit of payback to dole out. "Ain't that right, Tek?" he proposed and cupped Tek's dick.

Tek coughed on his drink, his eyes going wide, causing everyone to laugh.

What was that saying? Something about give a man enough rope and he'll hang himself? Yeah well, Jamie never did do things the conventional way. Give that man enough rope and I was the one hung.

Tek Cain

Roped

"WOW! THIS looks great," Blake complimented.

Jamie jerked, flailing momentarily as he tripped over his toolbox with the unexpected visitor. He caught himself at the last moment but cursed as the tools went scattering across the floor.

"Sorry. Didn't mean to startle you," Blake said apologetically and helped Jamie collect the tools.

"No problem," Jamie assured him. "I was daydreaming, and thanks."

Jamie had been working in the evenings doing light construction and painting for Blake and Ty. They were adding a private section off from the main club for members only. The private club had a large social area with heavy leather club chairs and tables in front of a stage. A large wood and stainless steel bar had been installed just the day before and looked amazing. But it was the side rooms that Jamie had been most fascinated with.

Each of the eight rooms had a private bath with walk-in showers and was heavily soundproofed and wired for security, including a panic button. Once the construction and painting was complete, the rooms would be furnished with armoires, king-sized beds, and various implements to satisfy certain kinks. It was the heavy metal rings he'd been bolting to the floors and ceilings in each room that piqued Jamie's interest, however.

They finished gathering up the scattered tools and then stood side by side to admire the completed room.

"I'll be glad to see this construction mess finished," Blake commented. "I hate all this disorganization."

"A little OCD, are ya?" Jamie teased.

Jamie really liked Blake Henderson. He was a hell of a nice guy and great to work for, but he was a little anal when it came to the workings of the club. And holy hell, was the guy a stickler for safety. Jamie wasn't the only one who noticed it. It was well known around the club, and Blake took the ribbing he got good-naturedly.

"One can never be too careful." Blake smirked.

"Everything on schedule for the grand opening?" Jamie inquired as he wiped the sweat from his brow with the back of his forearm and finished packing up the last of the tools.

"We've got two weeks to furnish and stock the rooms and bar, but I think we've got plenty of time to finish. We better," Blake chuckled. "I think Ty is ready to string me up."

"I'd pay to see that," Jamie laughed.

Blake wasn't a big guy, slightly above average in height, lean muscles. Ty, while shorter than Blake, was much broader in the chest and shoulders, yet as Jamie was learning quickly, size had nothing to do with dominance. Blake had an air about him that was pure alpha male. He didn't talk the bullshit most guys who thought they were alphas did. Blake didn't have to. He was confident without being overly cocky, and he simply commanded respect.

"Not gonna happen," Blake told him with absolute sureness. He patted Jamie on the back. "Keep up the good work and feel free to test your work," he said, glancing up at the steel loops in the ceiling. Blake must have noticed the stunned look on Jamie's face because he added, "Where do you think Bobby got the safety tips he gave you? Enjoy!" And with that, Blake stepped out of the room without waiting for Jamie's reply.

Jamie stared at the doorway long after Blake disappeared. He'd been a little shocked at first, but surprisingly, it didn't really bother him that Blake knew about his and Tek's meeting with Tackett, Bobby, and Rig. Everyone within the walls of the club seemed to accept everyone, which was one of the main reasons Jamie felt so at peace there. He didn't have to pretend to be something he wasn't, and no one asked him prying questions about his past. It was kind of cool.

Jamie studied his handiwork in the ceiling. His body heated as he imagined Tek suspended from the rings. Blake was right. A good handyman always tested the strength of his work. With a grin on his face, he pulled his cell from his pocket and hit the speed dial.

After the third ring, Rig answered. "Hello?"

"Hey, Rig, it's Jamie."

"Hi! How ya doing?"

"I'm good, thanks." Jamie glanced up once again at the ceiling, his smile growing mischievous. "I'm hoping you can give me some advice on where to get some supplies."

TEK WALKED into the darkened private club. After being out in the frigid New York temperatures, the blast of heat felt good on his cold face.

"Jamie, you in here?" Tek called out. He cupped his hands together and blew into them, trying to heat them up.

"Back here," Jamie called from one of the side rooms.

Jamie had called him earlier, sounding like a little kid. He was excited about the work he'd completed in the club and couldn't wait to show it off. Jamie was just too fucking cute when he was fired up about something. So, as much as Tek hated the cold, he'd bundled up and trudged his way over—on his day off, no less—to check out Jamie's handiwork. Tek shrugged out of his jacket and laid it on one of the workmen's tables and then made his way to the only room with a light on.

"Hey—" Whatever else Tek might have been going to say was forgotten as he spotted Jamie standing in the middle of the room. He was dressed in tight black leather pants and nothing else. Wrapped around his left wrist was a thick black nylon rope. He was stroking the other end with his other hand. Tek's pulse quickened at the sight of his man dressed like that, showing off all those luscious muscles.

"Shut the door and lock it," Jamie commanded. Tek didn't even hesitate, did exactly as Jamie asked without ever taking his eyes from him. "Now strip," Jamie ordered as soon as the door was locked.

"What the hell have you got up your sleeve?" Tek asked suspiciously, but he began unbuttoning the cuffs of his shirt. Tek cocked his head. "And where in the hell did you get those pants?"

"You like 'em?" Jamie asked, ignoring Tek's first question as he continued to run his hand along the rope.

"They're fucking hot," Tek assured him and waggled his brows lewdly.

"Thanks," Jamie responded, pushing his chest out, preening a little. "Rig hooked me up. Now will you strip already? Sheesh," Jamie complained.

Tek pulled his shirt off. After scanning the room and seeing nowhere to hang it, he let it drop to the floor. Tek bent and untied his tennis shoes and looked up at Jamie as he pulled them off. "Are you going to let me hold that rope while you pry those tight pants off?" Jesus, the things he could do to Jamie while he was bound. Naughty things. Things that would drive his lover out of his mind with lust. He'd been thinking about it ever since Jamie first mentioned ropes. Dreamed about it constantly. The fantasies kept getting hotter and hotter ever since Jamie had tied him to the couch. Now seeing Jamie with the black rope in his hands and dressed in leather, Tek was instantly hard and his skin tingled with anticipation of fulfilling some of his naughty dreams.

"Nope."

"What do you mean, nope?" Tek countered as he pulled off his socks and tossed them and the shoes aside.

"Just what I said." Jamie smirked. "Nope."

"If you say nope one more time, I'm going to spank your ass." A drop of sweat rolled down Tek's spine, and he shuddered. He'd gone from freezing his ass off to being cooked alive within minutes. "Why the hell is it so hot in here?" Tek complained.

"Wanted to make sure you wouldn't be cold, since I plan on having you naked for a while." It was Jamie's turn to cock his head and study Tek for a moment. "Are you going to bitch about everything tonight?" Under his breath he muttered, "Should have gotten a gag."

Tek heard it and rolled his eyes at Jamie without commenting on the jest. Tek slid out of his pants and boxers and added them to the pile of discarded clothes. Now he just had to figure out how to get Jamie out of his pants and the rope out of his hands. *Shouldn't be too hard*, he thought. He was very, very good at distracting Jamie. After knowing each other since birth, Tek knew all Jamie's weaknesses.

"So," Tek said conversationally. "Shall I assume the position?" He slid his hands behind his back and clasped them above his ass. He jutted his hips out, putting his erect cock on display.

Jamie eyed him suspiciously as he went to turn down the heat. Tek could tell Jamie was stubbornly refusing to look down any farther than Tek's eyes by the way his jaw was clenched and the fact that he wasn't blinking. That was fine with Tek. Jamie would eventually step up close enough for Tek to get his hands on him. For the moment Tek stood naked as a jaybird, swaying his hips. Trolling.

"It's not going to work," Jamie said knowingly as he moved back in front of Tek just out of his reach. He twirled the rope in his hand, holding Tek's gaze. "Turn around and keep your hands clasped."

"I'm sure I have no idea what you're talking about. What won't work?" he questioned innocently and added more swing to his hips, swaying back and forth seductively, his hard cock bobbing as he moved.

"Uh-huh. Sure, you don't," Jamie remarked. "I can see it in your eyes you've got something up your sleeves, and I'm telling you. It won't work. Now, assume the position."

"Nothing up my sleeve." Tek brought his hands to the front and held them up for Jamie's inspection. "See. I don't even have any sleeves."

Jamie took a step back and narrowed his eyes. "Dammit, Tek, would you stop it? I spent all afternoon setting this up. The least you could do is play along," Jamie complained and pushed his bottom lip out.

It was an honest-to-god real pout, which looked totally ridiculous on his big beefy lover, and Tek had to bite his tongue to keep from laughing. "Alright, fine," Tek conceded. He turned and clasped his hands once again behind his back.

Tek had no sooner turned around than Jamie pounced, grabbed Tek's hands in a tight grip, and leaned in close to Tek's ear.

"Obviously, my pout is more effective than your trolling," Jamie chuckled.

"Bastard," Tek grunted indignantly.

"Aww, don't be a sore loser, babe," Jamie teased as he wound the rope around Tek's right wrist. "I obviously know your weaknesses better than you know mine," he said against the side of Tek's neck and then kissed the sensitive spot just below Tek's ear.

Tek started to utter a snappy comeback, but Jamie spun him and smashed their lips together and short-circuited Tek's brain with a blistering kiss. Tek moaned into Jamie's mouth as his hard shaft came in contact with the soft leather pants. The material was cool against his heated flesh and he thrust his hips, looking for more of the tantalizing friction.

"You're so easy," Jamie said against Tek's lips when the kiss ended.

"Only for you," Tek reminded him breathlessly.

"Damn right," Jamie affirmed. "How does that feel? Not too tight?"

Tek opened and closed his hand a couple of times, testing the rope. It was secure, felt good against his skin. "No," he said, voice thick with growing arousal, and shook his head.

It still surprised him how quickly he could go from trying to outsmart Jamie to becoming passive, and he allowed Jamie to attach the rope to the rings in the ceiling and pull his arm over his head. He watched Jamie carefully as his lover lifted Tek's other arm and wound the rope around it. It was part of what made their sex so much fun. The playful battles between them to see who would end up with the upper hand kept it new and fresh and smoking hot.

"How's that?" Jamie questioned when he was done securing Tek's other arm.

Once again, Tek opened and closed his hand, testing the strength of the ropes. "I think you got me," Tek surmised with a grin and pecked Jamie on the cheek.

Jamie's smile turned brilliant. "Oh and the wicked things I'm going to do to you now that you're mine."

Jamie walked over to the far wall and bent to retrieve another rope. Tek watched him, Jamie's muscles flexing and rolling with each movement. Everything about the man ignited Tek's passion, and he licked his lips when Jamie went to his knees in front of him. Tek couldn't help but sway his hips seductively at Jamie.

"Any of those wicked things you're brewing up involve you staying in that position?" Tek asked hopefully. Those lips had wrapped around his dick so many times, and yet Tek could never get enough of that warm mouth and talented tongue.

"Maybe," Jamie said with a shrug as he wrapped the rope around Tek's ankle, secured it to the floor, and did the same with the other. "Now that's what I call a work of art," Jamie commented and sat back on his calves as he took in Tek's body with an appreciative expression on his face.

Tek's legs were only shoulder-width apart, but the rope was tight enough to keep him from going up on his toes, nor could he move them in either direction. Like the binds around his wrists, they weren't too tight, yet he was acutely aware of them. He liked the sensation. More so, he loved the look on his lover's face and his position.

"I'm your canvas to paint," Tek replied lewdly.

Jamie stroked his knuckles up and down Tek's thigh and then leaned in and pressed his lips to it. "I'm sure I won't be the only one doing some painting," he said against Tek's flesh.

Goose bumps bloomed across Tek's skin as the tingling sensation from Jamie's warm breath and soft lips rushed through him.

"But not yet," Jamie added, his voice a little deeper, rougher. He then slid his palm over Tek's other thigh before kissing it as well. "You can't come until I tell you."

"Well, he sort of has a mind of his own," Tek snorted.

"This might help him change his mind," Jamie announced and pulled a small black string the size of a shoelace from his pocket and held it up.

Tek studied the lace and gave Jamie a questioning glare. "What are you going to—" Jamie looped it around Tek's nuts. "Hey, wait," Tek sputtered. "That's some delicate equipment you're messing with."

"I know," Jamie purred and kissed the head of Tek's cock. His tongue lapped at the precum seeping from the slit.

Tek watched Jamie eagerly lick at the engorged head as he gently wound the string around Tek's sac snuggly and then around the base of his cock. "You.... Damn that feels good.... You sure that's safe?"

"Of course," Jamie assured him, his lips brushing along the length of Tek's cock as he spoke. "I'd never do anything to damage this." He followed back up the same path of his lips with tongue.

Tek was too consumed by pleasure to care that his cock was now bound. He liked the way it caused his erection to grow impossibly harder and throb. Or maybe that was due more to seeing Jamie on his knees with his mouth on him, but either way, he really liked the way heat fused through him and ignited his nerve endings. He rocked his hips, the pleasure intensifying.

"God, Jamie. Suck me," Tek moaned as the throbbing increased. "Stop teasing."

Jamie looked up at Tek, his blue eyes full of lust mingling with a hint of mischief as he swirled his tongue around the head of Tek's cock. "I'm not teasing. I'm building the anticipation," he corrected. "You always said it was half the fun."

Tek shifted in his restraints. *Shit!* He wanted to grab Jamie's hair and force his head down on Tek's straining erection. The ropes were both stimulating and frustrating as hell in equal measures. Instead, he could only stand there as Jamie continued to lightly lick at Tek's cock and moan as he tried to find a balance with the conflicting sensations and needs. For long moments, Tek's voice was too thick, brain too scattered to form proper words. And then he didn't need words, didn't need to beg or complain because Jamie was swallowing him down, his throat contracting around Tek's dick as he swallowed.

"Ah, fuck! That's it, Jamie. Just like that."

Tek thrust gently against Jamie. It was impossible to not move as Jamie began to suck him in earnest. His dark head bobbed as moaning and slurping sounds poured from Jamie while he feasted on Tek's cock. Seeing Jamie like this only added to the eroticism, and he thrust harder, wanting, needing more as the fire within his belly raged to an inferno.

"Damn I love to watch you suck me off," Tek praised huskily. "Almost as much as I love feeling it."

Tek gasped as Jamie took him deep into his throat again, swallowing around the head several times until Tek felt his orgasm rush down his spine. "Ja…. Oh fuck…. Jamie, I'm gonna…."

Jamie jerked back and fisted Tek's cock, making him whimper at the near-painful grip. "Not yet," Jamie growled, his voice sounding raw.

"Shit!" Tek complained and began to tremble all over as the need to come overwhelmed him, and yet he couldn't with the viselike grip on his cock. For long torturous seconds, Tek stood teetering on the edge, unable to leap off into orgasm nor step back and catch his breath.

"Deep breaths," Jamie encouraged as he nuzzled Tek's hip.

Tek hung his head, eyes squeezed shut, and clenched his jaw until the immediate need began to subside. The rush of blood in his ears drowned out sounds of his heaving breaths.

"That was mean," he grumbled, working to slow his labored breathing and pounding heart.

"Aww. Let me make it up to you," Jamie appeased. He went to his feet and pecked Tek on the lips.

"I don't think that is going to make up for it," Tek huffed. Christ, his nuts were so tight they ached with the demanding need to empty. "C'mon, man," Tek pleaded. "I need to come. Like, right-fucking-now before my sac bursts."

Jamie soothed his hand over Tek's rapidly rising and falling chest and kissed him again. "Soon," he promised and then walked away.

"Hey! Where the hell are you going?" Tek hissed as he looked down at his engorged cock and cringed. The black string looked obscene against his deep red color. "Get back here and finish this," he demanded, the sound coming out suspiciously like a whine.

"Keep your shirt on," Jamie sniffed. "Just going to grab a couple things."

"I would," Tek shouted. "But you made me take the damn thing off. You better be getting a condom and lube," Tek advised with a huff.

He was wound up tighter than a forty-year-old virgin in a whorehouse. His muscles were bowstring tight, and they trembled with the exertion. And, damn, he wanted to come so fucking bad. Tek was on the verge of begging, pleading, sobbing if he had to. Tek loved foreplay—hours of it—but their foreplay generally meant taking the edge off before the real heat was fired up. This was just torture after no sex the last couple of days. He pulled against his restraints; the movement caused his throbbing cock to bob painfully.

"And dammit, hurry up," he added pitifully.

Jamie came back to stand in front of Tek, blessedly with lube and condom in his hand, it was the chair in his other hand that concerned him.

Tek stared at him questioningly and nodded toward the chair. "What's that for?"

"You'll see," Jamie said with a wink.

Jamie set the chair down and the condom on top of it. It was no surprise when Jamie poured a small amount of lube onto his fingers. Tek figured he'd be feeling those slick fingers up his ass within seconds. However, Tek's mouth fell open in shock when Jamie shrugged out of his leather pants and reached around to press his fingers against his own ass. Jamie grunted, then bit his lip as he slicked himself up.

"Okay," Tek panted, rapt by the expression on Jamie's face. "I think that is one of the hottest things I have ever fucking seen. And trust me," Tek said adamantly with sly grin. "I'm not complaining, but, dude, you're doing it wrong. I'm the one bound here, remember."

Jamie raised his eyes and looked at Tek under his long dark lashes. "Oh, I know—" Jamie moaned loudly, the muscles in his arm bulging. "—and trust me, what I have planned will blow your mind."

"It's already nearly there," Tek admitted. "All you have to do is turn around, and I think you'll have succeeded in full eruption." 'Cause damn Jamie was hot, and he was so fucking turned on and... yeah. Full explosive eruptions were definitely possible without Jamie even touching him again.

"Patience," Jamie murmured wryly, removed his fingers, and snatched up the condom. He tore open the packet and stepped closer to Tek, his smile knowing.

"Ugh," Tek grunted. "I wanted a show!"

"There you go bitching again," Jamie tsked and rolled the condom down Tek's hard shaft. "I can always quit if you don't like what I'm doing."

Tek swallowed hard. Jamie's warm hands on him caused Tek's nerve endings to zing. "Jamie," Tek whimpered, no longer caring the word came out as a plea.

Jamie kissed him one last time, leaving Tek breathless and thankful for the ropes or he'd be on his ass with how weak his knees were. And oh Jesus, Joseph, and Mary, they did buckle and he had to lock them when Jamie turned and bent over with one hand propped on the chair and then reached around with the other to guide Tek's cock into his slick hole.

Tek rocked helplessly against that tight hole. He couldn't wait to be buried balls-deep in Jamie's ass. The ropes didn't allow for him to grab onto Jamie's hips like he wanted, to impale Jamie on his cock. But he could still push back and thrust forward with strength. Jamie's hand fell away, and he hissed as Tek entered him. Tek instantly went still as soon as the head of his cock breached Jamie and gave him time to adjust to the intrusion, but it was hard. Oh so very fucking hard when his body was screaming at him to move, to plow into that warm wet heat over and over. He clamped down on the urge. The way Jamie's ass contracted around Tek's cock made the struggle all the more difficult. His desire not to hurt Jamie the only thing keeping Tek's hold on the reins of his control, but it was slipping through his fingers quickly.

"Jamie," Tek hissed through clenched teeth. "Please tell me I can move. Please."

Jamie pushed back, and in one perfect motion, Tek was buried deep within his lover's body. Jamie's long pleasure-filled moan was loud in the room as he rolled his hips, giving himself time to relax and stretch yet providing Tek the friction he begged for.

"Ah…. Damn," Tek panted, pulling harder against his restraints as his toes curled. Not being able to touch Jamie was singularly the most frustrating thing he'd ever endured, and yet at the same time, he was more aroused than he'd ever been in his life.

Jamie leaned forward until once again only the head of Tek's cock was breaching him. "Do it," he growled. "Move."

The last of Tek's control shredded, and Tek pounded into Jamie, hard and fast. The moans and pleas of harder, faster from his lover as Jamie worked his own cock sent a jolt down Tek's spine.

Jamie had obviously been as turned on throughout the scene as Tek had been, because after a couple more hard thrusts, Jamie threw his head back and screamed Tek's name, the sound of it echoing around the room. Jamie's ass clenched even tighter around Tek's bound cock, ripping the orgasm from him in spite of the snug binding. Tek came longer and harder than he'd ever experienced, and his head spun as everything in his body went tight, shut down in the face of unimaginable ecstasy.

Finally, as the last drop of seed pulsed from his body, Tek gasped, panting for breath, still buried deep inside Jamie. Tek trembled with the exertion it took to keep himself upright, thankful for the strength of the binds or he'd be on his ass.

After several minutes, Jamie finally shifted—Tek slipping from his lover's body with a moan—and removed the restraints around Tek's wrists. Jamie held him and eased him down to the ground before freeing Tek's ankles. Jamie made quick work of the cleanup and then knelt next to Tek and rubbed the red marks on his wrist.

"You okay?" Jamie asked.

Tek slumped against him in a euphoric stupor. "Pow," he got out past his raw throat.

"What?" Jamie chuckled.

"You exploded my brain," Tek moaned and flopped down on his back.

Jamie stretched out next to him and laid his head on Tek's bent arm. "I take it that's a good thing?"

Tek closed his eyes and nodded.

"See, all that bitching for nothing," Jamie said lightly.

"I don't know," Tek countered sleepily. "I got what I wanted, didn't I?"

"I'll always give you what you want," Jamie murmured and pushed up closer.

Tek smiled weakly, too exhausted to move. He dozed off, not even questioning Jamie's words. He knew the truth in them. Hell, Jamie *was* what Tek wanted, and next time, he'd be giving Jamie a little of the want in return.

I'd always thought home was about bricks and mortar, walls and roof. A piece of property, a place where family gathered and they had to let you in and put up with your shit, because it was where you belonged. It was home.

I've been everywhere with Jamie. We've lived in hotels in towns I can't remember the names of. We slept in our truck, under the stars and hidden havens. Along the way, he taught me that houses and places hold memories, some good, and some bad, but they weren't home.

Home was wherever Jamie was.

Tek Cain

Home

JAMIE LEANED his shoulder against the wall and took in their small studio apartment. It wasn't much to look at, all mismatched furniture and thrift store décor. Tek had found some butt-ass ugly seventies-print lime green and neon orange fabric and made curtains to divide the space into a living and sleeping area. Jamie had laughed till his belly ached and tears rolled down his eyes watching Tek learn to sew. Tek had actually gotten pretty good at it, the curtains turned out well even if the pattern and colors were hideous. After spending what extra money they had on the small cabin—their must-have safe house farther upstate—they hadn't been able to afford much, but they'd made the apartment feel warm and cozy.

Jamie still loved to escape the city to their hideaway in the woods, which had been their home for nearly a year when they'd first come to New York. It had been one of the best years of his life. Just him and Tek hiding from a world that wanted to destroy them, but the small five-hundred square foot apartment was now home. His and Tek's home: the notion brought a fond smile to his face even if he did want to cringe at the décor.

The wariness he'd experienced since first coming to the city was always simmering just below the surface, always waiting for the other shoe to drop, though. It was a feeling he doubted he'd ever lose. One couldn't spend twenty-one years of their life amongst the lowlifes of society and not have it affect them. Jamie had learned to build a cautious wall around himself; he rarely trusted and had an edge with everyone. The exception was Tek.

"Earth to Jamie?"

Jamie blinked rapidly a couple of times, clearing the fog from his brain, and spotted Tek sitting on the couch, pulling on his boots. Jamie had been so deep in thought he hadn't even seen or heard the man come out of the bathroom.

"Enjoy your trip?" Tek asked with a smirk.

"As a matter of fact, I did," Jamie responded and sat down next to Tek. "I was just thinking about the cabin and this place," he said with a nod.

"Yeah? What about 'em?"

"I love being up in the woods, getting away from the noise and crowds, but this place... I don't know." Jamie shrugged. "Feels like home."

Tek finished tying his boots and stretched his long legs out. "It's the curtains," Tek chuckled.

"I'm sure that's it," Jamie muttered and rolled his eyes. "Do you ever miss it?" he asked somberly.

"What? The cabin? Sure I do, but we would have had to become mountain men if we continued living there. I don't know about you, but I really don't like foraging for my meals. I like fast food too much," he said, patting his belly.

"No. I mean home.... Chatom? I miss my dad," Jamie admitted morosely.

Tek leaned over till their shoulders were touching and took Jamie's hand in his. "Yeah, your dad's good peeps, I miss him too. I think about my mom a lot. What it was like for her when they told them I was missing, probably dead. I mean, she wasn't the greatest mom in the world, did a lot of fucked-up things, but she's still my mom. You know how I deal with it?" Tek asked, meeting Jamie's gaze.

"Lots of sex?" Jamie offered, trying to lighten the mood.

"Well, there is that." Tek smirked and pecked Jamie on the cheek. "But I also keep reminding myself it's better she just *thinks* I might be dead rather than actually having to bury me."

"I know," Jamie agreed. "I'm not saying I want to go back or contact them or anything. It would be suicide. Just...."

Jamie couldn't find the words to describe what it felt like. He loved his life here with Tek, no way in hell he'd want to go back, but at times, it was as if there was this invisible string tied to something inside him, tugging, trying to pull him back to his old life.

"It may never go away," Tek said as if he could read Jamie's mind. "But I can't, no, I won't go back there no matter what. I don't ever want to be that man again. The things I've done...."

The despair in Tek's voice tore at Jamie's heart, and he wrapped his arms around Tek and pulled him close. Jamie had done a lot of things he wasn't proud of: stealing, running drugs, lying. He'd even shot at men, but he didn't know if he actually hit anyone or killed them. The horrors Tek had endured, the things he'd done, been forced to do, weighed heavily on Tek, and Jamie wished he could bear the burden for him. All he could do was hold him and be there when Tek needed to talk.

"You're a good man," Jamie told him with utter confidence. Tek shook his head. "Yes, you are, dammit," Jamie growled, grabbing a handful of Tek's hair and pulling his head back until he was forced to meet Jamie's narrowed gaze. "You are, and if you keep arguing with me about it, I'm gonna have to beat your ass."

Tek opened his mouth, no doubt to argue, then snapped it shut. Sadness still filled his hazel eyes, but he smiled. "As long as you think so, I guess that's all that matters."

"Damn right," Jamie grunted. "And I'm going to keep telling you until I convince you."

The alarm went off on Tek's phone. They both jumped and then laughed at the mirrored shocked looks on their faces. "Time to get to the club," Tek announced, then pulled his cell from his pocket and turned it off.

"Shit," Jamie gruffed and grabbed Tek again. "I was hoping you would argue with me."

"I think you've been talking to Tackett a little too much lately."

"He's a wealth of information," Jamie countered and kissed Tek soundly before he could reply.

"I know what you're trying to do," Tek accused breathlessly when the kiss ended. "And it's not going to work."

It already had. Tek was smiling, and the guilt was no longer visible in his features. Still, Jamie didn't point it out, he simply responded, "Mmm-hmm."

"It's not," Tek said again and pulled out of Jamie's grasp. "Now stop thinking about my ass. We have a party to keep under control."

Jamie followed Tek to the door and grabbed their coats and handed Tek his. "I think about your ass twenty-four seven." As Tek shrugged into his coat, Jamie grabbed the ass in question and squeezed. "It's a damn fine ass."

"I know, and it's going to stay that way," Tek snorted. He opened the door and pointed out to the hallway. "Now go! I don't trust you to walk behind me."

They ended up walking side by side, laughing the entire way. Jamie sometimes forgot how hard it was for Tek when Jamie brought up the past. He'd have to be more careful in the future. It was, after all, the past, and it was sure a hell of a lot better to dream about the future rather than dwell in the past. He patted Tek on the ass and grinned at the playful glare Tek shot him. The present wasn't so bad either.

TEK AND Jamie rounded the corner, and Tek let out an unhappy grunt. The line outside the Guards of Folsom was halfway down the block, and he'd been hoping for a slow night. Blake and Ty were celebrating the grand opening of the members' only area, and Tek had hoped he'd get a chance to pop in and check out the party. Everyone was abuzz about the entertainment, but it looked like Tek and Jamie would be missing it.

As they made their way to the front of the line, people shying away from them as they approached, Jamie suddenly stopped at the entrance and Tek slammed into his back.

"Christ, that guy is as big as a horse," someone in line muttered in astonishment.

Hung like one too, Tek mused but kept that bit of information to himself.

As Tek waited for Jamie to move, the cold wind bit at Tek's ears and nose, and he shivered as it moved down his spine. He didn't know if he'd ever get used to the cold winters; the dampness in the air seemed to make it worse, seeped right into his bones.

Tek hugged himself and shifted from foot to foot, trying to generate a little heat as he continued to wait. It did no good. Finally, he growled impatiently, "What the hell is the hold up?" and shoved at Jamie.

Jamie turned and stepped sideways, and Tek spotted Rig and Bobby. He hadn't seen them since they'd gone to Florida a few months back, and from what he'd heard, they'd had a little surprise in tow when they returned.

"Rig, Bobby, damn, man, good to see you back. You here for the party?" Tek asked.

"Hey, Tek." Rig shook his head. "We were just leaving."

"You're going to miss a hell of a party. Tackett and Micah are the main event," Tek said slyly. Too damn bad he couldn't see it either. He was a little bitter about it, but he'd be bitter if he missed work and they didn't eat, so…. "Hey, is this Mason?" he asked, pointing at the smaller man looking up at him like a deer caught in the headlights.

The man was slight, couldn't be more than five seven. He was cute, actually adorable, and Tek could see the appeal for Bobby and Rig. Tek guessed his age to be not much beyond his own, but it could have been his size that gave that impression since he had lines around his eyes and mouth.

"Tek Cain, Jamie Ryan, meet Mason Howard," Rig said, the pride evident in his voice.

Rig then leaned down and said something against Mason's ear. It was difficult to make out what he was saying, but Tek thought he heard something about pussycats, which made Mason's dark eyes go impossibly wide and his Adam's apple bob as he swallowed hard.

"Hey, Mason," Tek said. Jamie echoed the greeting. Tek then added, "Welcome to New York."

Mason waved meekly but didn't respond. Tek had heard bits and pieces of conversations about Mason. He'd lost his Doms and had a hard time coping. It was good to see him with Bobby and Rig. They'd take damn good care of the smaller man.

Someone started to complain behind Tek, ripe curses about the cold. *Shit! Time to get to work.* "Good seeing you guys," Tek said to Bobby and Rig. To Mason, he added, "Nice to meet you, Mason," as he pushed past them. "Sorry, Blake will have my ass if I'm late again. We'll catch up soon," he tossed over his shoulder, Jamie right on his heels.

Tek hung up his and Jamie's coats in the employee area and went to the sink. He turned on the warm water and let it run over his cold hands. He was never going to get used to these damn cold temperatures. Considering it was only fall and he was already complaining, he and winter were so not going to be friends.

"Are you going to go watch the show?" Tek asked Jamie as he leaned back against the counter and dried his hands.

"Nah, looks like we'll have our hands full in the club tonight. It's packed."

"You know, you don't have to miss it on my account," Tek informed him. He tossed the towel on the counter and grabbed Jamie's T-shirt and pulled him closer. "You might learn something new from the Doms."

"I thought you said I was hanging around them too much," Jamie countered.

Tek slid his hand down Jamie's body, his fingers brushing over the ridges and valleys of his muscular stomach. "Yeah, ignore the ass-beating stuff, but maybe you can take some notes on the bondage," he suggested, his voice going a little deeper. "Things you'd like for me to do to you." He worked his fingers past the waistband on Jamie's jeans, seeking out the warm flesh below.

Jamie grabbed Tek's wrist and stopped his movements. "You're already late, and if you keep it up, you're going to miss your whole shift."

"Nag, nag, nag," Tek teased and pulled his hand free. "But seriously. If you want to go watch the show, I don't mind."

"Nope," Jamie said curtly and kissed him. "I'm sure watching your ass will keep me thoroughly entertained."

"You're so easy," Tek sniffed, then covered his ass with his hands and backed out of the room.

"Can't keep it covered all night," Jamie chuckled and stalked after Tek.

As it turned out, Tek didn't have to miss the entire show; in fact, he and Jamie both had the perfect vantage point leaning against the back wall across from the stage. Mark, one of the security crew hired for the private party, was called away on a family emergency, and Blake had asked Tek to stand in for Mark at the last minute. Tek was more than happy to oblige. The only thing that would have been better was if he and Jamie had gotten to see Tackett and Micah's performance, but they were there now.

"Got that notebook?" Tek whispered.

"Don't need it, man," Jamie responded and pointed to his head. "It's like a steel trap."

"Yeah, just hope you can open it later," Tek chuckled and then mumbled under his breath, "After I repay the brain explosion."

Tek's job was to keep an eye on everyone and everything within the club, yet he couldn't take his eyes from the man on the stage wearing black leather pants, a wide leather harness across his chest in the shape of an X, and heavy-soled boots. Tek didn't know who the man was, his face covered by a leather hood, but whoever it was sure as hell knew how to wield a flogger. The Dom was swinging it in a figure-eight pattern across a man's back who was tied to a St. Andrew's cross, down the guy's ass and thighs and back up. The Dom had worked up a sweat; his broad back glistened beneath the subdued stage lighting. No one made a sound, not a cough or clink of ice in a glass; everyone in the room seemed to be entranced by the show, the slap of leather to skin and the low moans flowing from the submissive, hypnotic.

The audience members weren't the only ones bewitched by the sight in front of them. Tek stared without blinking in complete awe of not only the Dom's controlled power but also the way the bound man took each blow. The sub not only seemed to take it, but the expression of bliss on his face where it rested against the St. Andrew's cross was proof he was not only taking the pain but finding immense pleasure in it.

Tek leaned in closer to Jamie's ear. "I don't get it," he admitted, never taking his eyes from the two men on the stage.

"Get what?"

"How can the sub look like… like you do after you've just blown a load?"

Jamie turned his head, his smiling lips brushing Tek's. "I look that good?"

"Better," Tek assured him. "But that guy's not getting nailed, he's getting beat. I don't get it."

"I don't either," Jamie said with a shake of his head and went back to watching the show.

Tek jerked his attention back to the stage when he heard a loud thump. The flogger was now at the Dom's feet, his chest pressed against the smaller man's back. Tek winced at the idea of someone pressing against flesh that surely felt as if it were on fire. But the sub obviously didn't mind, he had a sweet smile on his lips with his Dom's face buried in the side of his neck.

Everyone in the audience began to cheer and clap when the Dom bent and picked up a wide leather collar with an O-ring attached to it. Tek glance at Jamie who only shrugged and began clapping along with the others.

"What the hell are you clapping for?" Tek asked in confusion. Was he the only one in the room that had no fucking idea what was going on?

"The Dom is going to collar his boy," Jamie informed him and then put two fingers in his mouth and whistled.

Apparently, he was the only one who was clueless.

"He's what?"

Jamie turned and leaned his shoulder against the wall, giving Tek an exasperated look. "Collaring. It's a commitment ceremony between a Dom and his sub."

Tek stared at Jamie for long moments. "And you know this how?"

Jamie rolled his eyes. "What do you think I do all night while you're working? I pay attention to what's going on around me, talk to people."

Tek's brow furrowed. "I thought you watched my ass all night?"

"Don't pout, Tek. It really doesn't look good on you," Jamie teased and patted Tek on the cheek. "Now pay attention," he smirked and turned back to the show on the stage.

"I don't pout!" Tek crossed his arms over his chest, leaned back against the wall, and glared at Jamie. He did not pout, he glared, there was a huge difference.

Love? I've asked myself if that's what I feel for Jamie. Is that what it is when just the sight of his face makes me happy, or when I embrace him and my entire body tingles? I've heard it defined in songs and books, and I've agreed with some, but none of them truly encompass what I feel.

Even as I write this, I'm not sure. 'Love' is too small a word to define everything I feel for him, the meaning too simple. Too many intangible feelings for such a common four-letter word.

Tek Cain

Exposed

TEK STEPPED through the front doors of the Guards of Folsom, brushed the snow from his coat, and shook it from his hair.

"Hey!" Jamie snorted and shoved Tek.

Spotting the boss sitting at the end of the bar, Tek just laughed at Jamie's grumbling and made his way over to Blake. "Hey, boss man. How's it hangin'?"

"To the left." Blake smirked as he looked up from his paperwork. "You're early."

"Figured I'd make up for the last two times I've been late," Tek responded as he shrugged out of his coat. "Anything you need me to do?"

There was always stock to put away, boxes and equipment to move. His and Jamie's size made them the go-to guys in a club where the majority of the staff was... on the smaller size. Tek didn't mind. He liked to keep busy; it kept his mind from wandering to places he didn't like to go.

"Hey, Jamie," Blake said in greeting with a curt nod.

"How's it going?" Jamie asked without looking up as he struggled with his zipper.

"Actually, I'm glad you both are here. Would you two mind moving the cross from the stage?" Blake inquired.

"Sure thing," Tek said absently as he watched Jamie grow increasingly frustrated with his jacket. Tek slapped Jamie's hands away. "Would you stop? You're going to break it."

"It's stuck," Jamie complained.

"Where do you want us to move the cross to?" Tek asked Blake as he worked to get Jamie's zipper unstuck. The material of the liner was jammed in it, and Jamie had made it worse by trying to force it.

"In the corner on either side of the stage will be fine," Blake instructed.

"You're gonna have to pull it over your head, you dork. You stuck it but good." Tek grasped the bottom of Jamie's jacket and pulled it up.

"Jesus," Jamie spat as Tek tugged up on this jacket, and lost his footing.

Tek laughed as Jamie flailed and spun as he fought to get the jacket over his head. Finally, Tek pulled it free and laughed even harder. The static in the garment made Jamie's long hair shoot out from his head as if he'd stuck his finger in an electrical outlet, and his shirt was bunched up under his arms.

"You asshole," Jamie grumbled and ran his fingers through his hair, trying in vain to smooth it down.

"Whew," Blake whistled. "Hell of a tat."

Jamie's eyes grew wide as he stared at Tek with a panicked expression on his face and jerked his T-shirt down.

Tek gave a slight shake of his head. "It's okay," he mouthed and handed Jamie his jacket as he stepped past him.

"You know, I love Ty with all my heart and soul, but I don't know if I'd be brave enough to ink his name on my flesh," Blake confessed. "Guess he'll have to settle for his collar as proof. Do you have Jamie's name on yours?"

"Jamie's name?" Tek asked in confusion.

"Figured if Jamie had yours, you'd have his. No?"

Tek glanced at Jamie who suddenly seemed very interested in the opposite side of the bar. *Jamie has my name on his back?* "Uh.... No.... Not yet," Tek stammered, still staring at Jamie. *Since when?* "Yeah, so. We better get that cross moved." Tek grabbed Jamie's arm and pulled him along, tossing over his shoulder to Blake, "Just let me know if you need anything else done before shift."

The second they were in the private area, Tek shut the door behind them and spun on Jamie. "What the hell, dude? When did you get new ink?"

"I didn't," Jamie responded, averting his eyes.

"Then why in the hell does Blake think you have my name on your back? Let me see."

"It's always been there," Jamie muttered, his cheeks turning pink.

Tek studied Jamie as he tried to figure out what the hell was going on. He'd explored every inch of Jamie's body; hell, he'd been there when he got the fucking tattoo. How could he not know?

"Turn around," Tek demanded.

Jamie turned, and Tek shoved up his T-shirt. Across Jamie's upper back was the familiar Crimson VIII name with the logo beneath it. He studied it carefully but didn't find what he was seeking. Below it was "Truth & Knowledge," the letters he'd outlined with his fingers and tongue too many times to count. Tek took a couple steps back, scratching at his goatee. Another step back and just before Jamie pulled his shirt back down, Tek spotted it and gasped.

"Oh. My. Fucking. God!"

"Well…," Jamie said cautiously as he turned back around.

Jamie had always been the most honest person Tek had ever met. Jamie wasn't book smart, but he was always seeking knowledge from everything around him, just like he had about what was going on around the club. He soaked it up like a sponge. Tek had never once questioned Jamie's choice of inking "Truth & Knowledge" beneath the MC's logo, both words—no all three words—described what Jamie was all about. From a distance only the T in truth and the K in knowledge were visible and the ampersand was inked in a unique way, giving it the appearance of an E. Jamie lived for truth, knowledge—and Tek.

"Did you do that on purpose?" Tek asked around the lump in his throat as emotion swelled up in him.

"Yeah," Jamie admitted, sounding almost shy.

Tek wrapped his arms around Jamie and leaned his forehead on Jamie's shoulder. For long moments, he couldn't speak. The idea that Jamie had forever imprinted Tek's name on his flesh at such a young age was both insane and one of the sweetest things he'd ever done. Most people would certainly think it more the former than the latter. But for Tek, it made sense. From the moment of their birth, there had never been any question they were connected on a level that far surpassed something as simple as friends, brothers, or even lovers. Even after their confessions all those years ago when they became a couple, they'd never told each other they loved each other. The word was too... common, tossed around recklessly between people who didn't have a clue. He and Jamie didn't need words or ink or *common* terms of endearments. What they had went beyond physical, intellectual or even spiritual. It was more... indescribable....

Them.

Tek lifted his head and met Jamie's gaze with burning eyes. He blinked back any tears that might threaten. He wasn't sad, yet the damn things filled his eyes. *Bastards.* "Damn good thing you were thinking about me when you got inked," Tek informed him huskily, his voice betraying his sentiment. "'Cause I was thinking about you when I got mine. Cradle to grave. Me and you." Tek hugged him again and buried his face in the side of Jamie's neck to hide the one lone bastard that sneaked from his eyes.

Jamie hugged him back. Tek soaked in Jamie's warmth until he was better under control of his emotions and then patted him on the back. "All right, better get this cross moved."

Tek started to pull away, but Jamie held tight and smashed their mouths together. Guess Jamie still had one thing to say, the kind that curled Tek's toes and left him breathless when it ended.

"Now we can move it," Jamie said smugly.

As Jamie released him and walked by, Tek could tell from the little gleam in Jamie's eyes that not only had he known Tek had been struggling with his emotions, but Jamie liked it as well. Jamie, while not one to be mushy, certainly was the more.... Tek watched as Jamie sauntered over to the stage, a bit of a cocky swagger to his step. Tek rolled his eyes. Jamie wore his heart on his sleeve even though he tried to act all badass mofo most of the time. He also loved it when he was able to pull that—*Oh, God. Do I dare say, sweet side*—out of Tek.

I'm not sweet, dammit.

Tek tromped over to the stage, hands on his hips. "I'm not!" he insisted.

"You're not what?" Jamie smirked.

"Whatever it is you're thinking that's got you smirking and walking like you're the cock of the walk, I'm not!"

"Who said I was thinking of anything?" Jamie asked, trying to feign innocence. "Now, are you going to help me or not?"

Tek hopped up on the stage and pointed an accusing finger at Jamie. "I can tell by that cocky-ass smile on your face. Now knock it off. I'm not!"

"Not what, Tek? I'm sure I have no idea what you're talking about."

"Okay. That's fine," Tek grumbled and grabbed the opposite side of the cross. "On three," he instructed grumpily. "One...."

"Two," Jamie chuckled.

"Oh, just you wait till we get home," Tek threatened. "Three."

Tek heaved up on the cross. The thing weighed a ton, but it was manageable as soon as his laughing partner actually put some muscle into it.

Laugh it up, Tek mused as they worked to get the awkward weight off the stage. Tek had a few ideas popping into his head that would prove to Jamie he was anything but sweet, and he still had a six-hour shift to think about even more not-so-sweet things to torture Jamie with.

JAMIE EITHER had forgotten Tek's threat or hadn't taken it seriously as he casually strolled into the apartment and hung up his coat with his back turned to Tek. But Tek remembered. Oh, how he remembered. He'd spent the entire six hours of his shift, the half hour of clean up, and the twenty-minute trek home thinking about it. Before Jamie could take two steps away, Tek had his jacket off and thrown to the floor and had pounced on Jamie. Wrapping the unsuspecting man in a tight bear hug, Tek manhandled Jamie to their bed and shoved him down face-first, Tek then landing heavily on top of him.

"So you think I'm sweet, do you?" he hissed in Jamie's ear, and then he latched on to Jamie's wrists and pinned them to the bed.

"I never said that," Jamie responded, trying to sound innocent, but Tek wasn't fooled.

"No, but you thought it," he accused.

Jamie turned his head and looked up at Tek, a mischievous glint in his eyes. "Yes, I think you're as fucking sweet as a cute kitty cat," Jamie taunted.

"Do ya now?" Tek jeered.

"Uh-huh. Big ol' pussy cat, I believe Rig called you," Jamie chuckled.

"More like a lion, baby. Prepare to be mauled," Tek exclaimed and manhandled Jamie until he was stretched out on his back. It was easy, Tek barely having to exert himself with the way Jamie was giggling his fool head off.

Once he had him in position with Jamie's head pressed against the headboard and his size fifteens hanging off the end of the bed, Tek straddled Jamie's waist, then reached over and snatched the black nylon from the bedside table.

"Ooh, maul me, baby," Jamie got out in between snorts of laughter.

"Changed my mind," Tek drawled and waggled his brows as he held up the rope. "Prepare to be roped!"

Jamie put up a token effort to struggle away from Tek, but he was laughing too hard for it to be effective. As soon as Jamie's arms were bound to the bedposts, Tek crawled off him and ripped open Jamie's shirt.

"Hey!" Jamie protested.

"Serves you right for ripping the buttons off my good shirt," Tek retorted and undid Jamie's jeans. He worked them down Jamie's legs, pulled off his shoes and socks, and then tossed the jeans and briefs to the floor.

Tek grabbed another bundle of rope, his gaze drawn to where Jamie's cock was hard, curving up toward his belly. Tek licked his lips. He couldn't wait to get his mouth on it.

"Here, kitty, kitty," Jamie murmured and wiggled his hips.

Tek arched a brow but didn't respond to the taunt; instead, he wrapped the end of the rope around one of Jamie's ankles, down around the leg of the bed, and then back up. He pulled it taut and then wound it around Jamie's other ankle, tying it off to the other bed leg. He checked them, made sure they weren't too tight.

Satisfied, Tek went to his feet and rubbed his hands together. "Now, where should I begin?"

"I can give you a few suggestions," Jamie offered and wiggled his hips again.

"That's one option," Tek drawled and removed his shirt.

"It's the best option in this position."

"I don't know." Tek pursed his lips as he took in Jamie's magnificent body, laid out for him like a feast, as if he were contemplating his options. There really wasn't any better option than the one Jamie was hoping Tek would get to first, but that would come in time.

Tek tossed his shirt aside and ran the tip of one finger softly along the arch of Jamie's left foot. "Here?"

"A little higher," Jamie chuckled and jerked his foot.

"Oh, you must mean here," Tek asked as he slid his hand up to Jamie's calf.

"Getting warmer."

"Aha!" Tek ran his hand along the inside of Jamie's thigh, the soft hair tickling his palms. "This has got to be the spot."

Jamie shivered. "That's a good spot, but not the one I had in mind."

"You sure?" Tek inquired. "I would have thought for sure this was it. Better double-check," he said with a sly grin.

Tek bent and kissed his way across Jamie's muscular thigh to the sensitive skin on the inside. Tek teased the area with tongue and teeth, causing Jamie to shudder again.

Tek lifted his head and met Jamie's lustful gaze. "See, I was right. This is the spot."

Jamie bit his bottom lip and shook his head, his breathing a little fast as the flush moved up his body from belly to cheeks. "Close," he said breathlessly. "Very close, but not quite what I had in mind."

"Really?" Tek teased and cocked his head.

"I'm pretty sure," Jamie countered.

"But not positive. Better check again," Tek murmured and nipped the inside of Jamie's thigh again.

Jamie's back arched, and he hissed through gritted teeth with the sting. "Fucker," he growled.

"I can live with that," Tek said nonchalantly with a shrug of one shoulder.

Tek briefly considered giving in and going for the goods. He couldn't wait to get his hands and mouth on Jamie's cock, but the hopeful look on Jamie's face changed his mind. That would be way too sweet, and he was anything but. Mind made up, Tek ran his fingers up Jamie's thigh to his hip, barely brushing against Jamie's flesh. Tek tried to ignore Jamie's cock—he didn't touch it, but he certainly noticed it— hard and straining, bobbing with each movement Jamie made. No way could he keep his hands off it for long, but Tek wasn't ready to give in just yet.

"I think I may have figured it out," Tek drawled.

Jamie shook his head. "No! You missed it. You were hot and then went right on past," Jamie complained with a bit of a whine in his voice that had Tek biting down on the inside of his cheek to keep from laughing.

"Here?" Tek asked and swirled his finger around Jamie's right nipple.

"You know that's not it," Jamie grumped, but he pushed his chest up into Tek's touch.

"I know no such thing," Tek taunted and then teased the little nub with his tongue until it was erect. He blew on it, causing goose bumps to erupt on Jamie's skin. "See, I was right," he murmured and then sucked the nipple into his mouth hard and teased it with teeth and tongue.

"Damn!" Jamie cursed and arched his back harder when Tek pinched the other nipple. "I feel that all the way to my balls."

"I know," Tek responded wickedly. Jamie had very sensitive nipples, one of the reasons Tek couldn't keep his mouth and hands off them.

Tek continued to play with them until Jamie was squirming, his breath coming in short pants and loud moans. "You sure that's not the spot?" he asked as he brushed his lips over Jamie's, both hands now twisting and pinching Jamie's nipples. "I wonder if I could make you come by just playing with your nips."

"I'd rather it not be tonight," Jamie groaned. "My dick could really, really use some attention."

"Really?"

"C'mon, man, stop teasing," Jamie pleaded.

Tek nipped Jamie's bottom lip. "Baby, I have only just begun to tease you," he said seductively against Jamie's mouth before he took a step back.

Jamie's expression was wary, and he didn't look at all happy about the comment. Tek turned to hide his grin. "You see, there is a lesson to be learned here," Tek informed him and pulled open the top drawer of their dresser. He rummaged around beneath the socks and briefs until he found what he was looking for.

"A lesson?" Jamie asked, sounding suspicious. "What kind of lesson?"

"Well, for one, we are about to learn how fucking strong this bed is." Tek snorted as he stood at the end of the bed and leered down at Jamie.

"That's not funny, man," Jamie complained with narrowed eyes.

Tek flipped open the top of the lube with his thumb and poured a generous amount in his hand. Without a word or taking his gaze from Jamie's, he tossed the tube aside and rubbed his hands together, slicking them up with a naughty grin curling his lips.

"Dude, I'm serious. That shit's not funny," Jamie said and pulled against his restraints.

"I'm pretty sure I figured out that spot you were talking about," Tek informed him as he swaggered to the side of the bed. "Let's see if I get it right this time, shall we?" Tek wrapped one slick fist around Jamie's cock and pumped it a couple times. "Well?"

Jamie threw his head back and pushed up into Tek's hand. "Fuck yeah, that's it," he groaned.

Tek set a slow rhythm, keeping his fist loose as he stroked Jamie from base to tip. Before long Jamie started pushing his hips upward with more strength, looking for more friction. Tek loosened his grip even further and refused to quicken the strokes.

"Just get me off and you can play as long as you want," Jamie groaned. Still, Tek denied Jamie the friction he was seeking, keeping his fist loose and his movements slow. "Ah, c'mon, Tek, harder," Jamie pleaded and snapped his hips.

"Like this?" Tek asked, tightening his hand and stroking hard and fast.

"Yeah…. Fuck yeah. That's it," Jamie crooned. His eyes fluttered shut and he tightened his jaw as he strained to thrust up even harder.

Tek watched him closely. Jamie's breathing sped and he had a look of concentration on his face as he chased his orgasm. Jamie's cock was ruddy, throbbing against Tek's hand as precum seeped from the slit.

Tek had seen it a hundred times, knew each telltale sign in Jamie's body, and just as he reached the edge, Tek squeezed hard at the base of Jamie's cock and stilled his hand.

"Wh…. What the…. Fuck!" Jamie stuttered as his head snapped up and his eyes flew open. Tek's grin grew wider at the shock on Jamie's face that quickly morphed into realization of what Tek had planned. "Not cool, man," Jamie panted harshly and laid his head back down onto the mattress with a huff. "So not cool."

Tek sat on the edge of the bed and winced when his own hard cock was pressed against his thigh. He shifted, ignoring his own desire, and slowly began to stroke Jamie again. "You really are magnificent when you're about to come. Mmm," Tek purred.

"You should see me when I actually come," Jamie sighed.

"Oh, I'm looking forward to that as well," Tek assured him. He tightened his grip and quickened his movements. "Later."

Jamie lay there with his eyes closed as he did his best not to show any response to Tek's ministrations, but his body betrayed him. His teeth were sunk into his bottom lip and his muscles tense. He shook with exertion. Tek had to give Jamie credit for how long he resisted giving into the pleasure, but he couldn't hold back for much longer.

"Ah, hell," Jamie hissed and rocked his hips.

Tek once again clamped down on the base of Jamie's cock and with his other hand added pressure to Jamie's nuts.

"Fuck," Jamie hissed and then panted harshly. After a few tense moments, Jamie let out a long, low groan, the sound settling in Tek's groin. His dick twitched.

"Better?" Tek released Jamie's sac and ran his hand over his thigh.

"No I'm not better," he groaned. He took a couple of deep breaths in through his nose and blew them out slowly. He shook his head and then opened his eyes to glare at Tek. "I still need to come before my blue balls explode."

Tek made a point to study Jamie's sac, tilting his head and gnawing on his lip. "Hmm. They don't look blue. Red, a little purple maybe, but definitely not blue."

Jamie yanked on his restraints, the headboard protesting with a loud creak. "Dammit, Tek!" Jamie strained against the ropes, the muscles in his arms bulging. Jamie was one powerful son of a bitch, and Tek knew if he wanted free, the headboard wouldn't be good for anything but kindling.

"But, baby, I'm just trying to show you how much I appreciate your strength and control," Tek reasoned. "How sweet and gentle my touch can be," he murmured and stroked Jamie's cock softly.

"No, you're not," Jamie insisted. "You're trying to make both my head and my dick explode. There is nothing sweet about you. You're a mean mother fucker!"

Tek tightened his grip around Jamie's pulsing cock and slid the fingers of his other hand behind Jamie's balls, pressed against his opening. Tek waggled his brows and grinned. "And don't you forget it." He pushed one finger in and stroked the head of Jamie's cock hard and fast with the other hand.

"Oh! Oh fucking hell!" Jamie shouted, pressing down on Tek's fingers.

Tek pushed harder, found Jamie's prostate.

Jamie screamed.

The bed protested loudly, creaking and rocking as Jamie bowed his back, white-knuckled fists straining as the first burst of cum shot from his dick and landed on his chest. Tek watched in awe as Jamie gave into his pleasure. Sweat rolled down his temples, his hips thrusting and jerking through each wave of his orgasm. His deep rumbling moans echoed around the room. When the last contraction worked its way through Jamie's body, he shuddered and collapsed back against the mattress. He had a beautiful expression of bliss on his face. His chest, neck, and face were drenched in sweat and splattered with cum.

"That's a damn fine look on you," Tek praised.

Jamie grunted.

"No, really," Tek insisted as he went to his feet and began releasing Jamie from his binds. He didn't have to worry about any retaliation for his teasing. Jamie was a blissed-out pile of happy goo. "It's amazing the results a mean mother fucker can bring out in you."

Tek laughed when Jamie grunted again. Tek rubbed the red skin around Jamie's left wrist to help to get the blood flowing before moving around to the other side of the bed. Tek figured he had thirty minutes at best to remove the ropes and relieve a little pressure of his own before Jamie had enough brain cells for a little payback.

Tek shuddered, and his dick throbbed in anticipation of seeing just how fucking mean Jamie could be.

Good hands.
Talented hands.
Jamie's hands.

Tek Cain

Hands

TEK SAT at the monitoring station and whistled low. "Holy shit, this is impressive," he muttered.

"Normally, the video and audio feeds will be blacked out when the rooms are occupied," Blake informed him. "We believe in giving our members the utmost respect of their privacy. However, if a panic button is ever activated, you'll be able to open up the feeds to see and hear what's going on."

Tek studied the screens. Each room had a video camera positioned so the room was in complete view. From the desk, the security guard on duty could unlock rooms with a push of a button and deploy other guards through constant radio contact and intercom.

"Hell of a system," Tek complimented as he ran a hand over his goatee.

"Thank you," Blake responded and took the seat next to him. "You'll also be required to keep an eye on the main room and report any suspicious behavior or possible problems to one of the guards on the floor."

"I really appreciate the offer, but to be completely honest, I'm not sure I'd be able to make the distinction between possible problems and what's normal. This whole Dom/sub thing all seems...." Tek struggled to find a word that wouldn't offend Blake, but he faltered. "I just don't think I understand it enough," he settled on.

"You know the basics, you've learned quite a bit since you've been here, as well as from your dealings with Tackett, Bobby, and Rig." Blake leaned back in his chair and studied Tek for a moment. "I've watched you work the main club. Despite your size, people are comfortable around you. You're friendly, outgoing, and courteous to the clientele. More importantly, you are always aware of everything that's going on around you. You have this uncanny ability to see problems brewing and defuse them before they get out of control."

"Thank you for saying so, but—"

"You don't need to completely understand the relationship between a Dom and his sub to know if something is right or not. You can read people, Tek. It's almost as if you can read people's minds at times or at least their moods. That's very rare and a quality I value in my security team."

Tek felt a pang of guilt settle into his gut. Tek hated that Blake seemed to believe Tek was a good man. If Blake knew the real reason behind Tek's ability to read people, that it was born more from mistrust and a selfish need to protect Jamie from harm—if he knew about the lies, about Tek's past, he'd know his trust was sorely misplaced.

"Have you and Jamie considered exploring the lifestyle more in depth?" Blake suddenly asked, pulling Tek from his musings.

"No," Tek responded with a shake of his head and went back to studying the monitors. "Not really. Jamie and I don't have anything against it. Hell, we enjoy some kink, but if you're asking if either of us want to be like official Dominants with contracts and such, then the answer is no."

"Just play it safe," Blake reminded him. "And if you ever have any questions, don't hesitate to ask."

"Thanks, I'll be sure to do that," Tek said sincerely.

Blake leaned back in his chair and entwined his fingers over his stomach. "What do you think? This sound like a job you'd be interested in?"

Hell yeah, he was interested. Tek enjoyed working at the club, and Blake was offering him twice what he'd been making. It sure as hell would take a little pressure off him and Jamie financially. Yet that twinge of guilt just wouldn't let go of his gut. No matter how bad they could use the money, accepting the job seemed like a betrayal of sorts. Blake trusted him with the security of his club, and yet Tek couldn't trust Blake to be honest about who he really was and what he was running from.

"Like I said, I really do appreciate the offer, I'm just not sure I'm the right guy for the job," Tek said regretfully.

"I think you are, or I wouldn't have offered it to you."

"I—"

"You don't have to give me an answer right now," Blake interrupted. "I'd like you to give it some serious thought before you decide." Blake went to his feet, and as he walked by, he laid his hand on Tek's shoulder. "We all have a past, Tek, and a lot of us aren't proud of what we've done. It's what we learn from it and who we become in spite of it that defines us, not our past."

Tek sat staring wide-eyed long after Blake left. Was Blake making a general statement, or did he actually know about Tek's past? *Impossible.* If that were true, there was no way Blake would have offered him the job, and yet.... Tek rested his elbows on the desk and buried his face in his hands.

"We all have a past." Christ, didn't he know it. He wished to fuck he didn't. That he could just scrub it all from his mind. He didn't want to ever think about it, tried so goddamn hard not to remember. Tek's hands curled into fists, and he slammed them against his temples. He wanted to forget. Yet it was constantly nagging at him, eating away at his gut. Relentless. Always there, looking back at him from his reflection in the mirror.

Death.

He slammed his hands against his head again, a mournful sound spilling from deep inside him as he gripped his hair.

Destruction.

"Hey—"

Arms wrapped around Tek, familiar arms, as the first tears began to stream down Tek's face. Tek turned into those welcoming arms and just fucking lost it. He'd tried so hard for so long to fight it. To push all the pain, death, blood, sins from his mind. He wanted to purge himself of it, but it was part of him.

He sobbed for those who had lost their loved ones by his hands, the wives who would never hold their husbands, the children who would never know their fathers. For the countless lives he'd ruined by providing guns and drugs.

The lies.

The blood.

The deaths.

But mainly, he cried for the little boy lost who never had a chance.

Tek clung to Jamie as the despair in his soul became too much and his body tried to expel it in great heaving sobs. When the tears stopped, the bile rose and the retching began. But it was no use. He'd never be able to rid himself of the blackness that was forever seared upon his soul.

How long they sat together wrapped in each other's arms, Tek didn't know. He only knew when the sobs and retching finally stopped by the silence. He was exhausted, his throat raw, and his head throbbing. Blessedly, visions of the past were also silent.

"You ready to go home?" Jamie whispered, his hands running soothingly down Tek's back.

"Yeah," he responded with a nod.

Jamie removed his ball cap and set it on Tek's head, situating it low to shadow his red and swollen eyes. He then pressed both of his hands to Tek's cheeks and met his gaze. "It's about time you let your stubborn-ass wall down," Jamie told him with a soft smile and pressed a gentle kiss to Tek's lips. "Thank you for letting me carry some of the weight for you, even if it was only for a moment."

Ah damn! How could he regret breaking down, showing weakness when the one constant goodness in his life was thanking him for it? He had no idea what to say. Instead, he said nothing and allowed Jamie to steer him out of the club. The cold wind felt good on his face, and he tipped his head back and closed his eyes for a moment as he took deep, calming breaths.

"You okay?" Jamie asked cautiously and laid his hand against the small of Tek's back.

Tek turned his face and met those amazing caring blue eyes and smiled. "Yeah, I am now. Thank you."

Jamie returned the smile and ran his hand up and down Tek's back. Jamie's touch always made Tek feel better. Made him feel whole, connected.

Something that had occurred to Tek earlier popped into his head again as they walked arm in arm down the quiet sidewalk. "I think

Blake may know about our past," Tek admitted regretfully. "I think we may need to consider moving on."

"What makes you think that? Did you not get the job?"

"No, I got the job, that's not it. Just something he said made me think he knew a lot more than he should. Maybe he's setting us up?"

"I don't think so, Tek. Blake is a great guy. Honest to a fault and a man of his word." Jamie cocked his head. "Is that what happened back there? You're worried about our past being exposed?"

It was more than just exposure, but perhaps part of his meltdown was fear? He wasn't sure. Tek only knew he had to protect Jamie from the past at all costs, and he didn't have the money or the resources to live long on the run.

"I'm always worried about it. Have to," he finally responded.

Jamie was silent for the next block, but Tek could tell he was deep in thought by the expression on his face. As they waited at the corner for the light to change, Jamie said, "I don't want to leave."

"I know, neither do I. But we may not have a choice."

"I trust Blake."

Jamie never fully trusted anyone. The one exception was Tek, so it surprised him that Jamie would feel that way about Blake. "I know you don't want to leave, Jamie, but I'm not convinced we can completely trust anyone."

Jamie shook his head. "I do with Blake," he said with utter conviction. "Call it a hunch, a gut feeling, or whatever you want, but somehow, I just know he'd never betray us. I think you should take the job."

"Really?" Tek said uncertainly. "What if you're wrong?"

Jamie shook his head again, harder this time. "I'm not," he insisted.

Tek let Jamie's words sink in as they crossed the street and made their way down the next block to the subway. He'd been on edge the last couple of days, a little paranoid. Maybe that's what had set off the guilt and ignited his breakdown and it had nothing to do with Blake's cryptic words. *Fuck!* He hoped that's what it was. If Jamie trusted Blake as resolutely as he did, then Tek had to believe in the man too.

"Okay. I'll take the job," Tek finally agreed.

"Awesome!" Jamie exclaimed happily and pulled Tek tighter against him. Jamie slid his warm hand beneath Tek's shirt and rubbed along the side of Tek's body.

God, he hoped Jamie was right, that it was merely a coincidence and Blake had nothing to do with the fact that Tek had an uneasy feeling his past was coming to call. Maybe it hadn't been Rocco he'd seen watching them from a car parked outside the club.

SJD PETERSON, better known as Jo, hails from Michigan. Not the best place to live for someone who hates the cold and snow. When not reading or writing, Jo can be found close to the heater checking out NHL stats and watching the Red Wings kick a little butt. Can't cook, misses the clothes hamper nine out of ten tries, but is handy with power tools.

Visit Jo at:

http://www.facebook.com/SJD.Peterson;
http://sjdpeterson.blogspot.com/;https://twitter.com/SJDPeterson;

and http://www.goodreads.com/author/show/4563849.S_J_D_Peterson.

Contact Jo at sjdpeterson@gmail.com.

Guards of Folsom Series from SJD PETERSON

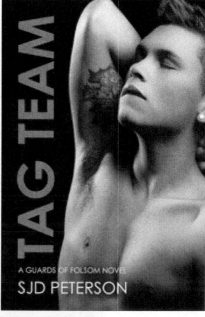

http://www.dreamspinnerpress.com

Whispering Pines Ranch from SJD PETERSON

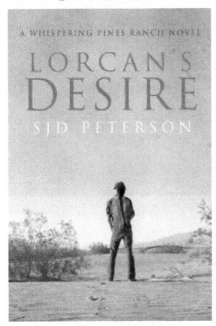

http://www.dreamspinnerpress.com

Whispering Pines Ranch from SJD PETERSON

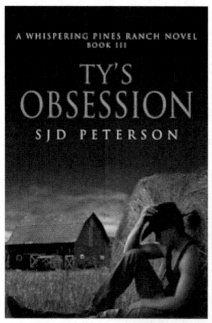

Also from SJD PETERSON

RIVETED

A WHISPERING PINES RANCH SHORT

SJD PETERSON

http://www.dreamspinnerpress.com

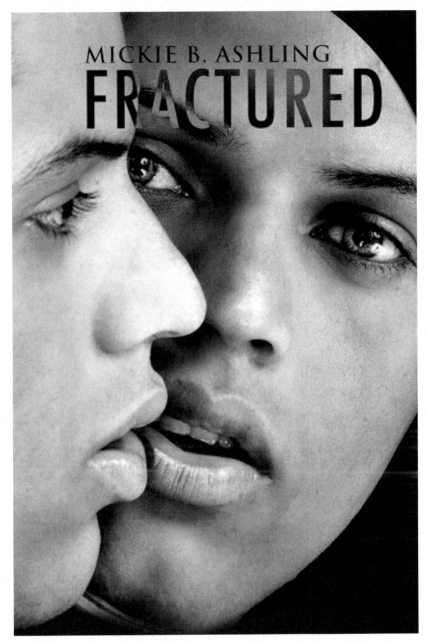

MICKIE B. ASHLING

FRACTURED

CPSIA information can be obtained
at www.ICGtesting.com
Printed in the USA
LVOW01s2007111016

508344LV00010B/140/P